HEART
QUEST.

PRAISE FOR CATHERINE PALMER'S BOOKS

"A *Victorian Christmas Cottage* is an engaging seasonal collection of novellas.
Entertaining."
  —*Library Journal*

"*Finders Keepers* is a romance that tackles deeper issues."
  —*Library Journal*

"*Prairie Rose:* Highly recommended."
  —*Library Journal*

"*Prairie Rose* begins with a bang and doesn't let up till the end. Expertly presents
the tragedy and triumph of the human experience. Also successfully illustrates
many eternal truths about God's character."
  —*A Closer Look*

PRAISE FOR KRISTIN BILLERBECK'S BOOKS

"With only her second novel, author Kristin Billerbeck has proven she's soon to
be a reader favorite."
  —*Romantic Times*

"Kristin Billerbeck's characters come alive with humor and compassion. Her
endings are more than happy; they are satisfying to the soul."
  —*Hannah Alexander, author*

"Her writing touches my soul. I look forward to more from Kristin."
  —*Lois Gladys Leppard, author*

"When I pick up a book by Kristin Billerbeck, I always know I'm in for a treat. I highly recommend all her books."
    —Colleen Coble, author

"If you're looking for an engrossing romantic story filled with true-to-life characters and emotional impact, pick up anything by Kristin Billerbeck."
    —Denise Hunter, author

PRAISE FOR GINNY AIKEN'S BOOKS

"Captivating. I became a part of the story as it was unfolding."
    —Jean Klusmeier, Pennsylvania

"Couldn't put it down! Ginny Aiken can tell a good story."
    —Carole McAllaster, California

"Terrific. I laughed and I cried. But mostly, I just fell in love."
    —Kay Allen, Oklahoma

"Wonderful. A novel with heart and soul involved."
    —Shirene Broadwater

"Helped me through a bad time. I needed your wit and fun to help bring me out of it."
    —KG

"Great book—thoroughly enjoyed each page! Easy to read, never slow, great plot."
    —Cyndy Roggeman, Michigan

"Loved your characters. So much heart and emotion, not to mention an engaging story line."
    —M

romance the way it's meant to be

HeartQuest brings you romantic fiction
with a foundation of biblical truth.
Adventure, mystery, intrigue, and suspense
mingle in these heartwarming stories of
men and women of faith striving to build
a love that will last a lifetime.

May HeartQuest books sweep you
into the arms of God, who longs for you
and pursues you always.

A Victorian Christmas Keepsake

CATHERINE PALMER
KRISTIN BILLERBECK
GINNY AIKEN

Romance fiction from
Tyndale House Publishers, Inc., Wheaton, Illinois
www.heartquest.com

Visit Tyndale's exciting Web site at www.tyndale.com

Check out the latest about HeartQuest Books at www.heartquest.com

Behold the Lamb edited by Kathryn S. Olson; *Far above Rubies* edited by Susan D. Lerdal; *Memory to Keep* edited by Ramona Cramer Tucker

Designed by Dean H. Renninger

Sripture quotations are taken from the *Holy Bible*, King James Version.

Scripture quotations are taken from the *Holy Bible*, New Living Translation, copyright © 1996. Used by permission of Tyndale House Publishers, Inc., Wheaton, Illinois 60189. All rights reserved.

Library of Congress Cataloging-in-Publication Data

Palmer, Catherine, date.
  A Victorian Christmas keepsake / Catherine Palmer, Kristin Billerbeck, Ginny Aiken.
   p. cm.
   ISBN 0-8423-3569-2 (pbk.)
   1. Christmas stories, American. 2. Love stories, American. I. Billerbeck, Kristin. II. Aiken, Ginny. III. Title.
PS648.C45 P36 2001
813'.6080334—dc21   2001002236

Printed in the United States of America

07   06   05   04   03   02   01
 9   8   7   6   5   4   3   2   1

CONTENTS

Behold the Lamb

CATHERINE PALMER

For Lindsay McClure . . .
beautiful young lady, dear friend,
and precious goddaughter.
I love you!

*The next day John saw Jesus coming toward him and
said, "Look! There is the Lamb of God who takes
away the sin of the world!"*
JOHN 1:29

PROLOGUE

"I won't forget what you taught me," the boy whispered as he looked up into his father's blue eyes.
Flakes of powdery snow drifted down like confectioner's
sugar, settling on the shoulders of the two figures
crouched in the shadows. Just over the top of an evergreen
hedge, a full moon gleamed as bright and silver as a new
shilling.

"And what did I teach you, Mick?" the father asked.

"That I must never be discovered."

"That's right, lad." The man bent and tousled his son's
thick brown hair. With grimy fingers, he opened a burlap
sack. "Now tell me again—what are we goin' to put in
'ere?"

"Silver forks and knives and spoons. Silver candlesticks.
Silver coins. Silver trays, teapots, and anythin' else we can
find."

"Good lad. Them silver things makes a bit o' noise, they
does, so you must be quiet as a kitten, eh?"

"Yes, Papa." Mick pulled his stockings up over his

3

knees, but an icy chill crept through ragged holes in the knitted wool. "I'm very cold, Papa. I want to go 'ome."

"Soon enough, Mick. But we've come all this way out into the countryside to do our work. Are you ready, my boy?"

"I'm ready, Papa." Mick peered around the corner of the tall hedge and studied the rambling manor house a short distance away. In the moonlight, its pale stonework gleamed a soft silver as it settled deep in the silvery snow. An icy pond stretched out—slick and coated with silver— in front of the manor house, and the boy wondered if rich people made everything they owned from that precious metal.

Shivering, he slipped his hand into his father's warm palm. Though he was proud to be considered old enough to work, Mick knew this was a dangerous business. His father had been home for only a month after serving a two-year sentence in the London gaol. Not long before their father was released, Mick's only brother had been captured by a constable while doing a job at a shop on Regent Street. Barely fifteen, he'd been shipped off to Australia to build a railroad. Mick didn't know if magistrates would send six-year-old boys away on a ship to Australia. But he didn't like the idea at all. He would miss his mummy.

"Now then, lad, you see them bars?" His father whispered the question against Mick's ear as he pointed out the wrought-iron grillwork covering the ground-floor windows. "See the way it curves round there? I want you to slip in through that little space until you're standin' on the windowsill. Then push open the glass pane and let yourself down inside the kitchen. After you make sure nobody's about, I want you to 'urry across and open the door where I'll be waitin'. You understand that, Mick?"

His father gripped his shoulder so tightly that it hurt. The boy nodded, though he didn't see how he was ever going to fit through that tiny space between the iron bars.

"And what did I teach you, Mick? Tell me again."

"Never be discovered." The boy repeated the admonition, silently reminding himself that he must be as quiet as a wee kitten, moving about on soft tiptoes, never making a sound.

"Go on then, lad. That's my boy."

His father gave him a rough shove, and Mick scampered through the snow toward the manor house. As he crouched beside the window, his heartbeat hammered in his head. Papa had assured him the family who owned the house had all gone out to a Christmas party and wouldn't be back until much later. But what if someone were still about? A small child might have stayed behind. Or a cook preparing a pudding for tomorrow's lunch.

Mick leaned his cold cheek against the frigid iron. Through a crack in the glass, he could smell something wonderful. His small, empty stomach gave a loud gurgle, and he caught his breath in fear. Glancing over his shoulder, he saw his father waving him onward.

"Never be discovered," Mick whispered as he slipped one leg through the curved place in the grille. He was going to do better than his brother, he decided. He was not going to be sent away to Australia. He would be so quiet that he would never have to build a railroad across the hot desert far away from his mummy.

Mick worked his other leg through the grille and then edged himself down into the cramped space beside the closed window. Holding his breath, he twisted one arm until it fit through. The other arm took more work. When his elbow bumped against the glass, he stiffened in terror.

If Mick was sent away, who would look after Mummy as she lay in bed coughing and coughing? Who would wipe away the blood with a rag? Who would stir the thin broth and keep coal on the fire? Papa was usually at the Boar's Head Tavern talking about business with his friends, or working his way along the riverfront where he sold his goods. Someone had to look after Mummy.

Taking a determined breath, the boy twisted and turned his head against the iron bars as he tried to pull it through the curve. One of his ears caught on a lump of jagged iron, but it tore loose as his head finally popped free of the bars. Mick imagined showing the wound to his mummy like a badge of honor . She would smile and pat his hand.

Bare fingers against the cold glass, Mick gave the window a gentle push. To his relief, it swung wide. Instantly, the aroma of a hundred magical delights wafted up through the air. The smell of freshly baked bread and apple tarts and roasted turkey and clove-studded ham and things Mick couldn't even name swirled around him like a dream. Catching himself before he exclaimed in wonder, he clung to the wrought-iron grille.

"Never be discovered," he mouthed again. Perched on the windowsill, he spotted a long table just below. A layer of fine, white flour covered the pine surface where a cook had been rolling out dough. Mick knew better than to tread in the flour and then track it across the kitchen floor.

Lowering himself down the wall, he balanced for a moment on the edge of the table and then leaped gingerly to the floor. The cavernous kitchen was dark, save the remains of a fire that glowed brightly in the grate. Though he ached to warm himself, Mick crept across the chilly black-and-white tiles toward the far door.

He was a kitten, he told himself, and far too clever to make noise. Reaching the door, he stood on tiptoe and drew back the bar that held it shut. Like a stealthy black cat, Mick's father appeared suddenly through the opening. He pressed his back flat against the kitchen wall and gave the boy's hair another tousle.

This was wonderful, Mick thought as he followed his father up a steep flight of stairs and past a green curtain of heavy felt. He was a part of the business now! He was doing quite well, too, copying the way his papa walked along the edge of the corridor, staying in the shadows, making not a single sound. They were a team, and soon they would have enough money to buy Mummy some porridge and a blanket. And they would buy a whole sack of coal for the fire. Maybe Mick would even get a new pair of stockings.

"Come in 'ere, now," Papa whispered against the boy's ear as he pulled him into a huge parlor. For a moment,

Mick could only stare, blinking in shock. The whole room was blanketed in warmth and richness. Heavy red velvet curtains hung over the windows, thick patterned carpets covered the floors, and immense tapestries draped the walls. Portraits and landscapes hung by cords from picture rails. Shelves of books stood sentry near the doors. Like the women who spent their evenings in the alleyways near Mick's flat, the furniture lounged about the rooms—brocade settees, wicker chaises, sumptuous chairs, tables covered by layers of silk and taffeta.

"The dinin' room will be that way," Mick's father whispered as he pointed toward a distant door. "I'll collect the silverware and the candlesticks. You stay in 'ere and gather up clocks and snuffboxes and anythin' else you find."

"Silver?" Mick clarified. He wanted to be sure he got it right.

"That's it." His father gave him a grin that sent a thrill of warmth right down to Mick's toes. "You're a good lad."

As his father crept away, Mick began to slip across the parlor in search of things to put in the burlap bag. He found a small silver box on a table, and he dropped it into the sack. Then he spotted a fine clock under a glass dome. Careful to make not a sound, he lifted the dome, gathered the clock into his arm, and set the dome down again. He was doing very well indeed.

On a desk, he found a silver pen. He slipped it into his bag as he stepped toward something silver that seemed to dangle in the moonlight. Stopping before the object, he studied it carefully. Egg-shaped, it was pointed at each end, and it twisted and spun gently in the cool night air. Gingerly, Mick put out his finger and touched the thing. It swung away and then danced back again.

How was this magical thing suspended in midair? Mick took a step back and peered upward into the darkness. As his eyes adjusted, he slowly realized the silver ball was hanging from the branch of a tree. And beside it hung a red ball. And a gold one. Tiny white candles, too, had been balanced on little clips all over the tree. The more Mick looked at the tree, the more he saw. There were strings of cranberries and long strands of crystal beads and tiny paper cutouts of a man with a long, white beard and a red suit.

Mick thought about taking one of the silver balls for his father's sack. Surely that would buy the finest wool blanket in all London. But what if Mick gave a pull and the whole tree fell down? And why did the rich people grow trees in their parlors? And why did they hang silver balls on them? And who was the man in the red suit?

Moving on, Mick found another silver box and a pair of silver scissors lying beside an embroidery hoop. He tucked them into his sack. He was almost back to the main door when he noticed a strange little house sitting on a table.

Mick peered at the house, wondering if tiny people might be living inside it—tiny people with their own silver boxes and parlor trees. As his eyes focused on the shapes, he realized that indeed it was filled with people. But they were only statues carved out of wood and painted in bright colors.

A mummy and a papa stood near a small box filled with hay. Their baby lay on the hay with a white cloth wrapped around him. The child looked sweet and kind, and something inside Mick longed to pick him up and hold him. Next to the mummy and papa stood three kings, who were also looking down at the baby boy. At the other side of the little house, Mick spotted a man carrying a long stick. He was standing next to a donkey and a cow. And right at his feet lay a tiny lamb.

"What did you get, lad?" The voice at Mick's ear nearly startled him into dropping his sack.

"I have silver, Papa."

"Let me see it, then." His father held out the burlap sack and peered into its depths.

"That's a clock," Mick whispered as he pointed out the prize.

"Good boy. And I got me a load of silverware and a couple of candlesticks."

"Can we buy Mummy a blanket now?"

"Aye, we can."

"What about some of that tonic from Mrs. Wiggins? It 'elps Mummy not to cough so much."

"We'll see. I've got to pay off some debts at the Boar's 'ead first." The father stared at his son a moment. "You've done good this time round, Mick. Why don't you choose somethin' for yourself, eh? I'll just take a peek at the master's desk while you decide what you want."

Mick held his breath as he watched his father walk away. Something for himself? A loaf of bread from the kitchen would be nice. Or maybe he should take a soft pillow from the settee. Either one would make his mummy feel better.

But Papa had told him to get something for himself. Mick looked across the parlor at the dark tree in the corner. Wouldn't he be the envy of the alleyway if he brought that silver ball out of his pocket and dangled it in the air for all his chums to see? Starting toward the tree, Mick thought of the boys' faces, their hungry eyes and rough hands. Someone bigger and meaner would take the silver ball away at once.

Across the room, Mick's father was rifling through papers and envelopes, eagerly stuffing some of them down into his bag. Maybe Mick wouldn't take anything from the house. He knew that all the things in the room belonged to the rich people. Even though Papa said the master of the house wouldn't even miss what was gone, Mick couldn't deny how bad he would feel if another boy stole his silver ball.

"Come on then, lad," his father whispered, taking the boy by the shoulder. "Let's go home to your mum, eh?"

Mick nodded, eager to slip back into his mother's arms and give her a warm hug. She would want to hear all about their evening's work. And she would be so proud of Mick—proud that he had not been discovered. But how could he prove he'd actually been inside the manor house? What sort of trophy could he show his mother? He needed more than a tattered ear to prove his bravery.

As his father hurried him toward the door, Mick spotted the strange little house sitting on the table. Again, he felt something pulling him toward the happy baby and his loving family. Pausing, he glanced at the carved figures, wondering if he should take the child. It would feel so good to pull the baby from his pocket now and then and stare down at that sweet face. But how could he take the baby away from its papa and mummy?

And then Mick's focus fell on the lamb. Small and gentle, it gleamed a silvery white in the moonlight. Legs tucked comfortably beneath it, the lamb lay curled on the table. It seemed to be smiling at Mick.

"Don't dawdle, lad!" his father hissed, giving his arm a jerk.

As he stumbled forward, Mick shot out his hand and grabbed the lamb. It fit perfectly into his tight, hot fist, and he clenched it with the thrill of possession. He followed his father down the long corridor and past the green felt curtain. He followed him across the kitchen with its sumptuous aromas. And he followed him through the door out into the snowy night.

As they staggered through the deep snow, across the lawn toward the hedge that rimmed the lane, Mick tucked the lamb deep into the pocket of his ragged shirt. The lamb proved that he was brave and smart. It showed that he had not been discovered, and he never would be. It was his own lamb now. His treasure. And no one would ever take it away.

CHAPTER ONE

"*P*apa, the post has arrived," Rosalind Treadwell called down the corridor of the two-story stone cottage. She set her tea tray on a niche table near the front door and picked up the three letters left earlier by a message boy. A smile crept across her lips as she read the name scrawled on a large yellowed envelope. "Lord Remington has written. Papa, you've had a letter from Sir Arthur!"

Her father, Lord Buxton, appeared in the corridor, his maroon, paisley-print dressing gown hanging to his ankles. "Has the post arrived, Rosalind?" he shouted. "Have I had a letter from Arthur?"

"Yes, Papa! I have it here." Setting the mail on the tea tray, Rosalind shook her head. Her father was growing more hard of hearing by the day. The doctor had recommended the purchase of an amplifying ear trumpet. But Lord Buxton refused to consider the extravagant expense. He informed his daughter that the horn would be a nuisance, and it would make him look foolish besides.

Rosalind felt she would far rather sit beside the fire and have a nice chat with her father—no matter how foolish he looked with an ear trumpet—than shout back and forth to him all day long. She lifted the tray and hurried back down the long hallway toward the drawing room. The autumn chill had crept along the uncarpeted granite floors of the old house, and she found herself wishing she had worn wool stockings.

"Where is Moss?" Lord Buxton grumbled as his daughter carried their morning tea into the room. "Why have you brought the tea? Didn't I ring for Moss? I'm certain I did."

"This is Tuesday, Papa," Rosalind said loudly. "Mrs. Moss always visits her son on Tuesdays."

"And she leaves you to bring the tea? That is a dreadful situation. Appalling." The elderly viscount seated himself in his chair beside the crackling fire and stretched out his legs. His long white nightgown barely covered his thin ankles, and the soles of his house slippers were worn through. "I wonder if the post has arrived. Did you think to look on the niche table in the corridor, my dear?"

Settling into the chair across from her father, Rosalind handed him the three envelopes. "You've had a letter from Sir Arthur."

"Aha. And I shall tell you who wrote these letters directly. Now let me see, let me see." He dug his spectacles from the pocket of his dressing gown and set them on his nose. "By george, I've had a letter from Arthur at last! And this one is from our barrister, Mr. Linley. Oh, dear, I hope it's not bad news."

Rosalind sighed as she poured the steaming tea into their cups. When Mr. Linley wrote, it was *always* bad news. Through a series of disastrous events, the estate had fallen on very hard times. Lord Buxton had been forced to sell off much of the land that had been in his family for generations. After his wife's death, he had moved his only child out of the grand manor house and into a large gamekeeper's cottage nearby, which was easier to heat and didn't require as many servants. Not many months ago, he had been compelled to discharge the whole staff save Mrs. Moss, the housekeeper, who had been with the family since her own childhood. Rosalind feared it would not be long before Mr. Linley suggested they sell the paintings and statuary that were all that remained of the Buxton wealth and legacy.

"I can't make out this name," Lord Buxton said, passing his daughter a small white envelope. "The hand is quite ill formed, don't you think? Obviously not an Eton boy. We were taught good penmanship in my day. Well, what does it say?"

Rosalind studied the writing. "He's got your title right, anyway, Papa. The Right Honorable the Viscount Buxton."

"Good, good." Her father was opening the letter from his oldest and dearest friend. "I wonder what Artie has to say. I hope his gout hasn't got the better of him."

"Papa, do you know a Sir Michael Stafford? A baronet from London?"

"Oh, dear. He's been unable to go to his club since Thursday last. The doctor gives him little hope for a reprieve. Poor Artie."

Rosalind opened the baronet's letter. "Shall I read this aloud, Papa?"

"Indeed, my dear. I shall take a cup of tea and say a prayer for poor Arthur. Gout. How very distressing."

"'My lord,'" Rosalind read as loudly as she could without shouting. "'I trust this letter finds you in good health. I pray the enclosed introduction from your friend, Lord Remington—'"

"Remington? Does this chap know Artie?"

"Apparently so, Papa. Sir Arthur has written him an introduction." She handed her father the note. Before he could interrupt again, she skimmed the remainder of the letter. "He wishes to come and meet you."

"Artie? But he's laid up with gout. Can't even get to his club, poor chap."

"Not Sir Arthur. The baronet, Sir Michael Stafford. He has written that he will arrive on Tuesday morning—" She caught her breath. "But that is today! He comes from London today, Papa. And you are in your dressing gown."

"Arthur has gout, my dear," her father pronounced very clearly, as though it were his daughter who was hard of hearing. "He cannot travel. I'm quite sure of it. There must be some mistake."

Rosalind let out her breath and took the introduction from her father's lap. "Lord Remington has written that Sir Michael Stafford is a man of excellent repute, vast wealth, and prominent social connection. He owns a stocking factory in Manchester and a lace manufactory in

Nottingham. He is a fine gentleman and most worthy of our acquaintance."

"Hurry with our paintings, did you say?"

"No, *worthy* of our . . . oh, read it yourself, Papa!" Exasperated, Rosalind put the letter in her father's hands and stood up. "How can we be expected to entertain this man today? Moss is away, and you are in your dressing gown, and we've only enough coal to keep one fire lit. The parlor is far too cold, and Papa, you're still wearing your nightcap. It's ten o'clock in the morning!"

"Clearly a parvenu," the viscount announced, setting the letter on the tea tray. "Baronet, ha! This Sir Michael Stafford most assuredly got his title by loaning someone a good deal of money. A peer, no doubt. Perhaps a royal. Shame the way things are going these days. Factory owners buying titles. Great houses falling to ruin. Where is Moss? This tea is quite cold, Rosalind, and you know how I feel about cold tea."

"Papa, you must take off your nightcap!" Rosalind reached for the offending item just as the knocker sounded at the front door. "Oh no, that will be the baronet, and we shall make a spectacle of ourselves. What if he has brought his wife? She'll tell everyone in London, and . . . oh, me!"

"Hot tea? Yes, indeed, that would be lovely, my dear." The viscount held out his cup. "Do you suppose Moss has returned from visiting her son?"

Rosalind grabbed the white cotton cap from her father's head and tugged the edges of his dressing gown together. "Sir Michael Stafford is here!" she shouted. "Sir Michael!"

Trying to suppress the edge of panic that rose inside her chest, she smoothed down her skirt as she hurried out of the drawing room. Although this man might be just a parvenu who had bought himself a title, he was a baronet all the same. He was a guest, too, and they hadn't had a visitor at Bridgeton Cottage in many months. Moss would not be back until this afternoon, and that meant Rosalind had only stale biscuits to offer, and even worse—the tea was cold!

Glancing at her reflection in a mirror as she raced for the door, Rosalind let out a groan. At best, her mass of curly brown hair was difficult to manage. Today, with the threat of rain, it positively had a life of its own. She pinched her cheeks, hoping to put some color into them, and turned the doorknob.

The gentleman standing in the morning mist might have stepped from an illustration in one of Rosalind's favorite novels. A dashing prince perhaps. Or a nobleman from some far-off land. Tall, elegantly dressed in a black frock coat, a white shirt, and a bright red ascot, he swept his top hat from his head. Thick, dark hair framed the bluest eyes Rosalind had ever seen. He had an aristocratic nose, finely formed lips, and a smile that seemed almost heavenly.

"Good morning," he addressed her, extending a gray-gloved hand to present his engraved card. "Sir Michael Stafford, at your service."

"Oh," was all she could manage.

"I have an appointment with Lord Buxton."

"I see, but . . ." She took the card. "But Lord Buxton is . . . he is occupied at the moment."

"Then I shall be pleased to wait for him in the parlor. Will you be so good as to show me in?"

Before Rosalind could move, the man stepped around her and walked straight into the front room. She covered her cheeks with her hands for a moment, imagining what he must think of the frigid parlor with its tattered curtains and empty fireplace. Had the room even been dusted in years?

"Sir Michael," she said, coming up behind him, "I'm afraid this is not a good day for a visit."

"Why not?" he swung around, eyeing her in mild displeasure. "I sent word of my arrival some time ago. Please inform your master that I have come."

"Yes, sir. Of course." Mortified, Rosalind hurried out of the room and raced down the hall to the drawing room, where her father waited. Sir Michael believed she was a housekeeper! Oh, it might as well be true.

In the past years of hardship, she had lost all hope of marriage and a family of her own. Nearly thirty now, she had learned to take joy in serving her aging father's needs, playing the small pianoforte in the parlor, and reading the countless books that had been carted over from the manor house library. Rosalind knew she would end an old maid, sitting by the fire with Moss or some other helper at her elbow. If only she could be allowed that peaceful existence. Instead, she must bear the humiliation of displaying her father's poverty before this handsome man who had so much money that he had bought himself a title.

"Papa," she cried as she burst into the drawing room. "He is here! Sir Michael Stafford has come. He wishes to speak to you. You must send a message telling him to go away. You must tell him you cannot see him today."

"Did you bring the hot tea, my dear?" Her father smiled peaceably. "If you will pop the cozy over the pot, I shall read you the letter from Arthur. He describes his gout in great detail. Such a dreadful situation. Do you know he cannot even go to his club?"

"Sir Michael Stafford!" Rosalind shouted at her father. "Stafford! He has come!"

"Thank you very kindly for the introduction, madam." The man himself strolled into the room and gave her a polite nod. Then he pointed to the mail on the tea table. "Lord Buxton, I see you received my letter. I trust it finds you in good health."

The viscount stood from his chair and gave his visitor a bow. "Stafford, is it? You know Lord Remington, I take it. Sir Arthur is a very good friend of mine. School chum, actually. Eton."

"Yes, sir. His son, William, is my closest companion."

"Aha." The viscount glanced at Rosalind for assistance.

"He knows Lord Remington's son!" she said, leaning toward him.

"Very good, very good. Do sit down, will you, Sir Michael?" Her father settled back into his chair, seemingly unaware that his white nightgown was showing again. "As you can see, we're a bit at sixes and sevens this morning. The housekeeper has gone out to visit her son, and the tea is quite cold. Rosalind, will you fetch another pot, please? There's a good girl."

Sliding the tea tray from the table between the two men, Rosalind stole another glance at Sir Michael. Well, he might be handsome, but he was also very proud. He stared past her as if she didn't exist, his attention focused wholly on her father. What the man thought he could get out of Lord Buxton only he and God knew.

As she carried the tea tray down to the kitchen, Rosalind realized that, in fact, God was the one she must turn to in this situation. In all her rush, had she thought to address him? In the midst of the humiliation born of her own selfish pride, had she considered her heavenly Father's will?

Repentant, Rosalind stood beside the kitchen stove and closed her eyes. God had given her a job to do. In the years since her mother's death, her father's health had withered. Rosalind's only desire was to take care of the man who had given her life and home and security. Tattered curtains and dusty mantelpieces did not matter. A dearth of servants and parties and carriages did not matter. And handsome young baronets certainly did not matter.

"Father, forgive me," she prayed softly as the kettle began to sing. "It doesn't matter that Sir Michael believes I'm a servant, because in truth, I am. I am your servant, Lord, and I want to do whatever you ask of me."

As Rosalind carried the tray down the corridor, she felt a sense of peace settle over her heart. She remembered that she had long since made her peace with the path God had set before her. Her introduction into high society had been

21

brief and of little consequence, and she had learned that the privileges of wealth mattered not at all. What counted was family.

"India!" Sir Michael was shouting as Rosalind pushed open the parlor door. "I was brought up in India! By my uncle!"

Smiling, she set the tray on the table again. At least the man was a quick learner. It hadn't taken him long to realize he'd get nowhere using his practiced and gentlemanly tone of speaking. Setting out two fresh cups, she poured the tea and then stepped aside to let the poor man bellow his mission.

"India, did you say?" The viscount stirred a lump of sugar into his tea. "Silk and spices, eh? Tea and curry. The Raj and all that."

"Yes, sir!"

"And how did you meet Lord Remington, my boy? I don't recall Arthur was ever in India. No, I'm quite sure of it."

"Actually, I met his son at a party."

"Artie?" The viscount nodded. "Yes, indeed, Artie was my old schoolmate at Eton. A fine chap, hails from Devonshire, but I'm sure you knew that. By george, we had some jolly good times together, Artie and I. And how did you happen to meet Lord Remington?"

Rosalind feigned disinterest as she watched Sir Michael shift uncomfortably in his chair. The baronet clearly had a mission in coming to Bridgeton Cottage, but would he ever manage to accomplish it?

"Artie and I used to slide down the steps on a silver tray," Lord Buxton said. "Good fun, eh? No, you could never have a warmer pair of chums than Artie and I. Well, with connections like that, my boy, you are in a fine position. Anyone who is a friend of Lord Remington is a friend of mine."

Beaming, he took a sip of tea and smiled at his guest. The baronet attempted a returning grin. By now his face was slightly flushed, and the tips of his ears had gone bright red.

"Lord Buxton," he said loudly, and then he cleared his throat. "Lord Buxton, I have come to speak with you about a personal matter."

"Personal, eh? Well, then, go on, go on."

The young man set down his teacup and adjusted his cravat. Then he leaned forward and shouted at the top of his lungs, "I have come to ask for your daughter's hand in marriage!"

Rosalind let out a gasp and sank onto the nearest settee. For a moment, she couldn't breathe. Certain she would faint, she grabbed the table next to her and clung to it for dear life.

"Marriage!" the man repeated, his blue eyes fixed on the viscount. "My lord, I will speak plainly. I have arrived at a time in my life when I feel it is prudent to select a wife. Lord Remington informed me that according to the original grant from the king, your estate and your title may fall to any of your heirs, whether male or female. Although I am landed and have a large fortune to my name, I have no family home nor any title that can be passed down. I propose, therefore, to marry your daughter, providing your estate with ample financial support and ensuring the continuation of your family's legacy."

Rosalind brushed a hand across her forehead. She had to breathe. She really must breathe!

"Do you understand me, Lord Buxton?" the young man shouted.

The viscount held up his hands, waving them slightly before his face. "I understand; I understand. You want my estate and my title for your heirs. In exchange, you will provide the comfort and social standing my daughter has never known."

"That is correct, sir."

"Well, it's quite a scheme, isn't it?"

"I prefer to think of it as an arrangement, sir. An arrangement for the benefit of both parties."

"Artie, eh? Good old Artie approves of it, does he? I suppose so, or he wouldn't have written the introduction." The viscount shook his head. "You'll have to give me a bit of time to think it over, of course. Could you come back next year, sir? Perhaps in the spring?"

"Next year? I have taken a room at the village inn, Lord Buxton. I planned to return for your answer tomorrow morning."

"No!" Rosalind cried, coming to her feet. "No, Sir Michael, you cannot come back tomorrow, and no, I shall not marry you. You must go away at once, sir, and never come here again!"

24

"I beg your pardon?" The man stood. "Who are you? But I thought you were—"

"I am Miss Rosalind Treadwell, daughter of Lord Buxton, and we are quite happy without your offer of wealth and social standing. Our lives here are most content, sir, and I assure you an arranged marriage to a perfect stranger would suit neither my father nor myself."

Sir Michael stared at her, his blue eyes blazing. He said nothing for so long that Rosalind began to worry that her manners had been perceived as utterly deplorable. She cleared her throat.

"We do thank you, of course, Sir Michael," she said. "Certainly your intentions were honorable. And we do trust that your journey back to London will be—"

"Pardon my bluntness, but you live in a gamekeeper's cottage, Miss Treadwell." The man took a step toward her. "You have one fire burning, no household staff, and cold tea. How dare you refuse to consider my proposal?"

She felt as though she had been slapped. Anger flickered to life inside her. "I turn you away very easily, sir. Our circumstances are not so desperate as to compel us to throw our fortunes into the arms of a man we do not even know."

"Your circumstances are more than desperate, Miss Treadwell. Your family estate has been sold away piece-meal. Your family home lies crumbling to dust. You have no reason to hope for a future that includes anything but empty hearths and empty stomachs and cold tea."

"The tea is hot, sir!" Rosalind clenched her jaw. She

didn't like this man, didn't like his determination to rub her face in her poverty. If he were any sort of a gentleman, he would do all in his power to make her feel at ease.

"Yes, it is hot," he said, "because *you* went to the kitchen, and *you* heated the water, and *you* made the tea."

"Mrs. Moss is out."

"Miss Treadwell, I have come here to offer you the service of a hundred Mrs. Mosses and the pleasure of hot tea at the barest nod of your head. I offer you fine silk dresses, blazing fires, a feast at every meal, and shawls that do not have holes in them."

"Oh!" Rosalind covered the offending patch on the shawl she was wearing. "You, sir, are very rude."

"I am very reasonable, Miss Treadwell, and I cannot fathom why you refuse to be the same."

"Because I do not wish for wealth."

"And what do you wish for?"

"For a quiet life with my father. And I have that already."

He glanced at the chair where the elderly viscount sat studying the situation through his spectacles. "Miss Treadwell, your father is the rightful heir to a grand estate, and he is entitled to the company of fine society. Do you love him so little that you would keep him in a gamekeeper's cottage in his dressing gown?"

"He is happy here."

"Would he not be happier in the company of his friend, Lord Remington? Would he not be happier with a roaring fire, warm clothing, and a good meal in his stomach? I have the means to provide your father with everything to which he is entitled—and more. I can restore the family home, fill the stables with the best horses, buy back much of the land that was sold away, and ensure that his line continues. You can have no possible objection to such a plan, Miss Treadwell."

Rosalind studied her father. He would indeed enjoy the company of old friends. He deserved good medical care and comfort in his waning years. But to trust their future to a complete stranger? What if this man had some wicked aim behind his proposal? He spoke temptingly, but what did they know of him? Nothing. Absolutely nothing.

"I do have an objection to your plan, Sir Michael," she said. "Were my aim in life the attainment of money and position, I would find your offer impossible to refuse. But I long ago gave up all hope of those things. My only wish is to serve my father. I cannot be certain that your proposal would benefit him."

"Why not?" he exploded. "I have told you what I will do for your father, and I have every intention of—"

"We do not know you, sir."

"You have a letter of introduction from Lord Remington. I can provide fifty more letters that would say the same of me. I am reputable, honorable, held in high regard in polite society."

"But we do not *know* you." She glanced down at her hands for a moment before lifting her head and meeting his eyes. "*I* do not know you, sir."

"But familiarity is the inevitable result of marriage, is it not? You will learn that I like roast goose, and that I prefer to go calling on Thursdays, and that I do not enjoy playing at cards. You will come to know me in time, and I shall know you."

"That is not the sort of thing I long to know about a husband. Before I could commit my father's legacy and my own future into any man's hands, I would hope to know him far more intimately."

"I do not wish to be known intimately."

"And why is that?"

"Because . . . it is not my desire."

He looked uncomfortable for the first time, and Rosalind wondered if she had discovered his single area of vulnerability. Sir Michael Stafford had built himself wealth and power and esteem. He had purchased a title. By marriage to her, he planned to gain a legacy and heirs. Around himself he had constructed an impressive edifice of prestige.

But who lived inside that edifice? What sort of man was he? And most important: why was he so determined to keep himself hidden?

"In consideration of the fact that you have proposed a business connection between our two families, I am certain you cannot object to an interview," Rosalind said, moving toward him across the thin carpet. "Are your parents living, Sir Michael? Have you brothers and sisters?"

"I have no family. My parents died when I was quite young, and I was sent to India to live with my uncle. When he passed away, I was left a small inheritance upon which I built my fortune. All of this is common knowledge."

"And whom do you love the most in this world, sir?"

"Love? Well, I have many friends and acquaintances." He ran a finger around the inside of his collar. "I enjoy an active social life."

"What is your greatest dream?"

"I've told you, have I not? An estate, a title that can be passed down to a son."

"Do you like children, Sir Michael?"

"Well, certainly. Of course I do. Not to mention that I own seven dogs—three Irish wolfhounds, two spaniels, and two setters."

Rosalind moved closer. "Are you a Christian?"

"Of course I'm a Christian. Everyone in England is a Christian. What sort of a question is that?" He took a deep breath. "Miss Treadwell, I can assure you, you have nothing to fear. Marry me, and you and your father will live in luxury and contentment for the rest of your days."

"Do you believe contentment arises from luxury, sir?"

"Of course it does. Poverty cannot bring happiness."

"Neither can wealth."

"My money has brought me a great deal of happiness."

"Has it?" Standing in front of him, she looked into his eyes—his disconcerting blue eyes. His noble stature and dashing elegance made her long to trust him. But she saw that his eyes belied his words. "True joy arises out of love, Sir Michael. Love for God. Love for family. Love for friends. I am happy already. You cannot give me that."

He stared at her. "I see I was mistaken in coming here.

I believed you would welcome my offer. Forgive me, Miss Treadwell. I wish you well."

"Good day, Sir Michael."

Rosalind steadied herself with a hand on the table as he turned away and started across the room. She had done the right thing, she knew. A life with a proud, unfeeling man who loved no one and wanted nothing of intimacy could bring only misery. She and her father would be warm and comfortable enough without his wealth. They could sell a statue and live for at least a year on the proceeds.

"Worked things out, have you?" Lord Buxton said as Sir Michael passed the fireplace. "Settled the details?"

"I beg your pardon, sir?" The man paused.

"The marriage to Rosalind. Have you set a date?"

"Your daughter will not have me, Lord Buxton. She prefers to continue her life with you in this cottage. My offer holds no interest for her."

"What? What are you saying, my good man? Speak up."

"She will not marry me!" he shouted.

"Oh yes she will." The viscount rounded on his daughter. "Won't marry him? What sort of nonsense is this, Rosalind? You most certainly will marry him."

"But, Papa, we know nothing about this man!"

"Artie recommends him highly. Brought up in India, what? A perfectly fine gentleman and the only offer of marriage you're likely to get." He grasped the lapels of his dressing gown. "My dear girl, do you think I would allow you to pass up the opportunity to better your circumstances? I love you far too much to deprive you of what you deserve. No, indeed, you shall marry this man, and the sooner the better."

He turned to Sir Michael and took him by the hand. "Grand idea, young man. Good scheme—provides the best for all of us. Well done, well done. Congratulations."

The baronet eyed Rosalind. She stared back at him, praying that he would walk away.

"I shall leave for London tomorrow," he said. "My carriage will arrive here at ten sharp to collect you both. I shall arrange for a coach to collect your luggage and transport your lady's maid."

"We have a housekeeper," Rosalind said. "I do not employ a lady's maid."

"You do now." Sir Michael gave her a smile. "Good day, Lord Buxton. Good day, Miss Treadwell."

CHAPTER TWO

S ir Michael Stafford studied his future wife as she sat across the carriage from him. During the entire journey to London, she had been staring out the window, and to his knowledge, she had not deigned to look at him a single time. Annoying, Stafford thought, for he was generally regarded as a rather good-looking chap. Any number of women batted their eyes at him or dropped their handkerchiefs in his path. Messages hinting at an interest in marriage had even been passed along to his friend, Sir William Cooper, the son of Lord Remington.

Did Miss Treadwell really find him so odious? And if so, why?

Stafford surveyed the turn of the woman's chin, the tilt of her nose, and the gaze of her large, gray eyes. She was pretty enough. Actually, she could be called lovely. But that did not give her any reason to put on airs. In fact, she had every reason to be humbly grateful to him for his proposal. Giddy with happiness. She was a poor woman with no prospects. He was bringing her wealth, society, family, a future. Yet, for all the regard she gave him, he might as well have gone to that gamekeeper's cottage with an insult!

"What a fair prospect," Lord Buxton remarked, looking out at the city through his own window. "London has always pleased me. I especially enjoy the parks. Did you say we would be staying in Grosvenor Square, Sir Michael?"

"Indeed, my lord. You and your daughter have been invited to lodge with Sir William Cooper and his wife during the weeks before the wedding. My own residence is not far."

"And you tell me Sir William is the son of my dear friend, Lord Remington? This is a happy connection." He reached over and patted his daughter on the hand. "Artie's son is Sir Michael's chum, Rosalind. Now, what do you make of that?"

For the first time since they had set off from Bridgeton Cottage that morning, she turned her focus on Stafford. "How very fortunate for you, sir. I'm sure you have taken full advantage of your association with that family."

"I beg your pardon?" he said. "I certainly—"

"Now then, Rosalind," Lord Buxton spoke up. "You are very dispirited today, my dear. Here we are driving into London, and you have not remarked on anything during the whole journey. This is quite unlike you."

"I have nothing to say, Papa. I think only of Bridgeton and of all that we have left behind us."

"A little kindness, did you say?"

"No, Papa. *Behind us.*"

"Indeed, you really should be kinder, my dear. Sir Michael has done us a great service with this plan of his. I had something of the sort in mind myself once, but nothing came of it. I have been thinking that a Christmas wedding would be nice. Your mama would approve, I daresay. Such a date would give you time to select your trousseau and to be introduced to your future husband's acquaintances. But it would not give you so much time that you could change your mind."

"I believe your daughter's mind is not at all settled on marriage, Lord Buxton," Stafford said.

"On the contrary, Sir Michael," the young woman spoke up. "My mind is perfectly settled on the matter. Marriage is the last thing I desire. I have no wish to wed a stranger and no anticipation of a happy future with a man who plainly states that he does not intend to be known by anyone, including his wife."

"Greater knowledge of me will not ensure your happiness in marriage, Miss Treadwell."

"Why is that, sir? Do you keep secrets that would displease me?"

Stafford glanced away. "Every man has secrets, has he not? But, of course, that is not what I meant. A wife's happiness cannot depend upon her husband himself, but rather upon the things he can provide her. Is that not true?"

When he looked at Rosalind again, he could see that her eyes were filled with distress. "My joy comes from within, Sir Michael. From my Christian faith and the hope that it promises. As for happiness . . . I had wished . . . long ago

. . . for a husband, children, a family. I believed that those cherished relationships might bring with them a great measure of happiness. But never have I desired a husband for the things he could provide. Never have I believed that objects could make me happy. And your statement merely illustrates the vast gulf that separates us."

Vast gulf, indeed! Stafford picked up his hat as the carriage turned onto Grosvenor Square and began to slow near the home of the Cooper family. This wife he had chosen was proving herself to be more than a little difficult, he realized. He had expected the woman to be quiet and grateful and obedient. Instead she seemed to have an opinion on everything he said or did—and none of her opinions were favorable.

His thoughts flashed back in time to the sight of his mother lying on her bed, a thankful smile on her face as she cradled some object her husband had brought. A silver teapot always made his mother happy. Even a saltcellar or a small silver box brought her great joy. She never complained at a lack of "cherished relationships." What utter nonsense this Rosalind Treadwell spoke.

As the carriage came to a stop, Stafford suddenly saw through to the heart of the problem. Clearly, Miss Treadwell had spent her life too far from good society. She had never known the pleasures of a fine silk gown, servants ready at the tip of a head, or a jewelry box filled with rubies, emeralds, and diamonds. Instead she took happiness in doting upon her aged father and reading the myriad books she had insisted on bringing with them to

London. She believed her Christian faith could bring her joy. What—trudging to church at Christmas and Easter so that one could be seen doing the appropriate thing? What joy could that bring?

No, Rosalind Treadwell did not understand what her future husband had promised her, and therefore she could not possibly appreciate him. So, it would be up to Stafford to teach her the true delights the world had to offer.

"Sir Michael Stafford," the footman intoned as he opened the carriage door. "Welcome to London, sir."

"Yes, indeed. London." Stafford climbed down from the carriage and turned to offer Miss Treadwell his hand. "I trust this will be the beginning of a pleasant new life for you, one in which the two of us will find common ground for amiability and contentment."

She set one gloved hand in his and lifted her skirt with the other as she stepped down onto the street. As she drew her hand away, she met his eyes. "I am determined, sir, to obey my father. I am, therefore, resigned to do my best at making you a good wife. In the coming weeks, I shall try to learn to like you. Failing that, I shall tolerate the situation as duty requires."

As she walked past him toward the grand house, Stafford could feel his jaw drop open. Try to learn to like him? Tolerate the situation? By all that was right, he should pack her into the carriage and send her back to her beloved cottage. How could anyone in her right mind take pleasure in such misery? And how could she find only misery in the great pleasures he had promised her through marriage?

"Stafford!" Sir William Cooper stepped out of a clarence that had stopped just behind the carriage. "What a pleasant surprise. We did not expect you until tomorrow. Lady Cooper and I have just been calling on my father."

Stafford's closest friend fairly bounded down the street toward the party that had just arrived from the country. His petite wife hurried along behind him, her cheeks pink with excitement.

"Sir Michael, you have accomplished your mission in record time!" she cried. "And what did I tell you? Did I not assure you the young lady would be delighted to accept your offer? Where is she? We must meet her at once!"

"Come, my good man, where is your blushing bride?" Lord Cooper and his wife peered into the depths of the carriage, as if in anticipation of discovering Cinderella herself.

"She is . . . over there." Stafford tapped his friend on the shoulder and gestured toward the young woman who waited with her father near the door. "Lord Buxton, Miss Treadwell, may I present Lord and Lady Cooper?"

"Pleasure, my good man!" Lord Buxton beamed at the pair. "And am I to understand that you are the son of my dear friend Lord Remington?"

"Indeed, sir. My father speaks very highly of you."

"And how is Arthur these days?"

"Not well, I'm afraid. Gout has all but incapacitated him."

"Wonderful, wonderful!" Lord Buxton clapped the man

on the back. "I shall go and call on him as soon as possible. Good old Artie. What times we had together at Eton!"

"My father does not hear well," Miss Treadwell said softly. "I beg you to excuse him."

"But of course!" Lady Cooper took her visitor by the arm and led her into the marbled foyer. "We shall all speak up when addressing him, shall we not, William? My husband adores his father, and I know he will do anything to assure the comfort and ease of Lord Buxton. Do permit the valet to see him to his room, where he might rest after such an arduous journey." She waved at a liveried man standing at the ready. "Jones, please see Lord Buxton to his rooms."

As her father was led away, Miss Treadwell gave the woman a smile. "Thank you so much, Lady Cooper."

"Don't mention it! We are delighted to have you with us, Miss Treadwell. I can promise you that William and Mick spent hours poring over the prospects—but your name was never dislodged from the top of the list, almost as if God himself had placed it there."

"Mick?" Miss Treadwell asked.

"Sir Michael, of course. Didn't he tell you? That's what his closest acquaintances call him."

The women entered the morning parlor and began divesting themselves of hats and shawls. Stafford handed his hat and greatcoat to a servant, though he felt he would like nothing more than to abandon the company and take his horse out into the countryside for a long ride. His life had been a carefully calculated series of moves along the road toward wealth and distinction. Had he now taken a wrong turn that could not be rectified?

"First we shall take tea with the men," Lady Cooper was saying as she seated herself near Miss Treadwell. "And after you've had a bit of a rest, we shall set out for town to visit my favorite milliner's shop. I am planning to host an engagement party for you and Mick within the fortnight, and you must have a new hat and gown for the occasion. You will not believe the hats at this shop! They are magnificent, Miss Treadwell. Oh, may I call you Rosalind? I feel as if we are dear friends already!"

"Of course."

"And you must call me Caroline. William, is she not the most beautiful creature?"

"Indeed, my dear. And that makes two of you gracing our home."

A peal of delighted giggles greeted the servants as they brought in trays of tea, cakes, steaming scones, clotted cream, strawberry jam, and tiny ham sandwiches. Stafford tried to concentrate on all of the company rather than on the silent young lady who sat across from him.

"Come now, Mick," Lady Cooper said when everyone had been served. "You must tell us all about your journey. Was Rosalind not surprised? Was she not utterly shocked to be made such an offer? And to such mutual advantage!"

Stafford sat back and gave his tea a stir. "*Shocked* might be the correct word to describe her reaction. Though I believe the arrangement has been agreed to without her acknowledgment of its mutual advantage."

"Whatever can you mean?" Lady Cooper turned to Miss Treadwell. "Are you not pleased, Rosalind, my dear? Is Mick not the most charming and handsome man you have ever laid eyes upon?"

Miss Treadwell gave him an inscrutable glance. "I would prefer to know his heart."

"His heart!" She laughed. "But women fairly swoon at his feet."

"Miss Treadwell is not enamored with the notion of an arranged marriage," Stafford explained. "She feels she cannot be happy, because she does not *know* me."

"But surely you have informed her of your merits," William said. "Brought up in India, left the legacy of a small fortune by your late uncle, educated at Cambridge. You have told her about your businesses, have you not? My dear Miss Treadwell, your future husband owns factories in Manchester and Nottingham, and he is connected with the highest—"

"Yes, he told me." She gave him a small smile. "Indeed, I am well aware of his excellent reputation. My father wishes his familial line to continue, of course, and Sir Michael's kind offer provides the means for that. As I have told them, I am willing to do my duty in this matter."

"Your duty?" Lady Cooper frowned for the first time. "But dear Rosalind, you will be so happy in this match. Did Mick not tell you about his London house—more than twice as large as this one? And he has leased a grand estate in the country where we enjoy the most marvelous parties."

"Miss Treadwell does not care for fine houses and parties," Stafford said. "She takes her joy from religion alone."

"And my happiness from many quarters, Sir Michael. I assure you, it is not the prospect of living well that dismays me. Rather it is the thought of a future without the joy of true familial companionship. To know and to be known . . . I believe this forms the foundation of a blessed and fulfilling marriage. I cannot welcome the thought of living with a man I am forbidden to know."

"Know?" Lady Cooper stood. "But what is there about him that you do not know already?"

"I do not know anything about him other than that he owns seven dogs and two fine houses, and he believes that joy derives from the accumulation of objects and from one's place in society. I do not know his passions— what makes him weep or laugh, what brings him night- mares, what gives his heart wings, what secrets he hides, or what dreams he cherishes. I do not know to what he has given himself heart and soul. How am I to be a wife—bone of his bone and flesh of his flesh— when he is but a stranger to me and has made it clear that he wishes to remain such for the duration of our marriage?"

Lady Cooper sat down again on the settee and gazed at her husband. Sir William stared back at his wife. Finally, she cleared her throat.

"Surely you are aware, my dear Rosalind, that marriage

is most commonly born of necessity. In time, a certain fondness may develop between husband and wife. Children are born, and this solidifies the bond of mutual affection. Perhaps the sort of blissful communion you dream of may become a possibility, but it is never required, and it is not to be expected."

Stafford watched as his future wife absorbed this information. He was relieved that his friends had so clearly expressed the truth about marriage. And yet, there had been something strangely compelling in Miss Treadwell's impassioned plea. Her face softened, and she gave a nod. "You are right, of course, Caroline. But I have never longed for mere fondness and mutual affection. I can share those emotions with a favored rat terrier."

"Terrier? Upon my word, Miss Treadwell, I am more than a dog." Stafford set down his teacup and leaned forward on the settee. "I am a gentleman, and I shall not be regarded as anything less."

"Of course," she said.

"I have come to believe that this woman has been away from enlightened company far too long." Stafford addressed his friends, while nodding at his intended. "She has read too many books and has looked after her father for so long that she does not know the true pleasures life has to offer. Rather than take her comments as an insult, I am determined to take them as a challenge."

"Good show," William said. "Bravo, my dear man. You intend to share your heart with her, then. To make of your wife a true soul mate."

"A soul mate? Of course not. I intend to shower her with every luxury that life has to offer, to so overwhelm her with the pleasures of wealth and fine company that she abandons her silly notions of becoming bone of my bone and flesh of my flesh. Whatever that means."

"Aha." William glanced across at Miss Treadwell. "There you are, then. You have set him a challenge, and I have never known Mick to fail at any challenge. Your husband will give you everything your heart desires, and you will become truly the happiest of wives."

"Thank you, I'm sure." The woman herself rose from the settee. "I shall ask the servant to show me to my quarters now, Lady Cooper," she said in a soft voice.

"But have you no response to Mick's plan?"

"He already knows I do not respond well to plans or schemes," she said. "If a husband of mine wishes to give me my heart's desire, he has only to provide me with one thing."

"And what is that, my dear girl?" Caroline asked.

"Love," Rosalind replied. She gave the party a curtsy. "His true, abiding love. Good afternoon, Lord and Lady Cooper, Sir Michael. Caroline, I shall be ready to visit your millinery shop within the hour."

✳ ✳ ✳

"Is this not the most divine color?" Lady Caroline Cooper smoothed a hand over her silk evening gown, two weeks later, as the two prepared for the promised engagement party. "I have never seen a purple of quite this shade, have you, Rosalind?"

"Indeed, I believe that in these past two weeks, I have seen every possible hue of purple available in London's shops." She sat before the mirror as her lady's maid arranged a decoration of blue ribbons and tiny white roses in her curls. "But it is a lovely gown, Caroline, and I greatly admire the sleeves."

"Your sleeves are far more beautiful than mine. That flare displays the fringe-and-tassel trim to great advantage. My seamstress was quite correct in recommending it. Honestly, Rosalind, have you ever known a better seamstress than my dear Mrs. Weaver?"

"Never." Rosalind wished for a fan to hide her smile. Before coming to London, she had known only one seamstress, and the aging villager certainly had no use for purple silk or fringe-and-tassel trim. Her tastes ran to common brown muslin, and Rosalind was comfortable with her simple wardrobe.

"I would wager that Mick will fairly swoon when he sees you tonight." Caroline stood back as Rosalind rose from the dressing table. "You have never looked lovelier."

"And who is this Mick fellow of whom you speak?" Rosalind asked. "Have I met the man?"

"Oh, don't tease," Caroline scolded.

"Caroline, during this fortnight, I believe I have come to know you far better than I know the man I will call my husband."

"Now, Rosalind, you know your future husband has been very busy arranging the wedding and putting his business affairs in order. Men don't have time to spend as we do, making calls and reading books and embroidering screens."

"But truly, Caroline, he has dined with us no more than three times, he has taken me to the theater only once, and he has managed to get himself to a mere handful of the myriad parties I've attended. He has never taken me for a carriage ride through the park or sat beside me at tea. He dances with me, certainly, but he is loathe to talk. We have not spoken more than five words alone in all this time."

"What do you want with talk anyway?" Caroline slipped her arm through Rosalind's and led her out into the wide corridor. "Men talk about the most boring things. Commerce, interest rates, trade agreements. If not that, they must converse on such ghastly topics as fox hunting or cricket or shooting tigers in India."

"India, there! I should love to know about Sir Michael's life in India. But every time I broach the subject, he gives me a polite smile and changes the topic."

"He doesn't like to talk about the past. He mourns his late uncle so greatly, you know. You must speak to him of the future, of your enjoyment of his gifts, and of the schedule of events you will attend in the new year. Why not tell him your dreams for refurbishing the family manor house at Bridgeton? That would please him very much, for I know he is interested in such things." Caroline broke off as the two ladies noticed the object of their speculation standing at the foot of the stairs. "Hello, Mick!" she called cheerfully.

"Lady Caroline." Sir Michael removed his hat and

stepped toward the women as they descended the long stairway. "Miss Treadwell, you are looking lovely this evening."

"What did I tell you?" Caroline elbowed her friend. "I knew he would adore your blue brocade and never even notice my purple silk."

"Your gown is enchanting, Caroline, of course."

"You have very elegant manners, Mick, but I see you can look at nothing but your dear fiancée. Is that not the most perfect neckline? Square is quite the fashionable shape this season, and it does show off her new pearls in a most excellent manner."

"The pearls are exquisite," Rosalind chimed in. "I have not had time to write a note thanking you for them, Sir Michael."

The man beamed. "You must not write me so many notes, Miss Treadwell. My footman is quite exhausted with running back and forth between our houses."

"Then you must not bestow so many gifts, Sir Michael. I am overwhelmed."

"As I had hoped." When Lady Cooper set off in search of her husband, Sir Michael took her place at Rosalind's side. "It has been my goal to so overwhelm you with plea-sures that your heart melts completely. Are you feeling a bit less put off by our coming nuptials, Miss Treadwell?"

"Would you be pleased if I told you that thirty new gowns, fifteen pairs of earrings, and seven necklaces of diamonds, pearls, rubies, and emeralds had transformed my heart? Or do you prefer that I be overcome by the sheer numbers of parties to which I have been invited? Or perhaps the endless array of succulent foods was intended to thaw my icy heart?"

"Well, I should hope that *something* in all that might have done it."

"I confess I was nearly done in by yesterday's potted partridge. I saw it, and my heart began to pound with passion for you."

"Potted partridge, Miss Treadwell?" He was chuckling as he escorted her across the crowded ballroom toward an alcove that contained a settee and several chairs. "I shall have to remember that. If potted partridge makes your heart pound, what might happen with stewed pigeon?"

"I am not at all fond of pigeon. Too many bones." She could feel heads turning as she and Sir Michael stepped into the alcove. As this was their formal engagement party, they were clearly the center of attention. "I believe this gathering to be unanimous in its admiration of you, Sir Michael," she said as she sat down beside him on the settee.

"I am hardly the object of their approval tonight, unless it be for my choice of companion. Do you not know how lovely you are?"

"You flatter me." Rosalind could feel herself flush. "But I do not qualify for such a compliment. My hair has a will of its own, and my fingers are frightfully—"

"Beautiful." He took her hand and kissed it. "Miss Treadwell, my attempts at wooing you with pearls and potted partridge may not have been completely successful.

But if my words could suffice, I should like to tell you how very much I have come to admire you since our first meeting."

"And how is that, when we have barely seen each other?"

"But I am told all manner of good things about you. You are said to be polite and witty and altogether charming. I know you are kind, for I have seen how you cared for your father for so many years. And your intellect is reputedly of the highest degree, owing, I suppose, to the great number of books you have read."

Rosalind thought about this for a moment. "But have you been told that I screech when I lose at cards, Sir Michael? And that when I embroider screens, one can never tell which side is the front and which is the back because both are all of knots and loops? Or that I like to take off my shoes and walk barefoot in streams?"

She could tell she had thrown him off course again, and she was pleased. This was a man who wanted controlled perfection in everything, including a wife. But real people weren't perfect. They were flawed and sinful, and she longed to be loved in spite of—and because of—all that made her real.

"Screech?" His blue eyes widened. "Have you . . . screeched . . . since coming to London?"

"I haven't had opportunity to play at cards yet. I've been too busy opening your gifts."

"I shall have to keep them coming," he muttered. "Miss Treadwell, have you any other *interesting* habits?"

"I'm sure I do. Let me think . . . ah yes. When I don't feel well, I must have someone read to me, someone dear and loving and warm. And what I want to be read is the book of Psalms, very softly."

"I see."

"And you might as well know that when I am angry, I weep."

"Weep?"

"Indeed. All my rage boils up and then spills over in tears. But surely you have some minor flaws as well, Sir Michael. Or do you not?"

He studied her for a moment, and she felt the intensity of his blue eyes. "I am not perfect," he said finally.

She let out a breath. "Well, of that I am mightily relieved! In fact, I feel myself more moved by this declaration than I did by your potted partridge. I declare, I am all atremble."

"Is it your practice to make light of everyone? Or only of me?"

"Forgive my teasing, sir. But it's true that hearing you acknowledge your shortcomings would move me more than receiving three pearl necklaces and seven silk gowns."

"Would it, indeed?" He leaned forward. "Then you shall hear that as a child I taught myself to swear most vilely by listening to the sailors on the docks of the Thames—but I have given it up since becoming an adult."

"I am glad of that."

"And I have a strong affection for garlic."

"Oh dear! I suppose you developed your taste for that flavor in India."

"Exactly right. Garlic and curry."

"But if you were in India as a boy, when were you learning to swear on the docks of the Thames?"

He swallowed. "Well, I was . . . it was before, of course."

"Before? Before the swearing or the garlic?"

"Dash it all, this is exactly why I never—"

"Oh, there you are, Rosalind!" Caroline rushed into the alcove, her purple silks aflutter. "I have been searching everywhere. You must come at once!"

"But what is the matter, Caroline?"

"Your father! Lord Buxton has fallen down the stairs just now. William sent for a doctor at once, but we cannot make your father move or speak. Oh, dear Rosalind, I fear for his life!"

CHAPTER THREE

*A*re you still in the library?" Sir William Cooper held a candle before himself to illuminate his path as he crossed the large room lined with countless leather volumes. "You've been in here for hours, Mick. May I inquire as to the object of your search?"

"A book. Poetry, I should imagine." He turned, aware for the first time how out of sorts he must appear in the eyes of his good friend. The engagement party had ended almost before it began, the entire assemblage returning to their homes on hearing the news of the Viscount Buxton's dire condition. A doctor had been summoned, Rosalind had vanished into an upper room to be with her father, and Mick had been left to wander the house—uncertain and confused for the first time in many years. "Lord Buxton. Is his condition much altered?" Mick inquired.

"No, I fear he is quite the same. My wife has visited the room, and she reports that he remains senseless and unmoving. The physician has determined that no bones were broken in the fall down the staircase. Yet, it may be that a blow to Lord Buxton's head has rendered him permanently . . ." He stared at the candle flame for a moment. "It is feared he may never recover."

Gritting his teeth, Mick strode toward the library's rolling ladder. "I must tell you I find absolutely no order within this collection of books, William. You have given your library no semblance of organization—neither by author name nor by subject matter. The volumes are shelved willy-nilly as though no one would ever think of actually reading—"

"Mick, are you well?"

He straightened and raked a hand through his hair. "Of course. I am simply . . ." He let out a breath. "No, I fear I am quite at sea in this matter. If Lord Buxton should perish as a result of this calamity, then I shall lose this opportunity of marriage. Left to her own choosing, his daughter will not have me, of that I am quite certain."

"But there were many other eligible young women on the list you and I wrote out. Rosalind is an intelligent girl and a good deal more than pretty. Yet I should think there are any number of—"

"No, William. No." Again, he crossed the room, unable to calm the agitation in his chest. "I selected Rosalind."

"It is not the loss of land and title that worries you, is it, Mick? You have come to care for the girl. You love her."

"Love her? Don't be absurd, man. Rosalind Treadwell is willful and impudent and far too free with her opinions. She is not beautiful, though I grant you her hair is very fine." He paused, thinking. "A sort of glossy brown, I believe, and the curls seem to shine in the firelight. Have you not noticed? And her eyes are bewitching. I cannot deny that. When she smiles, her eyes come to life with a sort of spark that I have been trying to identify. Is it mischief? or condescension? or mirth? or some odd mixture of all three?"

"And she does look fetching in her new gowns and jewelry."

"Indeed, she does. Lovely. I was not wrong to take the path I chose. Showering her with gifts has brightened her. But she makes light of such things."

Mick climbed the first rung of the ladder and ran his finger across a row of books, searching the titles. "She would rather hear my confessions of fondness for garlic than receive a strand of pearls from me. I cannot make her out, William. She intrigues and vexes me . . . and, I confess, she delights me." He stepped down and faced his friend. "As you well know, I am not a man of uncontrolled emotion. My life is planned and structured. I have long believed that one must keep one's affairs in perfect order. Symmetry, William. Symmetry."

"Yet Rosalind makes you laugh and fume . . . and pace about the library at all hours of the night."

"Yes." Acknowledging the fact that the young woman had thrown his carefully organized world into chaos gave him no comfort. He took the small carved lamb from his coat pocket and clamped it tightly in his hand. "I wish her father to recover . . . not because I hope to claim his lands and titles . . . but for her. For Rosalind. Because I know she loves him, and he is all she has."

William smiled. "She has *you* now, Mick. Why not go to her?"

"She will not wish to see me," he said, turning the lamb over and over in his palm. "I have blighted her life. I took her from her quiet home and her simple companions and her pleasant occupations. Perhaps she will blame her father's accident on me. If I had not brought them here—"

"I cannot believe Rosalind is that sort of woman."

"If I could find the book, I could take it to her. She mentioned it tonight, and I thought it might bring her some hope."

"Which book is that?"

"The book of Psalms, she called it. Have you heard of it?"

"But the Psalms are contained within the Holy Bible, Mick. How can you have forgotten that!" William walked across the room to a large bookstand on which lay an open Bible. "Here, take it upstairs, if you like. This one has been in my family for generations. I daresay it's quite complete, and you shall find an appropriate psalm for your lovely—if vexing—Rosalind."

As William left the room, Mick took the heavy book in his arms and turned through the crinkled pages. He had not "forgotten" the Psalms were contained in the Bible's leather binding—he had never known.

In all the ambition and busyness of his life, Mick had not given matters of faith much thought. Religion was something upon which the elderly might dawdle away their time. Church was a place to go at Christmas and Easter in order to be seen by the right people. And God . . . Mick wasn't sure about God. He thought perhaps there was a creator, someone outside himself who might have fashioned the world and might even hold some ongoing interest in it. He hoped there was a God. A heaven.

He looked down at the tiny lamb in his palm, remembering how he had longed to show it to his mother. She would have admired the intricately carved figure, small though it was. But when he and his father had returned to their flat the night of the burglary, they found her lying stiff and cold upon her cot. Consumption, a neighbor woman told Mick, had killed his mother. The angels had taken her away to heaven to rest in the arms of God.

Lifting his focus to the rooms overhead in the great house, he wondered what Rosalind Treadwell would have to say about angels and heaven and the arms of God. Tucking the lamb back into his pocket, Mick crossed the library toward the corridor that led to the stairway.

❀ ❀ ❀

"There you are now, Papa," Rosalind said as she slipped another pillow beneath her father's head. "That should make you more comfortable. Are you comfortable, Papa?"

She stared down at her father's unmoving face and felt hot tears brim in her eyes. Why could he not look at her? or squeeze her hand? Why did he say nothing? The physician suspected a head injury of grave consequence. But

Rosalind could not understand why her father seemed to breathe so easily and how his heart beat so strongly—and yet he remained unmoving.

"Papa," she said, touching his cheek. "Would you like something to eat? I could send to the kitchen for some cold beef." He didn't move. "Beef!" she said more loudly, hoping perhaps he simply had not heard her. "*Beef*, Papa! *BEEF!* Oh, why won't you say something? Why can't you—"

From behind, a pair of warm hands covered her heaving shoulders, lifted her, and turned her into the protection of a man's arms. "Miss Treadwell . . . Rosalind . . . I am so sorry."

"I don't know what I'm to do! He won't speak to me. He cannot say anything at all."

"Perhaps your father needs to rest. As you do."

Wiping her hand across her cheek, Rosalind became aware of the man who held her against his chest. "Oh . . . I didn't intend to . . . I'm very frightened, Sir Michael—"

"Mick. You must call me Mick, and you must allow me to seat you here on the couch. You seem very cold, Rosalind."

"But I must stay near my father," she protested as he led her toward a fainting couch near the window. He lowered her to the soft cushions and drew a woolen covering across her. "If he moves . . . if he opens his eyes—"

"I shall sit with him and hold his hand. If he stirs, I promise to call you immediately."

"But how can I rest?" she asked as Mick took a seat

beside her father and lifted the older man's hand. "My father is all the family I have. I'm not ready to lose him. I cannot bear it."

Rosalind shut her eyes and tried to stop the endless flow of tears. Sir Michael had come. But why? To assure the status of his future, of course.

She could think only of life without her father. How empty it would be without their lively discussions of Fordyce's sermons and their heated arguments over politics. How lonely she would feel with no one to look after, no voice calling to inquire on the arrival of the post or the status of the blooms on the honeysuckle hedge in the garden. Would she never again stroll along a stone path with her father by her side, his hand gently patting her arm as they debated the merits of Stilton cheese, or pondered aloud the movement of the planets, or discussed the impact of the Napoleonic Wars? Oh, how could she bear it . . .

"'I love the Lord, because he hath heard my voice and my supplications.'" The words spoken from across the room stilled Rosalind's thoughts. "'Because he hath inclined his ear unto me, therefore will I call upon him as long as I live. The sorrows of death compassed me, and the pains of hell gat hold upon me: I found trouble and sorrow. Then called I upon the name of the Lord—'"

"'O Lord, I beseech thee, deliver my soul,'" she whispered, reciting the psalm she had learned so long ago on her father's lap. "'Gracious is the Lord, and righteous; yea, our God is merciful.'"

"You know the words by heart?" Mick asked from his place beside the bed. "How is that?"

"My papa taught me." She swallowed hard. "You read from the one-hundred-sixteenth psalm, do you not?"

"I do, indeed. But why would you memorize this poem?"

"Because it is the Word of God."

"Word of God? What can you mean?"

Rosalind opened her eyes and stared at the man across the room. He sat with a Bible propped open on his lap and his hand carefully clasped around the fingers of the older man. Was this hunched figure really Sir Michael Stafford, the arrogant parvenu who had presumed to purchase her heritage with his wealth and high connections? Why did he seem suddenly so tender? so disconcerted? How could he not know that the Bible was the written revelation of God himself?

"God gave the Bible to us," she said, "so that we might know him. Know what he wants of us. Know how to pray to him. Know the history of his people, the promise of salvation, and the boundless grace of forgiveness and healing. Surely you have been to church?"

"Of course. Many times. But I—"

"'What shall I render unto the Lord for all his benefits toward me?'" she whispered. "'I will take the cup of salvation, and call upon the name of the Lord.' Papa taught me that the whole of the life of Christ is foretold in Scriptures that were written hundreds of years before his birth. Because we—as Christians—have accepted the cup of salvation, we now have the privilege of calling upon the name of the Lord. Which is what I cannot seem to do since Papa . . . since the accident. I try to pray, but then I only weep and dwell on all my losses and mourn the future without him. If I could only think of a prayer . . . of some way to tell God how terribly lonely . . ."

As her eyes flooded with tears, Mick left his place beside the bed and came to kneel at her feet. "I don't know anything about praying," he said softly. "But I know the sorrow you feel. My mother was ill for a very long time. I sat beside her bed when I was a child, and I begged her to get better. But she didn't. She couldn't. I understand that *wanting* . . . that terrible *pleading* you feel inside . . . and I know how helpless . . ."

"But we are not helpless in times of trouble. God is with us, Mick. The words of the psalmist go on. 'Precious in the sight of the Lord is the death of his saints.'" She paused, trying to compose herself. But as she continued to speak, the tears flowed down her cheeks. "'O Lord, truly I am thy servant; I am thy servant, and the son of thine handmaid: thou hast loosed my bonds. I will offer to thee the sacrifice of thanksgiving, and will call upon the name of the Lord.' Will you pray, Mick? Will you pray for my father and for me?"

"I don't know how," he said. "I'm sorry."

Rosalind took his hand in hers. "Oh, Father in heaven, I am your servant," she lifted up. "I bow before you, unworthy of your great sacrifice. I offer you now my own sacrifice—the sacrifice of thanksgiving. I thank you for my papa, for all the years we have enjoyed together, for the great love he has given to me. And I call upon your name, dear Jesus! Great God of healing, please make my father well. Please allow him to live—"

Choking on her tears, she allowed Mick to draw her back into his arms. "Rosalind . . ."

As she slipped her arms around him, she could feel his own chest tight with unexpressed sobs. "I, too, lost my mother at a young age," she confided. "I loved her so dearly, and I did not see how I could go on without her."

"Yes," he murmured. "Going on is . . . difficult. My mother had suffered many years from consumption, and I was away at the time of her death. She died alone. Alone without even a blanket to cover her . . . I never bought her a blanket . . . I didn't have . . . I couldn't . . . and I do not know where he buried her. My father took her away that night. When he returned, he told me I was a man, and I must make my own way in the world. We never spoke of her again."

"Then you must tell *me* about her. She must have been so good and kind."

He nodded, his dark hair feathering the side of her cheek. "She did everything she could for me. She held me in her arms and rocked me to sleep when the wind whistled through the window . . . and I was frightened . . . and she sang . . . hummed a lullaby . . ."

"Oh, I am so very sad for you. How you must have longed for her." She stroked her fingertips across his shoulder. "Mick, were you poor in your childhood?"

She could feel him stiffen against her. "It was long ago. I don't remember much." He pulled away. "I must see to your father. Excuse me."

Leaving her side, he returned to the bed. Sitting with his head bent, he seemed to read the Bible for long minutes at a time as Rosalind gazed at him through half-lowered lids. A drafty house, a blanketless bed, a mother dying of consumption, and a childhood spent among the dockworkers along the Thames . . . these images did not match with the man's supposed grand upbringing in the care of a wealthy uncle in India.

A curl of discomfort wove through Rosalind's chest as she closed her eyes and attempted to return to her prayers for her father. Who was this man she had agreed to marry? And why did the outpouring of his painful loss touch her so deeply?

Why did he not know how to pray? How had he never been told that the Bible was the holy Word of God? Who had he been, and who was he now? And why did she miss the comforting warmth of his arms clasping her tightly?

"O praise the Lord, all ye nations," Mick's voice echoed softly in the stillness of the room. "Praise him, all ye people. For his merciful kindness is great toward us: and the truth of the Lord endureth for ever. Praise ye the Lord."

※ ※ ※

"Mick's parents were killed in a terrible carriage accident when he was but a baby," Lady Caroline whispered as she sat with Rosalind in Lord Buxton's room the following morning. "His unmarried uncle took him away to India at once, and he was brought up there as though he were a young maharaja. It is a sad tale, yet I think he did not suffer greatly, my dear. The uncle employed many servants who cared for Mick almost as a son."

"And this is what he has told you?"

"Indeed, and he possesses many Indian items which now grace his London home. Sandalwood and teak chests, carpets of the most luxurious wool, and gold lamps inlaid with rubies and emeralds. I daresay he will show you everything when you are married. You will be quite overcome with the magnitude of the display."

"I'm sure that is his intention." Rosalind pondered this information. "And this wealthy uncle . . . was he well known in London society?"

"Not at all, for his own father had been a merchant in India, and the uncle was brought up there as well. Mick will not speak of the family at any length. He mourns his uncle so."

"I see." Distressed and confused, she leaned over her father and brushed a tendril of hair from his forehead. "And their trade? Surely you must know the nature of these prosperous enterprises."

"We know nothing." Caroline leaned a little closer. "Though it is thought the fortune might have been made in . . . opium." She paused a moment. "This might explain Mick's reticence in discussing the matter with you. I am aware you have been sequestered in the country, my dear, but surely you know of England's recent war with China over the opening of opium trade routes with India. I believe Mick's uncle may have been involved in the hostilities, and it is thought that he may have lost his life during—"

A soft knock on the door put a welcome end to Lady Caroline's speculations. A maid entered the room, bearing a silver tray on which lay a wooden box and a card addressed to Rosalind. "This was sent from the house of Sir Michael Stafford, mum, and the message boy was instructed not to delay its delivery for a moment."

"More pearls?" Caroline said as she took the box and handed it to Rosalind. "Mick is certainly determined to win you."

"I am sure it cannot be a necklace." Rosalind opened the clasp and lifted the lid. "Indeed not; it is an ear trumpet for Papa!"

The instrument, inlaid with mother-of-pearl and tortoiseshell, lay in a nest of finest silk. Her heart filling with gratitude, she removed the horn and set it against her father's ear.

"Papa!" she whispered. "Papa, can you hear me?"

His face remained unmoving.

"Papa," she said more loudly, "you must wake up, for you promised Lord Remington a game of chess today at the gentlemen's club. Sir Arthur will be looking for you this afternoon." She paused. "His gout is much improved, Papa. Indeed, he came to the party last night, and he was much distressed to learn of your unfortunate accident. Can you not . . . will you . . ."

"Rosalind," Caroline said, laying a hand on her friend's shoulder. "Come, my dear. Why don't you walk down to the parlor with me for tea? I have ordered a currant cake, and Cook is ever so clever at baking tea cakes. I realize this seems hardly the time, but you and I must take a moment to discuss the decor for your wedding. Mick has suggested that a Christmas tree might be the most lovely—"

"Aaah-rrry." The growl from the bed made Caroline gasp. "Rrrorind, wha Aaah-rry?"

"Papa?" Rosalind leapt to her father's side. He had managed to open one eye and was definitely attempting to speak to her. "Papa, I am here with you!"

"Rrrorind."

"Rosalind—yes, it is I!" She grasped Caroline's arm. "You must summon the doctor at once! Make haste!"

"Of course, of course!" The woman fled the room, her footsteps echoing down the long corridor.

"Wha Aaah-ry?" Lord Buxton groaned.

"I beg your pardon?" She shook her head in confusion. Why couldn't her father speak? His mouth seemed to hang slack on one side, and his tongue could hardly form syllables. She took up the ear trumpet. "Papa, you must speak more clearly. What are you asking me?"

His opened eye widened at the amplified sound. "Aaah-ry."

"Artie? Oh yes, he was hoping to play chess with you

today, Papa. At the club. But you . . . you had an accident. You fell down the stairs. Last night."

Her father took Rosalind's hand and proceeded into a lengthy discourse of words so mumbled she could not make any sense of them. But what did she care? He was alive!

"Papa, I cannot understand you," she said finally through the trumpet. "Do try to speak more slowly—"

"Is it true?" Sir Michael Stafford burst through the door into the bedroom. "I was leaving my house when the footman passed me on his way to fetch the doctor. Is your father conscious?"

"He is!" She came to her feet as the young man pulled her into his arms. "I believe your trumpet somehow penetrated the confusion in his mind, for I was speaking to him about Lord Remington, and soon after he began to ask for Artie. And oh, thank you, thank you! I cannot tell you how very grateful—"

"Say nothing. I rejoice with you, Rosalind." He looked into her eyes. "Your prayer . . . it was answered."

"Of course! But not all prayers are given such a happy response." She sank to her knees again. "Look, Papa, Sir Michael has come to see you. We must be so grateful to him for the ear trumpet he sent."

"And for the physician," the doctor said as he entered the room. "Sir Michael has spared no expense in your care, Lord Buxton. I was on my way to tend to an accident when I was given the welcome news that you have awakened from your deep rest. How are you feeling, my good man?"

Rosalind took the horn and leaned next to her father. "How are you feeling? The doctor wants to know."

"Taah-ba."

"Terrible, I think he said." Rosalind glanced up at the two men. "He cannot speak clearly."

"Will you allow me a moment alone to examine your father, Miss Treadwell?" the doctor asked.

"Of course, sir." As Mick led her out into the corridor, she let out a deep breath. "I realize he is not completely well, but he is alive. And for that I am so grateful to God—and you."

Leaning one shoulder against the papered wall, he regarded her in silence for a moment. "Rosalind, I know your thoughts are with your father. But I must beg the opportunity to speak with you concerning another matter."

"Caroline has spoken to me about the importance of making final wedding plans, but I really cannot—"

"It is not the wedding," he cut in. "It is something else. It is . . ." Clearly agitated, he walked past her down the hall. Then he turned and spoke again. "Rosalind, I must talk to you about . . . about me."

She reached out for the support of the wall beside her. Her thoughts flew to her unanswered questions about his past. Would he confess something now? Some terrible secret? Something that might separate them just when she was beginning to care for him?

"What is it?" she asked softly.

"Last night after I left you, I returned to my own house.

But I could not sleep." He began pacing again. "In the early hours of morning, I was roaming about my bed-chamber when I discovered that I had inadvertently carried William's Bible home with me. So I began to read it. I read until dawn, backwards and forwards, sometimes understanding what I read and other times completely confused at the meaning behind the words. I have not read it all, Rosalind. But I have read enough to know that I must tell you—"

"Miss Treadwell?" The physician stepped out into the corridor and shut the bedroom door behind him. "I beg your pardon for interrupting, Sir Michael, but I must speak at once and then be on my way. A young boy awaits me with a leg broken in two places."

"But of course, sir," Rosalind said.

"Miss Treadwell, the news is not good. Yet it is not as bad as might be feared. From my examination, I have concluded that your father suffers from apoplexy."

"Apoplexy?"

"Indeed, it would appear that a clot of blood formed within his brain—whether this occurred as a result of his fall or whether it actually caused the tumble, we may never know. At any rate, the clot seems to have dulled much of the feeling in the left side of your father's body—a common occurrence with apoplexy. Only with the most extreme effort can he move his left arm and leg, open his left eye, or speak through the left side of his mouth. Even his tongue, I fear, has been affected."

"But what are we to do?"

"Nothing at the moment. I have given him a sleeping tonic to allow him to rest." He covered her clasped hands with his. "Miss Treadwell, I regret to tell you that complete recovery is unlikely. Yet it is possible that—with time— your father may regain some of his former abilities."

"Thank you, sir," she said, unable to lift her head for fear he would see the tears brimming in her eyes. "I am grateful for the care you have shown my father."

"Take heart." He started down the stairway. "Your father is in good hands, Miss Treadwell. With Sir Michael soon to be his son by marriage, Lord Buxton will receive every luxury and necessity available."

Rosalind touched her cheek with her handkerchief. "I see now how wrong I was about you," she said softly to the man who stood beside her. "There is much good to be said for having the means to help people."

"Only if it is put to such use," Mick said. "I confess I did not accumulate my wealth for that purpose . . . but only for my own satisfaction."

She looked into his blue eyes and saw for the first time an openness, a vulnerability. "Perhaps the time has come for a change in more than your marital status. For that I am very warmly inclined . . . eager, in fact."

"Are you saying . . . Rosalind, are you saying the prospect of our union now pleases you? Do you tell me that you would come into the marriage willingly?"

"I am saying that I liked the man I met in my father's room last night. I liked him very much." As she was speaking, her doubts about his past slipped back into her thoughts. "But I'm not certain I know him fully. Only that the more I do know him, the less dismay I feel over this arranged union."

She reached out her hand for the door to her father's room. Then she hesitated. "You started to tell me something. Before the doctor came out to speak to me, you said you needed to talk to me about something you had read—"

"It was nothing." He gave her a dismissive nod, the openness in his eyes vanishing. "I am expected at my club. Good day."

"Good day, sir." Rosalind's hand closed on the icy doorknob as Mick hurried down the staircase.

CHAPTER FOUR

Mick could not have been more surprised to find Rosalind waiting for him in his parlor. Three days had passed since her father's return to consciousness, and she had spent all her waking hours at his side. Her obvious lack of trust in him had silenced his yearning to confess the truth about his past. Yet he could not will himself to stay away from her. Mick stopped by the house often, but they were never permitted to speak intimately, for the room was always occupied by visitors or medical staff.

"Rosalind?" He crossed the carpeted parlor as she rose from the settee. "Your father—is he not well?"

"Indeed, he is very well, thank you. I did not mean to alarm you." She was dressed in one of the gowns he had ordered for her, a soft pink skirt with a velvet jacket trimmed in French Honiton lace. A diamond collet necklace he had bought at Mappin & Webb, Ltd. on Oxford Street circled her throat. But it was neither the fabric nor the jewels that made him breathless.

Rosalind's gray eyes sparkled, her skin glowed with health, and her dark hair seemed alive with curl and movement. How could any woman be so lovely? And her smile! He had rarely seen her smile—but, my, what a glorious thing it was.

"I have come to express again to you my sincerest gratitude," she began. "The ear trumpet has made all the difference in my father's ability to understand me. And the nurses you employed to tend him have the highest hopes that he soon may be able to walk again. Even his speech becomes clearer as the phonetician you sent instructs him. Oh, thank you so much for helping us! Your generosity—"

"Please say no more." He lowered his head a moment, remembering the filth and hopelessness in which his own mother had passed her last days. "I am glad to do all in my power to help your father. I understand your great love for him, Rosalind."

"And this is the reason for your kindness? You do it for me?" She clenched her fingers together. "I confess . . . I feared your motives were more mercenary."

"That your father might live long enough to see us wed and allow me to become legally entitled to his estate?"

She flushed. "Perhaps."

"His death would free you from your obligation to marry me, of course. You know I have felt some concern over your lack of enthusiasm toward our union. But my assistance to your father stems from . . . well, I have grown to like him very much. More importantly, you love him. And I love you."

At his words, her head snapped up, and her eyes flickered. *"Love* me? How can you cast such a word about so lightly?"

"Lightly? I have never spoken of love to a woman in all my life. And I do not use the term merely in some vain attempt to win your affection." A swell of agitation filled his chest as he faced her. He had just expressed some of the most difficult words he had ever spoken, and yet she continued to doubt and question him. With this woman, he knew he could not mince words. He took the small lamb from his pocket and knotted it in his fist.

"Since I met you, Rosalind, I have been forced to . . . your forthrightness and determination to know me have caused me to look into my own heart for the first time in many years. I assure you I have done all within my power to ignore the stirring of emotion I feel. My whole life has been spent striving toward a single-minded goal—the accumulation of wealth, prestige, and power. You were intended to be simply a part of the accomplishment of that goal. But you came into my life with all the force of your will and your wit . . . and your total lack of interest in the wealth, prestige, and power I have managed to accumulate."

"I am sorry."

"No!" He rubbed the bit of carved wood under his thumb. "I have been compelled to look at my life from a new perspective, and what I have seen is emptiness. You have your love for your father, your devotion to your faith, and your utter determination to be truthful and loving in all that you do. I have this!"

He picked up a blue platter from the Ming Dynasty of China and sent it sailing across the room. It hit the wall and shattered into a hundred pieces. "What good has it done me? None! None at all."

She stared at him. "Not now, at any rate."

"What?"

"Well, you've broken it, you silly man." She marched across the room and regarded the fragments on the carpet for a moment. Then she lifted her head. "I once lived in a home with fine china platters. And when I was taken away to live at Bridgeton Cottage, I thought about them sometimes. And here is what I discovered. A fine china platter can be useful to serve a meal. Or it can sit in a home as a lovely, calming reminder of the beauty of God's creation. Or it can be sold to provide money when one can no longer afford to buy coal for the fire. There is nothing wrong with owning a fine china platter, sir."

"For the reasons you have stated, no. But I bought that platter for two hundred pounds from an elegant shop on Regent Street, and I put it in my parlor for the express purpose of causing all who might see it to think me a wealthy man."

"That is wrong."

"Indeed."

"Though you needn't have hurled it against the wall."

Mick let out a breath and tucked the lamb back into his pocket. "I have been filled with such anger these past three days."

"Anger at whom?"

"At myself." He sank down onto the settee. "Rosalind, if you should choose not to marry me, I can understand completely. I have seen the vileness of my own soul."

"Because you bought a china platter?"

"Because I am a man full of deceit and selfishness and greed, and all manner of wickedness." He rubbed his hand over his eyes. "I have spent these days and nights reading William's Bible, and I have come to understand that I am a man with nothing. All my wealth means nothing. My power means nothing. My status in society means nothing. I am the very worst of sinners."

Miserable, he stared down at the carpet. He fully expected Rosalind to walk out of the parlor and never to see him again. Instead, she sat beside him on the settee, folded her hands, and began to speak in the softest, most beautiful voice he had ever heard.

"My dear sir, I believe you have read only part of William's Bible," she said. "You have seen your sin, but you have not welcomed God's love and forgiveness. You must read how Jesus took the punishment you deserve—all of us deserve—by allowing himself to be crucified. Like a sacrificial lamb, he paid for our sin with his own death. And when he came back to life, he brought with him the assurance of eternal life for us."

"Heaven," Mick muttered, thinking of his mother.

"You don't have to spend the rest of your days on this earth smashing china platters and despising the wicked state of your soul. You have merely to accept God's forgiveness and begin to walk in his love."

"Accept it?"

"It's very simple," she said, taking his hand and bowing her head. "Dear God, you know all the blackness in this man's soul. Do forgive him now and welcome him into your kingdom. Amen."

"That's it?"

"Well, you might want to do the asking yourself."

Mick studied his knees. Was it really so easy? Could he rid himself of the blot of evil in his past and claim the promise of a new life?

"Dear God," he said, and as he spoke, he recognized a strong sense of someone listening. Someone present in the room with him and Rosalind. "I have read the Bible, though not all of it. And I have come to see that my motives and my actions are not all they should be. No, that is stating it too mildly. I have been a sinful person since the earliest days of my life. I ask you now . . . I beg you . . . to forgive me. Accept me. Love me."

"Amen. There you are, then," Rosalind said. "A new man, completely forgiven of all your sin."

"It seems too easy."

"That is its beauty." She stood. "But I assure you that the forgiven life you now lead will not be easy. Our God has a bitter enemy, and it is the enemy's greatest delight to tempt us back into sin. You should go to church more than at Christmas and Easter, sir. Church is the place where we can worship God and gain strength and wisdom. I recommend it highly."

Mick came to his feet and walked beside her toward the

parlor door. "Rosalind, now that you know all this about me—all my failings—do you wish to be released from our agreement? I cannot blame you—"

"No, indeed." Her eyes shone as she met his gaze. "For I find that I am in grave danger of falling in love with you, sir." She dipped her head. "Do excuse me now. I must return to Papa."

Before he could respond, she had fled across the foyer and out the front door.

❋ ❋ ❋

"This is a capital idea, indeed!" Lord Remington clipped a small, white candle to the branch of the towering fir tree that stood in the front parlor of Sir Michael Stafford's house in Grosvenor Square. "William, was this your notion? Or do I detect the distinct touch of my dearest Caroline?"

"No, Father, for it was Mick himself who conceived the plan." William was stirring a bowl of hot cranberry punch. "He said that a Christmas Eve wedding called for a tree and all the trimmings."

"And what could be more enjoyable than gathering friends and family for a decorating party?" Mick asked as he hung a red glass ball on a limb. "All of you have played an important part in the union that is to take place tomorrow morning. Miss Treadwell . . . Rosalind . . . and I are very grateful."

Rosalind smiled as Mick cast a warm glance in her direction. How could it be that in such a short time, her heart had transformed from a solid block of suspicion and resentment to this buttery, flip-flopping, giddy lump that danced about in her chest every time he looked at her? She took her father's hand, seeking an anchor.

"Mick is thanking everyone," she said through the ear trumpet.

"Ahh." Lord Buxton nodded sagely. Though his speech was not completely clear, he was able to sit up for long periods of time, and he was making every effort to learn to stand again.

"Artie!" he called, beckoning Sir Arthur with his good hand. Lord Remington hobbled across the room on his gouty legs, and Rosalind gladly gave him her place on the settee. The two men had discovered that their chess playing abilities had not suffered in the least. Rather than making the effort to go to their gentlemen's club, they simply visited each other's abodes, and their cries of victory or defeat could be heard echoing down the corridors at all hours.

"The tree is lovely," Rosalind said as Mick stepped toward her with a cup of punch. "Caroline said you ordered all the trimmings yesterday from a shop on Bond Street."

"I've never put up a tree before." He gave her the cup and took her free hand in his. "I hope it will be a tradition we can enjoy for many years to come."

"Indeed."

"Children," he added, "would very much enjoy a tree."

Rosalind couldn't force away the blush she could feel heating her cheeks. "I always loved Christmas when I was a little girl. But I suppose you had no fir trees or cranberry punch in India."

He glanced down. "Rosalind, I—"

"What is this?" Caroline exclaimed over a collection of boxes near the door. "These ornaments are not new, Mick. Oh, how lovely! Wherever did you get them?"

She lifted a silver ball of blown glass high into the air. Rosalind gave a gasp of joy. "Those are *our* ornaments!" Leaving Mick, she fairly danced across the parlor in delight. "Papa must have ordered them to be sent from the great house at Bridgeton. Look, Mick!"

"How very pretty," he said.

"They've been stored in the attic for many years, but I would know these balls at once. My grandpapa bought them in Bavaria before the turn of the century. He told us they were all hand painted by a wee man in a shop on the side of a mountain. Oh, how delightful!"

Her heart singing, she hurried to her father's side and gave his cheek a kiss. Lord Buxton patted her arm. "Mick, please may we add them to the tree?" she implored. "I know they are old, but—"

"Of course, Rosalind." His face softened. "It is your tree now . . . and your home . . . as much as it is mine."

"Thank you. Thank you so much!"

"Look at this!" Caroline cried as she unwrapped an angel with spun-glass wings, and Rosalind could not bear to miss a moment. She raced back to the boxes and eagerly took out one cherished object after another—a wreath made of gilded pinecones, angels and Father Christmases of embossed paper, tiny lace cones spilling with silver ribbons, and countless glass balls from the mountains of Bavaria.

Never had she thought she would spend the days before her wedding in such joy. Caroline and William had become her dear friends, unabashed in their happiness at the growing attachment between Mick and herself. Her father's health was steady. Her acceptance into London's highest society seemed assured. But most of all—she couldn't keep herself from glancing in his direction—most of all, she had come to adore her future husband.

How could it be that God had seen fit to bless her with more than she had ever dreamed of in a man, Rosalind wondered as she unwrapped an old nativity set her grandfather had carved. Mick was more than handsome, she had decided. With his broad shoulders and thick hair and warm blue eyes, he was . . . well, he was a masterpiece! She loved the shape of his hands, the hint of beard that shadowed his face each evening, the fine angle of his nose, the turn of his ear . . .

"Who are these people?" Caroline asked, holding up a small picture frame that emerged from the bottom of a box.

"It's Mama and Papa!" Rosalind cried. "How did it get put into the Christmas decorations? One of the servants must have thought it was an ornament." She took the portrait and gazed at her youthful parents. Then she scrambled to her feet and hurried to her father. "Look, Papa, it's you and Mama!"

At the sight of the portrait, he let out a cry of joy. "Maude!" he said, so clearly there could be no doubt of the depth of love they had known. "My Maude."

Her heart flooding with pleasure, Rosalind looked around for Mick. Surely he would wish to see how her parents had appeared in their youth. Indeed, Papa had often told Rosalind she was almost a copy of her mother. With her masses of brown curly hair and her slender figure, she could see the resemblance so clearly now.

"Where is Mick?" she asked, looking around the room.

"He stepped outside for a moment," Caroline said as she began setting up the nativity scene. "Oh, look, it's snowing! I do hope he doesn't stay out long."

Remembering how Mick had spoken of his desire for children, Rosalind felt determined to show him the portrait of her mother. What if their daughters had the same curly hair? Would he be pleased? She thought so, as she pushed open the long French door that led onto a croquet lawn. He had admired her curls just that evening, and he had stated that she must purchase all the jeweled combs and pins she desired so that her hair might be displayed to its fullest advantage.

"Mick!" she called, spotting him near the far edge of the lawn. She lifted her skirts and ran through the heavy flakes that had begun to fall. "Mick, you must come back inside, for Caroline has found a portrait of my parents, and I want you to see it. I am quite sure you will recognize how strongly I resemble my mother—"

She gasped as he caught her suddenly in his arms.

"Rosalind, I love you more than words can express!" he exclaimed. "As I watch you, I feel so undeserving of you. You are good and kind and so beautiful!"

"And you are generous and witty and very handsome!" she returned, laughing with pleasure. "Oh, Mick, I cannot think when I have ever been so happy."

"Nor I. God has given me such a gift in you." He bent his head and touched his lips gently to hers. "I have longed to kiss you."

"Kiss me again," she said breathlessly. "For I am dizzy with joy."

He drew her more closely into his arms and this time permitted his kiss to linger. "Rosalind, I spoke to you of my past," he said, his breath warming her ear, "and I feel that before we marry, I should make a confession."

She drew back a little, but she could not see his expression in the darkness. "Mick, does your behavior of the past continue into the present?"

"No, of course not. Absolutely not, but I—"

"Then I do not wish to hear it. God has forgiven you, and tomorrow we shall begin to build our new life together. The only confessions I will hear from your lips are confessions of love."

"Rosalind!" he whispered, clasping her tightly.

"Oh!" she exclaimed, feeling a small object in his breast pocket. "What do you have in your coat, Mick? Is it that little thing you take out when you are troubled? Let me see it."

He pulled the lamb from his pocket and set it in her hand.

"Come, we must go back to the parlor, or we shall begin to freeze." He slipped his arm around her. "I keep that little toy in my pocket as a sort of comfort. It reminds me of when my mother was still alive . . . when hope lived in my heart . . . I'm not sure what it is, really. A lamb or something, but I treasure it as the anchor to which I have clung when all the world seemed falling down around me."

"Mick, it is so tiny," Rosalind said as they stepped back through the French door into the lighted parlor. "It is a lamb, a small carved lamb. Indeed, it—"

Her voice caught as she looked across the room at the nativity scene that Caroline was arranging. Unable to speak, Rosalind walked to her side and stared down at the small carved figures. There were Mary and Joseph and the baby Jesus. The three kings and the shepherd with his hook. And there were the donkey and the camel. But the lamb . . . the tiny lamb had gone missing on one terrible Christmas Eve.

Feeling that she might faint, Rosalind clenched the lamb in her fist and started for the door. She had to get out of this house, she thought as she ran across the foyer. She had to pack her bags and send for a carriage and have her papa brought—

"Rosalind!" Mick's voice seemed to echo in her spinning head as he caught her arm. "Are you ill? What is the matter?"

She turned slowly and forced herself to face him. "This lamb," she said, her words barely audible in the deserted foyer. "I have seen it before."

85

"But that's impossible, for I have had it since I was a child."

"Many years ago," she began, unable to look at him, "my papa decided to convert all his liquid assets into bonds. I was but a small child at the time, but I remember how he worked day and night to sort out the ledgers before the new year began. One evening, we went out to a Christmas party, and he left his ledgers and the bank notes on a table in the parlor. When we came home, they were gone. Most of our good silver was stolen, too." She swallowed hard. "But what I wept for was the desecration of the small nativity scene my grandpapa had carved and painted by hand. I had played with it, loved it, cherished it. And that night . . . that night, someone had stolen the lamb."

Mick reached for her, but she pulled back. "Rosalind, I—"

"My family never recovered from that loss. Our fortunes continued to fall, and my father was forced to sell much of his land and other holdings. My mama died, broken-hearted and rejected by her own friends and family. In the end, Papa and I moved into the gamekeeper's cottage, where we were forced to peddle the family statuary and paintings in order to keep coal in our fireplace and food on our table." She opened her palm. "The night this lamb was stolen, we were ruined."

"But how can you be sure—"

"I know this lamb!" she cried, her heart tearing in two. "My grandpapa carved it, and it is a perfect match to the set in your parlor—the set that is missing its lamb! Mick, please tell me you did not take this from my house. Please say you had nothing to do with the crime that destroyed my family!"

He stared at her, and his face grew hard. "I see that my past does matter after all."

CHAPTER FIVE

*H*e ruined us!" Rosalind knotted her fists as she paced before the small fire in her father's bedroom. The only relief in her heart was that she had escaped Mick's house. On learning that she was unwell, the decorating party had dispersed. Sir William and Lady Caroline returned to their home with Rosalind and Lord Buxton. Lord Remington's carriage took him back to his town house. And Mick was left alone.

"Ros-ind," Lord Buxton said, holding up his ear trumpet.

"Mick ruined us!" Rosalind stepped forward and fairly shouted into the horn. "It was he who stole your money that night so many years ago, Papa. He is a deceitful man with a wicked past. All of his great wealth has been gained from thievery. And he professed himself to be a Christian!"

Taking her handkerchief from her sleeve, Rosalind pressed it against her eyes. She walked to the fireplace and stared down at the glowing coals. "All that I believed in

was a lie! Indeed, he is a parvenu. Sir Michael Stafford—
oh, that is a good joke! He probably got his title by some
underhanded means. And then he thought he could marry
me in order to carry out the final workings of his evil
scheme! He stole your money, Papa, and then he tried to
steal your land and all your titles. Abominable man! Insuf-
ferable, horrible, revolting man!"

She grabbed the poker and gave the fire a prod. "I don't
know how I was so easily tricked. I was lulled into thinking him handsome and good and . . . well, he did tell me
he had a wicked past . . . but I had no idea it was so frightfully evil! I thought perhaps he had taken advantage of a
business partner or violated a trade agreement or something so much less . . ."

Rosalind glanced over at her father, who was attempting
to write on a sheet of paper. A letter, perhaps. A document
freeing her from the marriage agreement. Her father had
always said, "Sin is sin," and by that he had meant no evil
was greater than another.

But Mick's sin had been against her! Against her dear
papa! How could she see that as anything but the worst,
most unforgivable wickedness? And to think how close
she had been to marrying him.

She had been such a fool! She had come to believe Mick
was truly a gentleman of the first order. He had cared for
her father with the greatest of kindness. He had paid for
doctors, nurses, the phonetician, even the ear trumpet. He
had visited day and night during Lord Buxton's gravest
hours. And he had done all in his power to provide Rosa-

lind with every comfort and luxury a woman could dream of. But now she understood—all this was merely a part of his plan to secure her hand in marriage, and with that, to gain the prestige of her father's titles for himself!

"He is a vile man!" she shouted, crossing to her father and speaking into his trumpet. She picked up the carved lamb that had been lying on the table where her father was writing and shook it in his face. "Mick took this from us, Papa. That Christmas Eve when all your money was stolen, Mick was in our house, and he stole this lamb. Do you not recognize it? Grandpapa carved it! It went missing from the nativity scene on that very night. Sir Michael is a thief, Papa, a lying, horrible, despicable thief, and we should do all in our power to—"

To what? What could they do to recover their losses? He had ruined them, but what power did they have to . . .

Rosalind stared at the lamb. "We must ruin *him!*" she cried. Grabbing the wide end of the trumpet, she spoke into it. "All Mick's acquaintances have seen him holding this lamb from time to time. Everyone knows it is his. We shall therefore prove to one and all that it was stolen from our home, Papa! We must expose him for the man he is. All his past will be revealed—his childhood on the docks of the Thames, his wealth gained from breaking into the homes of wealthy families, and his lies about . . . about that rich uncle in India, his education at Cambridge, and . . ."

And he had said he loved her! She slammed the lamb back onto the table and crossed to the fire again. Surely, he had meant those words, that passion! His eyes had been so full of adoration. He had clasped her so tightly. And oh, how she had welcomed every whispered word from his lips . . . his wonderful, magical lips . . .

"Ros-ind!" The growl caught her as she was blotting the tears that had fallen down her cheeks. She turned to find her father beckoning.

"I believed he loved me, Papa," she wept. "And I loved him. I loved him so dearly . . ."

Her father picked up the paper on which he had been writing and waved it at her. She took it and read the spidery letters he had penned.

"John 1:29." A Bible verse. "What does it mean?" she demanded. "Why have you written this?"

The viscount took the paper away from her, picked up the little lamb, and set it firmly on top of his written words. He gave her such a significant look that she dropped down into the chair beside his.

"What, Papa?" she asked. "I'm sorry, but I can't remember that Scripture verse."

He let out a raspy note of exasperation.

"Fine then, I shall go to the library and look it up!" She started for the door but returned and spoke into the trumpet. "It is our duty to expose him. He has risen to his position by wicked means, and all his friends and business associates are deceived in him. We must draft the letter in the morning."

As Rosalind hurried down the staircase, she heard her words echoing in the corridor. In the morning . . . in the morning she had planned to be getting married! She would have put on her gown of white silk, woven strands of pearls through her hair, and given her heart to the man she had grown to love as dearly as life itself.

Oh, how could he have betrayed her so? Had he known from the moment he chose her that it was her father's wealth he had stolen? Had he selected her as some kind of a joke—the final *coup de grâce* to the slow destruction of their family that he had begun so many years before?

"Ma'am?" A small boy standing in the shadows startled her. "I've been ringin' and ringin' but nobody comes. I've brought a message to Miss Treadwell from Sir Michael Stafford." He stepped forward and extended a silver tray. "Can you see that she gets it? He gave me a whole shillin' to do the job, and I don't want to lose me wages."

"I'll see that she gets the letter," Rosalind said, taking the tray.

"Thanks, ma'am, and a happy Christmas to ye!"

"Happy Christmas." Rosalind sighed as she walked toward the library. Of course she had known this would come. Mick would try to explain himself. Or make some offer of apology. Or perhaps he would guess that she had no course but to expose him. Might the letter contain a bribe?

Stepping into the library, she broke the seal and opened the letter.

"'Miss Treadwell,'" she read softly. His ill-favored penmanship bore testimony to the fact that he had never attended Cambridge. Why hadn't she known from the beginning that something was amiss?

93

"'I have nothing to offer you now but the truth,'" she read.

> *I was six years old when my father and I entered your manor house one Christmas Eve whilst you were out. It was the first time I had assisted him in a burglary, but it was not the last. After collecting most of your silver, we prepared to leave, when my father noticed some items on the desk in the parlor. As he took the papers, I was drawn to the small set of figures on a side table. From among them, I selected the lamb, which became my constant companion during all the years that followed.*

There it is! she thought. *He has convicted himself!* This letter would be all that was required to bring about his downfall. She returned to reading.

> *My father took the money he had stolen from your home and spent most of it in a manner that made it unable to be reclaimed. When I was twelve, my father died violently. Having lost my mother some years before—the very night we invaded your home, in fact—I was compelled to see to my own fortunes. It was at that time I determined that the only road to security lay in the accumulation of property, prestige, and power. I took what little money my father had not gambled away and began to invest it in small enterprises. I educated myself through the reading of books, and I erased all trace of my early speech patterns.*
>
> *By sheer determination, I found myself growing wealthy and gaining in both reputation and power.*

Realizing that I could not hope to further myself if anyone learned of my wretched past, I invented a fabulous tale of a wealthy uncle in India—which to my great surprise was willingly believed by one and all.

"I knew it!" She wadded up the letter. "He never lived in India! It was all a lie. No doubt he grew up in some wretched rookery on the East Side!"

Stalking across the library to the stand where the Bible was displayed, Rosalind suddenly thought of the night Mick had sat beside her father and poured out the story of his mother's death. That hadn't been a lie, of that she was most certain. He had loved his mother dearly, and she had died of consumption without even a blanket to warm her.

"Oh, God!" she cried, lifting her head as if she might call her heavenly Father to come at once—and in person. "I don't want to feel any sympathy for him. He is wicked!"

All the same, she smoothed out the letter and resumed reading.

By the time I purchased the factories in Manchester and Nottingham, which I still own, I had washed my hands of every trace of the guile that had given me my start. I had erased my past, I felt sure. I wanted nothing more than to continue along the path to wealth and power, vowing to myself that I would never again be forced to live like a common thief.

I provided valuable services to a certain member of Parliament during the recent wars, and I was rewarded with a baronetcy. But I had begun to dream higher still.

My goal became absolute legitimacy. I determined to marry a woman whose titles and lands I could obtain as my own and pass down to my sons—as though I were a true peer and not the son of a criminal whom I hardly knew because he had spent most of my childhood in gaol.

"Oh, dear!" Reaching for the arm of a chair, Rosalind lowered herself weakly to the seat. This was more dreadful than she could have imagined. But it was not Mick's clawing ambition that dismayed her. Instead, she saw him as a ragged little boy whose papa had taught him the ways of thievery, and a mama—dearly loved! —who had died a terrible death and left him all alone.

My good friend, Sir William Cooper—who has not the slightest idea of my background, I assure you—set about to help me find the perfect woman to be my wife. She must be the sole heir to her father's estate, we decided. Ideally, she must be compliant, weak-minded, poor, and easily wooed by the promise of wealth. We chose you.

"Well!" Rosalind snapped. "Imagine that!"

Of course, you were exactly the opposite. You have a mind of your own, a wit as sharp as any blade, a heart rich in faith, and no interest in my showers of gowns and jewels. In short, you are nothing like the woman I wanted, and everything like the one I need. I have fallen deeply in love with you, Rosalind, and I know that

*losing you will be a grief as great to me as any loss I
have ever suffered.*

*Let me close by assuring you that until tonight, I had
no idea it was your family that my father and I had
victimized. I am grieved and sorrowful beyond words
for the pain this crime inflicted. If I could do anything
to change my past, believe me, I would do it gladly. I
can only thank you for showing me that I am forgiven
by God. Now I am prepared to pay for my sin in the eyes
of all England.*

Rosalind started to lower the letter, then she noticed a
small sentence scribbled at the bottom beneath his signa-
ture. She held the paper to the light.

I am sorry I stole your lamb.

Choking down a sob, she folded the page and clutched it
tightly in her hand. *Oh, Mick!* Why had it turned out this
way? She had no choice but to expose him. Knowing what
he had done, she could never marry him. But if she didn't
marry him, she would have very little means to provide
for her father in the last years of his life. Perhaps Mick
would offer to pay for her silence. But, no, he hadn't done
that in his letter, and he never would. Such a thing would
be as wicked as stealing. Mick had clearly stated that he
had put all his underhanded dealings behind him long
ago. Indeed, he had begged forgiveness from God for that
past.

But oh, how her family had suffered at his hand! Each
time her father had sold off another parcel of land, she had

believed it might kill him to do so. And when they had dismissed their servants and moved into the gamekeeper's cottage, her papa had closed himself into a room for nearly a month. Rosalind had feared he would lose his mind! In fact, she often blamed his many ailments on the transition to poverty.

Suddenly remembering she had abandoned her father in his chair upstairs, she felt a rush of guilt. She must help him into bed at once, for it was surely past midnight! Rising, she started for the door before remembering her mission to the library.

"St. John, chapter one," she said, turning through the old Bible's pages. "Verse twenty-nine. 'The next day John seeth Jesus coming unto him, and saith, Behold the Lamb of God, which taketh away the sin of the world.'"

Rosalind turned away. The Lamb of God was Jesus himself, the one who had taken away the sin of the world. Why had her father been so determined that she recall this Scripture? He had placed the little stolen lamb on the notation. *Behold the Lamb of God, which taketh away the sin of the world.*

The Lamb . . . the Christ child who had come to earth so many years before . . . had sacrificed himself to take away sin. All sin. Even sin as wicked as Mick's.

Feeling broken and weary, Rosalind climbed the steps back to her father's bedroom. As she had feared, he had fallen asleep in his chair. With some effort, she managed to wake him and help him stagger into bed. It had been a long night, one filled with the ecstasy of love and the bitterness of betrayal. She could hardly imagine how she would survive the day to come.

She stepped into her own silent bedroom and shut the door behind her. From her window, she could see the corner of Mick's house across the square. What was he doing now, alone in the darkness? She could almost imagine him staring at his darkened Christmas tree—the only tree he'd ever had! And nearby, the small nativity set would be sitting on a table, a reminder of the holy child who had come to earth to give his life for the salvation of one and all.

For Rosalind.

For William and Caroline.

For Lord Buxton and Lord Remington.

For every person in every house on Grosvenor Square, and every person in every squalid rookery in the East End.

And for Mick Stafford, too.

Christ had given his life for everyone who would beg forgiveness for sin and accept that gift of salvation . . . just as Mick had done in his parlor when she sat with him on the settee and helped him to pray.

"Oh, Father God!" Rosalind cried aloud again as she jerked the curtains shut and began to tear off the fine evening gown and pearls she had worn for that special evening. "Father, please help me know what to do! He ruined my family, and by rights he should pay for it. I have the means to destroy him!"

She grabbed the little lamb and the letter Mick had sent. "By all that is just, this letter should be published in every newspaper from London to Manchester. This lamb is the proof of his guilt. And he is guilty! Horribly, despicably guilty!"

Kneeling down beside her bed, she wept into the downy coverlet. Her heart ached for the man she had learned to love. And her heart broke for her family, whose fortunes had been destroyed by that very same man. What should she do? Expose him before all the world—ruin his businesses, demand reparation for the wealth he had stolen, drag his reputation through the muck, and strip away every measure of goodwill he had labored so hard to earn?

Or should she hold her tongue—return to the gamekeeper's cottage and live out the remainder of her years in the manner in which she had always planned? Should she extend to Mick the forgiveness that God had granted her? Should she rise above all that would seem right and fair and just in the eyes of the world—and give this man the undeserved blessing of grace?

"I don't know what to do," she whispered into the coverlet. "I'm tired, so very tired."

Unable to think or plan, she folded her hands and began the prayer she had said every night since early childhood:

> "Jesus, tender Shepherd, hear me,
> Bless thy little lamb tonight,
> Through the darkness be thou near me,
> Keep me safe till morning light."

She crawled up into the bed and drew the coverlet over her chilled shoulders. "Jesus, tender Shepherd, hear me," she whispered again. "Bless thy little lamb tonight . . . bless thy little lamb . . ."

✳ ✳ ✳

Mick stood inside the apse of the church and studied the black-and-white marbled floor beneath his feet. He did not know what the coming hour would bring, but he fully expected it to be the worst of his life. Just past dawn, a breathless footman had arrived with a note from Rosalind.

I shall see you at church in the morning, ten sharp—R.

Of course, that was the hour they had set for their wedding, and the church was filling rapidly with friends and acquaintances, members of Parliament, lords and ladies of London's highest society, and even a cousin or two from the royal family. Everyone wore his or her finest Christmas garb—red and green velvets, burgundy silks, shimmering gold and silver, and sparkling diamond tiaras. And all of them would be sitting in the church, listening intently, when Rosalind Treadwell exposed him as a liar and a thief.

Mick let out a breath that turned to vapor in the chilly morning air. He couldn't blame her—and he would not run from the humiliation. He deserved the public reprimand, and he might as well have it all done to him at once. He knew Rosalind too well to doubt that she would choose a bold manner in which to have her victory. She was very clever, and this would be a death knell from which he could not possibly recover.

"Have you got the ring?" William asked, hurrying

across the floor. "Rosalind has arrived in her carriage, and they've already brought Lord Buxton to the front of the church."

"Never mind about the ring," Mick said.

"I beg your pardon? Have you lost it?"

"Let's just get on with this." He brushed past his friend and moved out into the sanctuary, where the choirboys were singing in their high-pitched tones. After Rosalind read the letter condemning him, he would speak a few words confirming its accuracy. He would then return to his home to meet with his accountants and prepare whatever sort of remuneration Rosalind felt was appropriate to restore herself and her father to their former position. Following that, an extended trip would be in order. Perhaps he would finally go to India.

Mick clasped his hands behind his back as the music swelled and the guests turned to look at the woman coming down the aisle. This was going to be the most difficult part of the whole matter. Seeing Rosalind. Seeing the hatred in those beautiful gray eyes. Knowing he had lost her forever.

He felt as though he were a man condemned to the gallows as he lifted his head to meet her. And there she stood—in her bridal gown! Rosalind laid her hand on his and knelt to the altar. Mick could hardly breathe as he forced his knees to bend.

What sort of trickery was this? What did she mean to do to him?

"Dearly beloved," the minister began.

Mick tried to listen. But he could hear nothing save the loud pounding in his ears. His heart felt as though it might bolt right out of his chest. What was she doing? What was happening?

He stole a glance at Rosalind. She had bowed her head and closed her eyes, and Mick realized suddenly that everyone was praying. Praying? Rosalind was supposed to be reading the letter he had sent her! She was to stand before the assembly and destroy him—not kneel beside him and . . .

"Wilt thou, Michael John Stafford," the minister was asking him, "have this woman to thy wedded wife, to live together after God's ordinance in the holy estate of matrimony? Wilt thou love her, comfort her, honor, and keep her in sickness and in health; and, forsaking all others, keep thee only unto her, so long as ye both shall live?"

Mick stared at the man.

Rosalind nudged him with her elbow.

Mick swallowed and tried to make himself speak. "I will," he managed.

"And wilt thou, Rosalind Elizabeth Treadwell," the minister continued, "have this man to thy wedded husband, to live together after God's ordinance in the holy estate of matrimony? Wilt thou love him, comfort him, honor, and keep him—"

"And I forgive him," Rosalind inserted.

The minister cleared his throat. "Yes, well, indeed . . . as I was saying . . . in sickness and in health; and, forsaking all others, keep thee only unto him, so long as ye both shall live?"

"I will," she replied in a firm voice.

"The ring," the minister whispered.

In a daze, Mick dug in his pocket and took out the ring he had bought so long ago. Rosalind held out her hand, and he slipped the ring onto her finger. The minister let out a breath of relief, said several more long speeches that Mick couldn't begin to decipher, and began to offer the final blessing. "'Our Father which art in heaven, hallowed be thy name,'" he said. "'Thy kingdom come. Thy will be done in earth, as it is in heaven. Give us this day our daily bread. And forgive us our debts, as we forgive our debtors.'"

"Yes," Rosalind said softly as she squeezed Mick's hand. "Oh yes."

"'And lead us not into temptation, but deliver us from evil: For thine is the kingdom, and the power, and the glory, for ever. Amen.'"

As they stood together, the minister placed his hands on them. "Forasmuch as Michael and Rosalind have consented together in holy wedlock, and have witnessed the same before God and this company, and thereto have given and pledged their troth, each to the other; I pronounce that they are man and wife, in the name of the Father, and of the Son, and of the Holy Ghost. Amen."

Mick barely had time to blink before Rosalind was in his arms and kissing him ardently on the lips. In the next instant, they seemed to be flying down the aisle and into a carriage. Before he could catch his breath to speak to her, she had floated out of the carriage and into his house. Mick followed behind her until he discovered himself in his own parlor—where his Christmas tree glowed with a thousand white candles.

"Jolly good show, old man!" William cried, giving him a slap on the back.

"All the happiness in the world, Mick!" Caroline pecked him on the cheek. "Did you know you've given William the sudden inspiration to woo me until I have fallen madly in love with him?"

"What?"

"We're going to the Continent on an extended holiday—just the two of us. We shall stay at a chateau in France, where he has promised to take me dancing every night until I have worn out three pairs of shoes!"

Giggling, Caroline slipped her arm through her husband's and hurried away to greet the throngs of visitors arriving at the house. Mick gazed around him as a towering white cake was cut and passed out. Hundreds of gifts were laid on tables set up about the room.

Seemingly every member of the peerage stepped forward to wish him well . . . him and Rosalind, for somehow she appeared at his side in the most enchanting gown of soft pink velvet. She smiled at everyone, chatted in the friendliest manner, and all the while kept her hand firmly clasped in his.

Finally, Mick could bear it no longer. He left her side and caught up with William, who was kissing Caroline under a sprig of mistletoe in the foyer. "Listen, William," he said, taking his friend by the arm, "I must know what is going on here."

"Mick?" William frowned at him. "Are you unwell?"

"I'm quite well, thank you."

"Indeed, I should hope so on your wedding day!"

"William, do not play games with me." Mick could hear the growl in his voice. "Did she not tell you about the lamb?"

"Who? What lamb?"

"Rosalind, of course. Did she not tell you about the lamb . . . about India . . . about that Christmas Eve when I was a boy and—"

"Mick, what are you jabbering about, man? Rosalind said nothing to us this morning but 'A happy Christmas Eve to you both' and 'I can hardly wait to be married to Mick.' Now get back in there to her. Your guests will soon be going away, and you've stood about all morning as if someone had transfixed you."

She hadn't said anything? Mick wandered back into the parlor, still trying to reconcile reality with the certainty that by this time he was to have been utterly undone by Miss Rosalind Treadwell. Instead, she had married him. Married him?

He looked across the room at her, and his chest swelled with joy. She had married him! Her words before the minister came back to him in full force: *"I forgive him."*

"Rosalind!" He crossed the room and swept her into his arms. "Rosalind, is it true?"

"Of course," she said, laughing. "I love you, Mick! I shall love you always."

As he swung her around, the remaining guests began to applaud. "Good show! Well done! Cheers!"

Mick took Rosalind's hand and circled the room, pumping everyone's hand he could grasp. "Happy Christmas to you!" he cried out. "God bless you!"

Rosalind chuckled, dancing along beside him as they said their farewells to everyone. And then she was giving her papa a kiss and seeing him off in his carriage. William and Caroline dismissed the servants, and then they, too, were gone.

As the door shut on the last of the crowd, Rosalind pulled Mick by the hand back into the parlor. "Come on," she said. "It's not Christmas until tomorrow, but I cannot wait to give you your present."

"Present?" Mick followed her across the room to the small table where the nativity scene stood. "Oh, Rosalind—"

"Look," she said, slipping the tiny white lamb from her pocket and setting it beside the manger in which the Christ child lay. "Now it is home again . . . where it belongs."

"Rosalind," Mick said, taking her in his arms, "I thought you would . . . I expected this morning to be . . . do you really wish to be my wife?"

She smiled and tapped him on the nose. "I believe that's what I promised God in church just this morning, silly goose."

"But I . . . the things I did to you. I destroyed your family. How can you ever forgive that?"

"When I was praying last night," she said, turning her gaze downward, "I realized that you and I are no different. We are both sinners, both in need of the tender Shepherd's blessing, guidance, and protection. I forgive you," she said, looking into his eyes, "because I have been forgiven."

"Oh, my love. My dearest love." He took her in his arms and kissed her until all the uncertainty had fled from his heart.

"You and I," Rosalind whispered as they gazed down on the baby in the manger, "are just two little lambs . . . forgiven and loved by the Lamb of God, who takes away the sin of the world."

A Note from the Author

Dear Friend,

As I ponder the keepsakes and treasures God has given me over the years, one of the first blessings that comes to mind is you! I cannot imagine writing my books without the knowledge that you, my dear reader, are supporting my ministry with your encouragement and prayers.

Thank you for writing to me and for being patient until I've had a moment to write you in return. I cherish your letters, saving them in a special file and taking them out to read and reread. I love the little things you send me— pictures of yourself and your family, photographs of your church or home, cards to lift my spirits, funny little stickers that make me smile. You tell me the stories of your life, the names of your children and grandchildren, the places you have been, and the joys and sorrows you have known. You are very real to me and, as I write, you are in my heart.

Thank you also for sharing with me the depths of pain you have suffered in your life. How I wish I could reach out and hug away your hurt! I cannot tell you how I praise the Lord when you write that something in one of my books has helped to heal you. That lets me know that God is at work, and I'm doing what he wants me to do. Bless you.

My friend, I lift you up to the Lord, thanking him for the great treasure he has given me . . . in you!

Blessings and peace,
Catherine Palmer

About the Author

CATHERINE PALMER lives in Missouri with her husband, Tim, and sons Geoffrey and Andrei. She is a graduate of Southwest Baptist University and has a master's degree in English from Baylor University. Her first book was published in 1988. Since then she has published more than twenty-five books and has won numerous awards for her writing, including Most Exotic Histori- cal Romance Novel from *Romantic Times* magazine. Total sales of her novels number more than one million copies.

Her HeartQuest books include the series A Town Called Hope (*Prairie Rose, Prairie Fire,* and *Prairie Storm*); *Finders Keepers; Hide and Seek;* and novellas in the anthologies *Prairie Christmas, A Victorian Christmas Cottage, A Victorian Christmas Quilt, A Victorian Christmas Tea,* and *With This Ring.* Her first suspense novel, *A Dangerous Silence,* was published earlier this year, and her first hardcover book, *The Happy Room,* is scheduled for release early in 2002.

Her original HeartQuest books, *The Treasure of Timbuktu* and *The Treasure of Zanzibar,* were rereleased last year as the Treasures of the Heart series. The first two books are now titled *A Kiss of Adventure* and *A Whisper of Danger.* Also look for the never-before-published third book in the series, *A Touch of Betrayal.*

Catherine welcomes letters written to her in care of:

Tyndale House Author Relations
P.O. Box 80
Wheaton, IL 60189-0080

Far above Rubies

Kristin Billerbeck

This book is dedicated to my husband, Bryed.
He is a man who walks with integrity,
lets his love of Christ shine through,
and who shows me every day how
I am worth far above rubies.

CHAPTER ONE

EMPIRE CITY, CALIFORNIA, 1890

*J*ack Grant clasped his hands behind his back and nervously paced the train platform. He could hear the familiar whistle blowing through the cedars, but never before had its piercing cry caused his heart to pound so vigorously. Katherine was nearly here. Katherine, his beloved fiancée. The woman who had traveled nearly a continent for their binding love. He smiled to himself when the black steam engine came into view. Positioning himself outside the luxurious Pullman, he waited, his breath halted in anticipation.

She appeared as if in one of his dreams, with her fair hair lit by the afternoon sun and her periwinkle gown cinched tightly at the waist. As she stepped down to the platform, it was only when her nervous smile met his that he realized it was not Katherine at all but her elder sister, Emma. Her hair suddenly seemed a shade darker, her height a smaller stature. He silently chastised himself for the mistake, counting it as folly because he had missed

Katherine for so long. After all, she and Emma did share the same light and sparkle to their eyes.

His gaze was now caught and reined in by those eyes. An unnaturally beautiful hazel, Emma's eyes reflected more than Katherine's mere beauty; they also reflected a knowing countenance that bespoke a marked intelligence.

It was all folly, of course. A natural mistake, that he would find another woman so attractive. Nearly three months had passed since he'd seen either sister, and they did share many similarities.

"Emma, is Katherine still on the train?" he asked, searching around her.

❋ ❋ ❋

Emma Palmer smiled in response. As fearful as she had been about coming, something in Jack's expression soothed her frayed nerves. Jack Grant's rugged appearance would have caused the hardest of women to soften. His dark, wavy hair was combed to Sunday perfection, and his Christmas green eyes held her rapt attention. *Katherine is a fool*, Emma thought.

Jack held a ring in his hand, a gorgeous emerald-cut ruby worthy of anything she had seen in the Boston shops. His disappointment was apparent when he slowly pocketed the exquisite piece. He straightened, his broad shoulders expanding. How she hated to dash the expectation she saw in his expression, yet she wondered how Jack could have fallen victim to Katherine's coquettish giggles and flirtatious manner. He appeared far too intelligent for such frivolity.

Emma had little doubt that her sister's feelings for Jack, however fleeting, had been real. At least, they had been before Jack had disappeared to California, and Katherine had quickly turned her diminutive attention span elsewhere. What a pity. Jack Grant was everything a woman could hope for in a husband. Instead, Katherine would marry a banknote, and she, Emma, would marry Jack. *If* he would have her.

Aunt Mabel stepped up next to her. "Jack, I've come as Emma's chaperon. And to explain."

"Explain? Explain to me where my bride is?"

Emma closed her eyes. Her father's words echoed in her memory. *"Mr. Grant is not in a position to be selective, Emma. He has a steady stream of investors visiting that mine operation of his. And I never promised him Katherine; I promised 'my daughter' in marriage. When you step off the train, he'll know exactly what's happened, and if he wants to avoid any scandal, he'll marry as scheduled."*

Emma's pleas had been useless, and here she stood before this incredibly handsome yet confused stranger, offering herself in marriage. Had her mother not exacted a promise out of their father—that neither daughter would be left a spinster—Emma might be happily attending a tea in Boston at this very moment.

"Is someone willing to offer an explanation? Where is Katherine?" Jack's tone wasn't angry, but Emma could tell that recognition was seizing him with an unsavory flare.

Aunt Mabel started to speak, but Emma silenced her with a gentle squeeze. How would Emma explain Katherine's lighthearted ways to a man who had seen only what he wanted to see? Jack Grant had come to Boston and courted Katherine like no other. They had gone to the theater, on carriage rides . . . and Katherine had given him the mitten without a second thought.

"Emma," Katherine had said with a flip of her blonde ringlets, "men in Boston are plentiful—especially the bankers. I could scarcely care who I marry as long as I live in one of the best houses along Mansion Row. Besides, you could hardly expect me to live in California without today's modern conveniences and entertainments. Mr. Grant called his home the 'cottage.'" Katherine had frowned with distaste.

And so it was Emma who had inhabited the private Pullman car to California. Complete with Chippendale furniture, a sitting area, a gaming table, and even a small bedroom paneled with mahogany, it was a luxury in travel such as she'd never known. Elegant, cut-glass hurricane lamps along the wall and red crushed velvet upholstery everywhere only served to remind Emma that it did not rightfully belong to her. Her aunt had begged her to stop fretting. She had reminded Emma that Katherine was only a passing fancy to Jack and that he'd soon be over such a whim. After all, in retrospect, were there not many happily married men in Boston who probably felt the same way?

Now, standing in front of Mr. Grant himself, Emma wasn't so sure. Jack surveyed them both. "I didn't realize

Miss Katherine was bringing her entire wedding party. Well, good for her. We shall have quite the celebration. You must be their Aunt Mabel." Jack stretched out his hand and shook hands with Aunt Mabel.

"Yes, and I'm afraid I don't have the news you wish for, Mr. Grant." Mabel smiled gently.

Emma put her hand on her aunt's arm to quell the forthcoming speech. "No, Aunt. I shall tell him. It will be the least of my humiliations." Emma cleared her throat. "Mr. Grant, my sister is not coming. It seems she has plans to marry another."

Jack stepped back and watched as the porter shut the door to the Pullman car. "I don't understand. Why would your father send the bridal party without the bride?" He laughed at first. He was obviously thinking this was some kind of joke. Then the evergreen of his eyes slowly disappeared as he comprehended the scheme unraveling before him.

Again, Aunt Mabel tried to save the situation, but Emma stopped her. She might as well be honest. Her reputation with Jack Grant was poor at best. She had nothing left to lose. He might as well know she found the idea as ridiculous as he soon would.

"My father said that he'd only promised you a *daughter*, not Katherine. His plan was that you would marry me and Katherine would stay in Boston."

Jack's brows lowered. "Your father arranged our marriage without consulting me?"

"It appears as such." Emma smoothed her skirt

nervously. "I would appreciate passage back to Boston and, I assure you, this whole thing will be forgotten. I'm sorry for the trouble." Emma didn't look to his eyes, not with the disappointment so evident in his voice. Her presence wasn't appreciated. She hardly needed the confirmation in his expression.

Victorian society had refined visions when it came to taking a wife. A beautiful woman of means and eloquence was sought when a man of stature settled down. Emma, although taught in all the right ways, compared herself to a piece of functional furniture—comfortable, yes, but sturdy and practical, too. She performed her household arts with the utmost care, but she would never be something looked upon with reverence.

Katherine, in contrast, was the consummate choice of better homes, a fine furnishing with curved legs and expensive craftsmanship. By the time Katherine married, it would be too late to see that fine hardware had hidden her true nature: a spoiled woman with a fiery temper.

Emma felt Jack's stare boring down on her, and she stuttered her words. "W-we'll just stay in town until the next train and be on our way."

Jack let out a short laugh. "Your father certainly knows how to strike a deal. I suppose I should give him credit. He knew I was entertaining investors this week, didn't he?"

"I'm not sure, sir." Emma felt herself scrutinized, as she anxiously awaited the moment when he would approve passage back to Boston and free her from this embarrassment. She could put up with his harsh stares until then. But his next comment sent her heart racing.

"Well, Miss Emma, it appears we are to be married tomorrow."

Emma looked up sharply. "I beg your pardon, sir?"

"I can't afford a scandal. Your father knew that, I suppose." Jack's expression faded into a strained grin. "I have three possible investors visiting in the cottage clubhouse. They're planning to attend my wedding tomorrow. And a wedding they shall have. You are familiar with genteel society?" he questioned. "Although I'm not sure how genteel society feels about fraudulent representation."

"Yes, sir. I was trained at the finest finishing school in Boston. My father has entertained some of the city's most prominent bankers and lawyers with me as his hostess." Emma's heart raced at the possibility of staying. She couldn't explain why, but suddenly being Jack's wife felt like a much better life than heading back to Boston. She couldn't deny that her heart caught in her throat when she looked at him.

"Good. I'm sure with your father's business practices, he'll be in need of those lawyers at some point."

Emma swallowed hard. "I'm sorry, Mr. Grant. Truly I am."

"Your sister said nothing of me before your journey?"

"No." How could she tell him Katherine had only laughed at their infatuation?

"Harley will get your trunk. Come along." He walked resolutely ahead of Emma and her aunt. The discussion was over, and they rode to the cottage wordlessly.

❋ ❋ ❋

The drive leading into the estate was beautiful, through some of the most majestic trees Emma had ever seen. It was like being surrounded by the joy of Christmas all year round. Judging by their height, they must be as old as the hills themselves, and the lush greenery surrounding her filled her with a new kind of peace. Emma tried to imagine herself as mistress of this place, decorating a freshly scented cedar to celebrate the Savior's birth. It was hard to think about Christmas, however, in the temperate fall of California.

Jack passed up the carriage house and continued on the winding drive until they came to the foot of a mansion that put those of Boston to shame. Emma's eyes opened wide at the sight. Its sprawling walls seemed to have no end, and she wondered what kind of people lived in such a grand home.

The great house was an English manor of brick and serpentine stone. Stately and castlelike all at once, it appeared to go on forever, so that the ancient redwoods appeared to be normal-sized trees standing next to the home. Emma tried to maintain her composure, knowing their cottage would be on such a dignified estate.

Jack stopped the carriage in front of the mansion and looked to her. Again, she witnessed his disappointment. He had probably hoped he would turn and find her more pleasing than before, but the same brown-haired, hazel-eyed woman looked back. She prayed he wasn't recalling the luminous, golden ringlets of her sister at the moment.

He turned away. "Here we are, the cottage."

"Th-the cottage?" Emma stared at the mansion. Beside it, a rose garden glowed with all the colors of the rainbow. Large, healthy roses played off the sunshine, and hummingbirds hovered over them, making a romantic buzzing sound. Although the chill of fall could be felt in the air, it was like a spring day in Boston. A grand fountain like those in Europe trickled in the background. And behind the house was another structure that appeared as large as the house itself. "Where is the cottage?"

"You're looking at it, Miss Emma." Jack unloaded her trunk. "There is a bathtub with running water within the house and electric lamps, plus heating, so I think you'll be quite comfortable here."

Emma felt the corners of her mouth turn up. If Katherine had known the "cottage" was an exalted mansion with creature comforts, Emma had little doubt it would have been Katherine who would be marrying tomorrow. Just for a moment, she felt giddy.

Until Jack's terse tone continued. "Your maid is Mary. She's waiting for you at the door. I'll see you tomorrow at the wedding. Not a word of this to anyone, do you understand?"

"Yes, Mr. Grant."

"Jack. You may as well call me Jack. We're not big on formality here in California, and since we're about to become man and wife, you may start by calling me by my Christian name."

CHAPTER TWO

*J*ack toured the grounds of his estate and pondered his dilemma. He hadn't slept a wink, though his racing mind didn't notice. This very afternoon he would take a wife. Not the beautiful, enigmatic Katherine, who made him feel alive; but her sister, the woman Henry Palmer couldn't marry off to a man in Boston.

Jack sighed aloud. Wasn't this always the way? He planned his steps so carefully, and God sent something completely different. Something he didn't want. Californians would always be considered barbarians by city society. Emma's arrival was only confirmation of that fact. No amount of money would ever impress society's upper crust, or his father, for that matter. Jack thought he might cheat the system by marrying a wife of culture, but now it would take that much longer to prove he was a business voice to be reckoned with.

He tried to tell himself it didn't matter. A wife was a necessity for entertaining prominent businessmen, especially in the West, but being handed a pale copy of his true love was like a knife to the chest. What was God asking of him? He'd wrestled with the question countless times, wondering if he should go through with the ceremony regardless of who would attend. He found solace in the fact that his family wouldn't have attended even if Katherine was his bride. They'd never understand his infatuation with California, or its dirty business of digging through the ore for gold.

He pulled a handkerchief from his Levi's and unraveled the contents: a sweet, angelic picture of his beloved Katherine. Although she wore no hint of a smile in the photograph, it was as though her violet eyes looked only at him. They pierced the paper and spoke to him. Her expression conveyed a message he so badly wanted to hear. *I love you, Jack. We belong together.* Could he so easily toss that aside?

The ruby ring fell to the ground. He bent, picking it up mournfully. His grandmother's ring. His grandfather had purchased it in England on his way to America, only to succumb to the fever on his way. His grandmother treasured that ring and had given it to Jack on his last Christmas. *For his bride,* she'd said, *because the price of a virtuous woman is worth far above rubies.*

Jack shook his head. "How could you do this to us, Katherine?" He unfolded the handkerchief further and held a lock of her golden hair. "How could you let this happen? Why didn't you fight for me?" He closed his eyes and dreamt of her. Katherine had *kissed* him. Not allowed herself to be kissed, but had actually kissed him with a fire he'd never known. Nothing would ever compare to that.

Canceling this fiasco of a wedding was the only possible route. No investment was worth throwing away that kind of love. He would go to Boston and fight for Katherine. He squared his shoulders, marching to the cottage.

Over the crest of the lawn, he noticed Emma. She sat in the rose garden with her Bible open upon her lap. Seizing the opportunity to speak with her alone, he strode toward her. However, her shaken appearance stopped him in his tracks. Tears streamed down her face, but she wiped them away with a delicate linen cloth and continued with her reading, oblivious to his presence.

She bowed next to the brick bench, clasped her hands, and prayed in earnest. Something about her quiet presence stilled him. Looking down at the photograph, he was struck by the contrast in sisters: Katherine, so blonde and delightful; Emma, so serene and filled with unanswered questions.

He wadded the handkerchief and pocketed it, drawing a deep breath. Emma never saw him advance, and he could hear her muffled cries as he approached. He couldn't imagine what could have upset her. She was making a profitable marriage that very afternoon. Or so she thought.

"Is something the matter, Miss Emma?"

Her head shot up, and her tear-streaked face shone up at him, a single tear glistening in the morning sun. She patted her soft brown hair, magically spun with highlights of gold, and sniffled. "No, nothing at all, sir. It is bad luck to see the bride before the wedding."

"I think we've had our share of bad luck as it is, Miss Emma."

She sniffled again. "Yes, sir."

"Please, Emma, call me Jack. You make me feel like your employer."

"Yes, of course. I'm sorry, Jack."

"Emma, will you permit me to ask, why are you here?"

"In the rose garden? I didn't realize—"

"Not in the rose garden, here in Empire City. Why are you here?" Jack watched her for signs of deception, but he saw only honesty. A purity that drew him despite his resolve.

She paused for a moment. "I'm here to marry you, Jack, because my sister, Katherine, is marrying another." She straightened her shoulders just a bit. "My father thought this best because you needed a wife, and he feared I needed a husband. If you'd like me to leave, only say the word. I shall take the blame with your investors."

He felt his heart leap at the prospect. "Will Katherine come in your place, Miss Emma? If you go back to Boston, will Katherine come to me? Would your father allow her?"

A bewildered look crossed her face. She peered at the extensive grounds before speaking. "Perhaps, if she knew about the cottage, she would come."

Jack felt his face flush with rage. "Katherine would not care of my holdings." But even as he said the words, he wondered. No, he had to believe this was their father's doing. "Katherine is not such a shallow creature as that. You only say these things to flaw my memories. I love your sister! Your father did wrong by sending you in her place."

"I agree." She looked up again, her face rosy from her extensive sobbing. Under the morning sun, he saw the hint of green and gold in her eyes that sparkled over the simple brown he'd noticed yesterday. Then a bit of fire flashed in her eyes, lighting her expression. "What is it you want of me, Jack? If you don't want me as a wife, I cannot blame you, but send me home. Do not torment me with your angry words. Do you not think I've felt their sting? I've left everything behind, Jack—my teaching, my friends, my family. You are not the only one who suffers."

His breath left him at the thought of how he'd hurt her. Regardless of their circumstances, his actions were not of a genteel nature, and her crying now made sense. He'd been cruel and uncaring, not worthy of the title *Christian*. He spoke softly, "You're right, Miss Emma; I had only thought of myself. I'm sorry."

"If you want to believe Katherine is sweet and good, I'll not tarnish your memories, but know this. She didn't come, Jack. And unless I tell her of the electricity, the tennis courts, and the sheer size of the cottage, she won't come."

"I cannot believe that!" Jack heard his teeth grind in anger.

"Then send me home and find out. Unlike my father, the idea of spinsterhood appeals to me. Especially now that you've made our married future clear. Think ill of me if you will; I have nothing to lose. I had a fine life teaching the children of Boston, and I should like to go back to it if I'm not welcome here."

He watched her curiously. Her challenge was real. Not a hint of insincerity emanated from her. He reminded himself that trusting Emma made Katherine a liar. "You have a lot to gain by making me think evil of your sister. The property, the grounds, the mine itself—all yours if this wedding goes as planned."

She laughed through her tears. "I do not care of *possessions,* Mr. Grant. I've watched goods control my family for far too long. You cannot serve both God and money."

"You accuse your sister again with your quotes! All while you hold a Bible in your hand. Do you not know the Christ as your Lord, that you could lie so easily?"

With this accusation, she stood, her whole body trembling. "I do know my Lord, sir. I speak only the truth. Katherine may have loved you once, but she is not here. I am here. I'm not asking you to love me. I'm only asking you to send me home, or make the best of this awful situation. The apostle Paul said he could be content in all situations, and I'm willing to try if you are. But do not play with my feelings anymore. I fear I cannot stand it."

"You ask me to forget Katherine," he said incredulously.

"I ask only that you not blame me for her actions." Again, he saw the tears well in her eyes. "Or my father's. If you wish to be married this afternoon, send word to my aunt. Otherwise, I shall pack my trunk and leave for Boston on the next available train." Emma flung her skirt around and marched toward the house.

Jack stood aghast. Emma was either the consummate actress, or she really didn't want such a marriage. Was it possible? When he had everything in the world to offer such a woman? Everything, that is, except his love. The sight of her walking away made his mouth go dry. Why should he care if she left? But in an odd way, he did care. Perhaps it was just the thought of another rejection that plagued him.

"Wait!" Jack called after her. There was the possibility Emma spoke the truth, but Jack couldn't deny Katherine's kiss in Boston. The tenacity with which she gave it could only amount to love.

Emma turned back, waiting. He held out Katherine's handkerchief to his would-be bride. "Would your sister give a lock of her hair to a man she didn't love?"

Emma glared at him. "I suppose that is a question for Katherine."

Jack seethed at her intimation, but there really was no choice. Jack needed a wife and, regardless of the true reason, Katherine was not here.

❋ ❋ ❋

Emma disappeared into the cottage in a flurry of blue silk. Jack picked up the Bible she'd left in the rose garden and opened it. It was filled with flowered notes and letters. He softened at the knowledge that she evidently spent a lot of time with this sacred book. He hoped she did indeed know her Scriptures, because perhaps that meant God had saved him from himself. Katherine's faith, he reasoned, could not have been nearly as strong as he'd thought, if she had so easily abandoned her commitment to him.

Jack promptly put the Bible under his arm, his mind still reeling. What *was* the truth?

"Jack!" Seth Trainor, one of America's prominent bankers, walked toward him. Seth's approval of the Gold State Mine could make or break Jack's future. The older man glanced at his pocket watch and deposited it back into his vest. "I wanted to let you know I'd met your bride earlier this morning while touring the grounds. She was in the rose garden, studying her Bible. Lovely girl. I'm quite impressed."

Jack was speechless. Had Emma been in the garden all morning? He finally found his tongue. "We met in Boston. I had business with a friend of her father's. We were introduced at a small dinner gathering."

"You're lucky to have found love with such a genteel woman. It is hard to find a woman of society willing to move to California. She has a very graceful carriage. Most young men your age find the pretty little ornaments instead of a proper wife who can manage a great home such as this. It shows discretion that you selected such a fine, young woman of character. I hope you run your mine with the same good sense."

Was it possible men of society might actually think Emma a proper choice? With his tunneled view of Katherine, he had not allowed himself to pursue the notion. "What did you discuss with her, Mr. Trainor, if you don't mind my asking?"

"Call me Seth. Emma seems quite interested in your work, Jack. She says she heard that vicious pounding noise all morning, and I explained the California stamp in detail to her. Most women give you that blank stare when you discuss business."

Jack shifted uncomfortably. Emma's interest in the mine could only mean her noble speech about material possessions was simply an act. It was not natural for women to be interested in such things.

"A worthy wife is information I can take with me to the bank. A man never understands the asset of a good wife until he marries," Seth continued jovially.

Jack's chest deflated. Excuses, rather than a wedding ceremony, would be folly. If Seth approved of Emma, that could only be good news for the mine. Was this meeting perhaps part of God's plan, too?

"Why don't we head to the mine, Seth?" Jack slapped the elder man's back. "They're going to be blasting tomorrow, and it will be too dusty to enter. We've found a rich vein of gold we're following. I imagine you'll be quite pleased with the quartz we've taken out this week."

"That sounds like a fine idea," Seth agreed. "I take it you're not planning any kind of wedding getaway?"

"The mining business never stops. No time for frivolity. Let me just leave word with Emma, and I'll be ready."

"Most assuredly, my boy. Take your time; I'm just enjoying the gardens. I'm thinking of staying on through Christmas. I'd like the wife to see the place. I feared it would be too rugged for her. How wrong I was. And the train ride wasn't taxing either."

Jack thrilled at the prospect of Seth staying on. Jack could learn a lot from such a profitable businessman. He sprinted up to the house and bypassed Emma's maid altogether. He pounded on Emma's door. "Emma! Emma, open the door."

Emma peeked through the cracked doorway, her face blanched. "Yes," she answered calmly.

"The wedding will take place this afternoon as scheduled. Four o'clock in the rose garden under the trellis."

Emma simply nodded and shut the door quietly. Surprisingly, his heart sank at the disappointment he had seen in her eyes.

CHAPTER THREE

A lock of Katherine's hair, indeed, Emma thought, frowning to herself. *There are probably enough locks of Katherine's hair out there to wig half the balding women of Boston.* Emma gazed at her reflection in the mirror. Her wedding gown was the latest fashion with the finest lace, fashioned into one huge, high bustle in the back. The style cut scandalously close to her figure and flared at the bottom. She felt unchaste in it.

Thankful for the long veil, she surrounded herself, wishing she could disappear altogether underneath the lengthy lace train.

"You look beautiful." Aunt Mabel came up behind her in the mirror, caressing her shoulders.

"I look ridiculous. Did Katherine fashion this gown? I feel like the mythical mermaid of drunken seamen's tales."

"Emma, it is *your* wedding day, and you are thinking only of Katherine," her aunt chastised.

"Well, that makes two of us, I suppose. I'm sure Mr. Grant has thought of nothing else either."

Aunt Mabel whirled Emma around. "Emma, this dour outlook will only serve to harm you. You must forget the circumstances of this wedding and focus on your future. You did not happen here by chance, despite what you think." Aunt Mabel looked at her gently.

Emma's frustration melted into fear. "He despises me, Aunt. I am to be married, not just to a man I don't know, but to a man who loves my sister."

"And so Leah must have felt, my dear, but her legacy lived on in the lineage of Christ himself. Who are we to judge how God might intervene on your behalf?"

Emma clung to her aunt's hope. "You always see the silver lining, Aunt Mabel. What if there isn't to be one this time?" Emma gazed at her bridal reflection. "I have been second to Katherine my entire life, and so shall I be on my wedding day."

"Your position is the same as it always was with God, my dear. You must ask yourself which is more important. This is not like you, Emma."

Guilt enveloped her. "I have been feeling dreadfully sorry for myself, haven't I?"

Aunt Mabel straightened Emma's veil, ignoring the question. "Arranged marriages happen every day, Emma. It is not the end of the world. You and Mr. Grant will work out a nice agreement. Focus on the Lord. Please God, and eventually your husband will see the light."

Emma drew in a deep breath, trying to imagine why God might have placed her here on this day. Christmas was coming, and she would be responsible for this great house and its festivities. Surely with all the activities to plan, she would hardly have time to worry about Jack.

"Thank you for being here with me, Aunt Mabel. I should never be able to go through with this without you." *And you, Lord,* she added silently. *What would you have me do?*

"You are like my own daughter, sweet Emma. I would not have missed it, even if you were betrothed to a man in England. And I'll let you in on a secret." Mabel's head touched her own. "Katherine would never be able to live in this lavish lifestyle, Emma. You must remember, she does not know how to take responsibility for a large household. Don't ever repeat this to anyone, but I daresay God has protected our Mr. Grant from Katherine. I love you both, but I have little doubt your father saw to Mr. Grant's best interests when he sent you here."

"I shall miss working with the children in Boston and teaching them to read. Why couldn't Father let me be?"

"Your father never did approve of that, Emma. It wasn't proper for a young woman of your stature to be in the seedy part of town alone, no matter how noble the cause."

"Perhaps that is one silver lining. If Mr. Grant pays me little mind, I should like to teach the miners' children." Hope resonated in Emma's voice. Her true calling had always been teaching, although her genteel birth prevented such an occupation. Any occupation other than marrying.

"You must focus on your husband now and seeing to *his* needs." Aunt Mabel's gentle voice reminded Emma that after today, life would never be the same. Her life would now be alongside a handsome stranger.

❄ ❄ ❄

Awash with color and sweet scent, the rose garden was a romantic setting for a late-fall wedding. In Boston the cold snap would have stung in the air, but here in California there was only a pleasant breath of heaven in the light breeze. With the birds' gentle songs, Emma drew in the magical surroundings, believing, if only for the moment, that love filled the garden.

White silk fabric swept deep from the trellis, dotted with several cut roses. Wooden chairs, placed along the path, held staunch businessmen with callous expressions. Emma wondered if any of them cared a whit for Jack or had any connection to him other than the mine. But what did it matter? The marriage was as much a sham as the guests' concern.

The man she'd met earlier, Seth Trainor, walked her down the aisle and lovingly took on his role. His steady, fatherly ways gave her a sense of peace amid the turmoil. Emma quivered down the makeshift path as the focal point of strangers' eyes. As she neared her future husband, she was struck by his dashing appearance once again.

He truly defied the image of a Californian. He was dressed in the finest black suit with tails, a white tie and vest completing the refined ensemble. Even in the suit, his muscular build spoke of long hours in the mines. Against the backdrop of his tanned skin, his evergreen eyes sparkled. His face broke into a friendly smile, and she felt her shoulders relax at his softened demeanor.

He whispered as she came closer, "I'm glad you made it. I was worried you wouldn't come."

She only smiled in return, but her knees weakened beneath her at his warm words. For the first time, she saw a hint of what Katherine must have seen—a disarmingly charismatic gentleman who knew how to make a woman swoon. Not just the handsome facade, but the warmth within his heart. *Oh, Lord, please help me! Will he ever treat me this way again? Or will the romance end as soon as the ceremony does?* His harshness may have been easier to endure than his gentleness.

The preacher, a staid man, acted as though he conducted a funeral service rather than a wedding. His voice expressionless, he stated the vows without looking up. Jack, however, never took his eyes from her during the ceremony. With breathless anticipation, she answered "I do" when prompted. The solemn vows rolled off her tongue with wonder. She felt as though she were in love.

Emma anticipated receiving the exquisite ruby ring she'd seen yesterday at the train station. It wasn't that she cared much for jewels or treasures; it was that Jack Grant had pledged himself to her, and not Katherine. She held her ring finger out, and Jack slipped a plain, gold band onto her finger.

She exhaled unnaturally and looked to her new husband. His smile hinted that nothing was wrong in his own mind. Where was the ruby? Had he sent it to Katherine? Would Katherine know that Jack's heart still beat for her? Emma felt her eyelids sink shut. The humiliation unbearable, she prayed for strength and smiled at her new husband, avoiding the dark thoughts that plagued her.

"You may kiss your bride," the preacher stated.

Jack bent down and brushed her lips with his own. Her heart pounded at his touch. So much so that she forgot the audience of strangers before them. She returned his short kiss woodenly and turned to face the small congregation.

"Allow me to present Mr. and Mrs. Jack Grant." A round of polite applause burst forth, signaling the end of the wedding. She was married.

The reception line was short yet cordial. Introduced to each of the attending businessmen, she did her best to make small talk. The mine, still in business for the day, didn't allow the miners to attend, and Jack had no family present. He dismissed her questions about his parents, and she didn't press him. A lavish banquet feast was set out on the lawn.

After the men were well cared for, Jack looked to her with kind eyes. "Emma, do you mind if we take a walk? I'd like to discuss something privately with you."

"Not at all." Emma brightened at his invitation.

Jack gave a friendly wave to his investors and friends. Then he walked alongside her with his hands clasped behind his back. When they were safely away from the crowd, he spoke solemnly. "I'm sorry we've gotten such a rough start, Emma, but we shall go forward. What's done is done."

"It's to be expected, Jack. We shall make the best of things." Emma was encouraged by his kind overture. She hoped he'd take this opportunity to present the real wedding ring—the ruby ring she'd seen yesterday—so she'd know Katherine would not be receiving what was rightfully hers now. "I will be a good wife to you, Jack. I've already learned a bit about the mine, and I expect to help with the miners' children and their education."

His expression gave nothing away. Would he pay her any mind whatsoever when they began their marriage? If only she could read his dark eyes. If only he'd look at her now as he had during the ceremony. She waited patiently for him to continue.

"This conversation probably should have taken place before the nuptials. It should come as no surprise, however, and I did not care to embarrass you."

"What conversation?" And what could possibly embarrass her more than marrying him when his feelings were abundantly clear?

He strolled ahead of her. "Emma, I want sons. Sons to carry on my name and this mine. Sons to earn the respect my own father never gave to me. The gold veins in the rock will go on long after my death, and I'll need someone to leave them to. Of course, I'll give you time to get used to the idea, since our courtship was ill conceived."

Emma gulped in a burst of air and tried to hide her raging blush. Did he expect an answer? She attempted a reply, but words would not form.

"That is all I wanted to say, Emma. We should get back

to our guests. They'll wonder where we've disappeared to."

"Yes," Emma agreed. "Jack?"

"Yes, Emma."

She looked straight into his eyes, willing herself to be strong. "We'll have a fine family."

CHAPTER FOUR

*T*he great white quartz sparkled in Jack's hands. "There must be thousands of dollars in this one rock." He studied the gold veins carefully, shaking his head in wonderment. "And to think this area has already been mined so many times before."

"Perhaps it is a wedding present." Seth Trainor's bushy eyebrows rose and fell.

Not likely, Jack thought. *I deserve no present.* Jack and his bride, though married for one week, had managed only casual greetings to one another in the grand hallways and at formal dinners with clients. Jack, knowing he'd done nothing to make his wife feel welcomed, smiled sheepishly at Seth. Consumed by his own waning confidence over the loss of Katherine, he didn't know how to be a husband to this foreign woman. Emma always offered him her hopeful smile, which only made Jack feel the brunt of his guilt more.

"Why don't you take the rock to Emma?" Seth suggested.

"Why?" Jack asked.

"Ah, dear boy, it's apparent you've only been married a short time. Courtship doesn't end at the altar. One must continually show his wife affection if he has any hope of a prosperous marriage. It's the small things that make a wife feel loved. . . ." His voice trailed off.

"What would Emma want with a piece of quartz? Especially one that hasn't even had the gold stamped from it?" Jack laughed at the notion. "Emma is a practical woman. She doesn't care about such romantic notions. She's already started some sort of project in the carriage house. I fail to see how an unstamped rock from the mine would impress her."

Seth's well-worn face broke into a hearty grin with wrinkles lining his eyes and mouth. "Son, there is no such thing as a practical woman. Have you ever read Proverbs 31? Where it describes the ideal wife?"

"Yes, of course." Jack swallowed, trying to wish away his guilt. One of the verses was the very one that caused him to think of Katherine as the ideal wife, because she was worth more than precious rubies. Any man could see the sparkle that emanated from her eyes and would desire it for himself. Jack chastised himself for still thinking of Katherine as *his*. But what could he do with his feelings? His marriage was a sham, like a panful of fool's gold. It shone on the outside for all the investors to see, but it offered no hope and no future riches.

"Tell me the verse you're thinking of," Seth prodded, like an overzealous preacher.

Jack sighed, annoyed with the conversation. " 'Who can find a virtuous woman? for her price is far above rubies.' " Jack kicked the soil beneath his feet, biting his lip to keep his frustration from offending Seth.

Rubies. The very word prompted thoughts of his grandmother's precious Christmas ring, still loose in his vest pocket. It belonged on a vibrant woman, one who characterized the vivacity of its bright red color. Perhaps the precious stone was meant for a future daughter and not for his wife, as his grandmother had once said. His wandering reflections ended at the sight of Seth.

Jack cleared his throat. "So that's why you think I should give Emma this quartz rock? You think her price is far above the gold inside it?"

Seth laughed again, and Jack suddenly felt like an ignorant schoolboy who had missed the joke. "No, son. You're reading into the wrong part of the verse, just as all young men do. The Bible asks, Who can find her? because she is not to be found. She is to be created."

Jack humored the older man. "There is but one woman for every man," he said, surprised his thoughts came out audibly.

Seth shook his head. "God gives us a wife as a gift, and it is up to *us* to make her feel as worthy as rubies."

Jack nodded his head in mock agreement. What any of these ramblings had to do with this rock he held in his hand, he had no idea, so he placated the respected banker. "Well, luncheon will be served soon. We'd best be heading back." Jack flipped the rock onto the California stamp, where it would be ground for its precious gold. *Rocks and rubies, Lord. What do you make of that?*

❉　❉　❉

As the two men approached the house, Emma greeted them on the stone walkway. She had her hair pulled up into a loose knot, and the cinnamon highlights glistened under the light and captured Jack's attention. Emma had a blush to her cheeks, like the softest rose in his garden. Jack was struck by her beauty, both in a physical and emotional capacity. He'd never noticed how the green in her eyes sparkled when she spoke. Now he wondered how he possibly could have missed it.

"Jack! I've just had the most wonderful news." She clapped her hands together, then remembering herself, addressed their investor. "Hello, Mr. Trainor." Emma practically burst with excitement, and Jack couldn't imagine what could have gotten her in such an agitated state.

"Well, do not keep us waiting." Jack looked to Seth, hoping the investor wouldn't be bothered by his wife's exuberance.

"Yes, do tell us, Mrs. Grant!" Seth said enthusiastically.

Breathless, Emma continued. "The new overseer has a family with three children who are school-age but have never been to school. Oh, Jack, his wife had several ideas for creating lovely Christmas gifts this year. She's brought gossamer ribbon, shiny paper, and lace from San Francisco to purchase."

"Emma, might we discuss this later?"

"I'm sorry, I digress in my excitement. Her children have never been to school, Jack. Mrs. Willow thought teaching the children would be a great help to her. I've already converted a room in the carriage house and filled it with books and—"

"Emma, the overseer is our employee." Jack watched Emma's face twist in confusion, and he hoped to quell any further nonsense in front of Seth. "We'll discuss it later." The light from her eyes evaporated and was clouded over by moist tears.

"I need to dress for dinner." Seth grinned, as if understanding something deeper, and made his way to the cottage. "Gardens were meant for newlyweds."

Jack felt his jaw flinch. "Emma, need I remind you who Seth Trainor is in society? Domestic issues should never be discussed in front of clients. Your finishing school should have taught you such manners." As Emma sniffled away a tear, Jack tried to change his tone. "Emma, a wife must learn to keep matters of the home within the confines of the manor. I daresay Seth Trainor cares little for our Christmas plans."

A lone tear escaped down her cheek, and Jack sucked in a deep breath at his outburst. As the old banker shut the door to the cottage, Jack realized too late what Seth had been trying to say about Jack's treating Emma with great care and esteem. How he wished now that he'd heeded the advice.

Emma straightened her shoulders, her enthusiasm long since dead. "I'm sorry, Jack. I should have spoken with you privately. I was overzealous in my estimation of your interest in such matters. I'll see to them myself in the future, as you wish." Emma turned to leave.

"Yes, with the exception of teaching. It is not appropriate for you to teach. Should you want to set up a schoolhouse, that is fine, but what will my investors think if they see my wife *working?*" He didn't wait for her answer. "They shall think I don't make enough on the mines to support her in a proper lifestyle, and thus, the mine is not a good investment."

"Perhaps they might think you believe education important for the children of your staff." Emma stalked off.

"Emma!" He called, running after her until he finally grasped her arm. "Women of culture do not *teach*. Society frowns upon a wife of station working. It is for the common and certainly not for a woman in your position."

Didn't Emma understand he'd made it possible for her to have idle, leisurely days? Her sister, Katherine, had loved to hear about such a life. If only Katherine had believed that, he could have provided it. . . . The sting of her disbelief still rattled him.

"Emma, what did your Boston connections do with their day? Certainly, there must be something of interest to you?"

"My friends met for tea in the afternoons, did the theater in the evenings, and took their family pew on Sundays. Empire City appears to have no one available for tea and only one theater, which plays questionable entertainment. I'm assuming this is why you came to Boston for a wife. I presumed my responsibilities would include church and finding something to do here at the mine."

"You do have responsibilities for the mine. Seeing to the house and our guests!" Jack paced to keep his wits about him.

Emma faced him directly. "If you desire the children of the mine growing up ignorant, that is your right, I suppose. Nothing like raising a city full of feebleminded people to make a man more powerful." Emma's sharp tone caused Jack to grind his teeth together.

He shouted after her, "Katherine would never think of teaching as a daily occupation!" He saw what the mention of Katherine's name did to her. It struck her with the force of any fist, and he cringed at his behavior.

Her complexion was flushed with emotion. "My sister didn't know children breathed, Jack. Her life existed only for tea cakes, the latest fashions from Paris, and the trail of men who paid their homage to her beauty."

Jack clenched his hands. "You shall not teach," he stated simply. "That is my final word on the matter." An Easterner would always feel a level above a Californian, no matter how much money he dug out of the ground. Well, *his* wife would be different.

"What is it you thought Katherine would do here, Mr. Grant? Did you think my sister would be content in this society? With a complete lack of genteel women to pass the time with and entertainments to keep her busy? I think you're quite fortunate I've come instead. Even if you fail to realize it." Emma's usually calm waters took on a storm Jack wouldn't have imagined possible. She appeared so quiet, so placid, and yet she harbored such an intense wave of anger.

"I expected your sister to come as my wife, wear her fine dresses, and enjoy the beautiful estate I've built. Look around you, Emma. There is plenty to manage with this great house and all its guests. Boston society may look down its nose at California, but I have more than the lot of them." Jack's laughter smothered the truth. Society, and all its bondage, had won again. Jack didn't have a coveted Boston society wife. He had an arranged marriage with a woman barely salvaged from spinsterhood.

Emma's pained expression forced his eyes away. "I must see about dinner. That is my *duty*."

It had felt so right when he flung those evil words at her, but now they just made him sick. Seeing her pain held no victory. He prayed for strength, looking to the Lord to take away his resentment. *Father, I don't know how to be a proper husband to this woman. What can I do to make things right with Emma?*

A moment later, the idea came. "I'll be in shortly." Jack inexplicably ran back to the stamping mill and grabbed the chunk of quartz containing the ribboned streaks of gold. He stared at it and shrugged. He would give it to Emma. . . . What did he have to lose?

Making his way back to the house, he found her in the kitchen, directing the servants in the latest serving techniques. He juggled the large rock in his hands, uncertain of how to give her the peace offering.

"Jack!" Emma wiped her hands on a cotton towel and approached him. "Is something the matter? I'm perfectly capable in the kitchen."

"Here!" He thrust the rock toward her, unable to come up with intelligible words. Seth Trainor's idea now seemed more ludicrous than ever, but Jack had nothing to lose. If he and Emma couldn't make things work, there would be far more disgrace from a dissolution of marriage than from a simple arranged marital union.

"A rock?" She studied it. "A rock with stripes? Is there something I don't understand?"

"It's a gift," he said numbly. *Women are supposed to like presents, aren't they, Lord?*

Her eyes lightened and, with the evening sun shining through the kitchen window, he saw their green flecks once again. "It's a wonderful gift, Jack. Thank you." She paused, biting her lip. "Is there something I'm supposed to do with this rock? Is it decor? or a doorstop?"

Jack smiled, coming toward her. She flinched at his approach. He felt her tremble as he took her hands, holding the rock between them, their hands melded together for the first time since their vows. "This is gold, Emma. These dark stripes . . . look at them in the light." He held the rock up to the window, and it shimmered like a hummingbird's wings.

Emma gasped, her large hazel eyes blinking quickly. "Oh, Jack, it's just beautiful. Will you use the California stamp to crush it?"

"You are a quick study, aren't you, Emma? No, I'm not planning to get the gold from this one. I want you to have it. I thought it might look pretty on your nightstand and remind you of the mine, to pray for it. And for me. It's a paperweight worth thousands."

149

"Really? It's for me?" The hope in her eyes again struck him full force. "I need no reminder to pray for my husband, though, Jack."

It was apparent she wanted to believe in him, that she wanted to be a proper wife, but how could he ever make her so? He recalled their awkward conversation about starting a family, and he just couldn't imagine following through with his plan. Making Emma his wife felt like a reality that would never come.

"A peace offering, Emma. I'm sure I owe you more. If you need more to do around the estate, I might be able to use some help with the ledgers at the mill. I'm so busy all day. I forget what it must be like for you with so little to do. In the office you'll be protected and away from the employees." *And none of my investors will see you*, he added silently.

It was a small sacrifice, but it was far more appropriate that Emma be seen improving the mill rather than teaching the employees' children. Jack had struggled so long for the respect of bankers and business investors. He wasn't going to sacrifice his hard-won reputation by allowing his wife to teach.

If Emma had more to do, perhaps she'd expect less from him, and then slowly, he might be able to love her. Not passionately, perhaps, but out of respect as any husband should.

"Jack, really? The ledgers? I'm quite good with numbers!" Emma clasped her hands together. "I can hardly wait to begin. What time shall I be ready tomorrow?"

"There's no hurry, Emma. Just whenever you can find time in your household management. It would be nice to have you at the office."

"I'd like to go with you," she answered softly.

"Very well. I'll come for you at eight."

CHAPTER FIVE

*H*e gave you a rock?" Aunt Mabel's confused expression was priceless, and Emma laughed aloud.

"It's not just any rock, Aunt. It's full of gold, real gold. Jack says thousands of dollars' worth! But there's more!" Emma's energy level took on a life of its own. Joy bubbled up in her soul. She reeled across the bedroom in a ball of her own making. "Jack thought it inappropriate for me to teach the overseer's children, but he did agree to let me set up the school!"

"Emma, that's marvelous."

"In time, perhaps he can be persuaded to see the advantage of my teaching the children. In the meantime, he's asked for my help on the ledgers. I shall go to the office this morning, so we'll be together during the day. Oh, Aunt, maybe if I spend some time with him . . . maybe . . ." Emma's voice faltered. "I'm glad to help Jack, even if it's in a secretarial capacity. Katherine would not have understood the ledgers." Emma felt a tinge of pride burst forth.

Mabel clicked her tongue in annoyance. "Emma, I must confess I do not understand this cross-country competition with your sister. Katherine is in Jack's past, and that is where she shall stay. Why must you torment yourself with this ridiculous rivalry?"

Has there ever been a time when I have been free of such competition? Emma traced her finger along the raised, lilac wallpaper. "Everything in this estate was prepared for her. Just as Father always made things right for Katherine at home, Jack has done so here. I must live in this romantic, mistress's bedroom, decorated in her favorite color, swathed with the finest fabrics, and scented with the most expensive perfumes, all for Katherine. I know she is in Jack's history, but I find myself wishing she were in *mine*, and wondering if she ever will be."

But Emma decided not to allow Katherine's ghost to steal the day's joy. Emma had the gold rock to remind her that things were going to be different from here on out. Jack was willing to make an effort, and Emma would make the most of it.

Selecting her finest reception gown, Emma spread it across the canopied bed. "Do you think Jack will like this?" Shiny, bright peacock blue fabric fanned out across the spread. The gown was the latest fashion, designed with a high neckline, broad shoulders, a tightly cinched waist, and a scant train that traced Emma's steps. She allowed her maid, Mary, to fasten the gown, and she looked hopefully into the mirror.

"Oh, Emma, it is simply beautiful. Your figure is divine in it," admired Aunt Mabel.

"I had it fashioned before I knew I would be marrying.

Father insisted I wear gowns like this, which were less appropriate to wear for teaching. I supposed he hoped to quell my desire to see the children by making me feel out of place in the wrong dress." Emma broke from a moment of reverie. "Do you think Jack will like it, Aunt?"

"Of course, my dear. I believe it with my whole heart."

"I'm content to be useful." Emma announced wistfully. "I was useful in Boston, and I shall be useful to my husband here."

Aunt Mabel looked away. "You shall be more than useful, Emma. Just give God time to work."

The richness of the parquet flooring shone to the point that Emma could see her pale reflection in it. Emma swayed with delight as the gown lit up the room with color. "I do hope the dress pleases him."

"*You* will please him." Aunt Mabel walked to the dressing table and picked up a small pot of rouge. "You have always been such a pretty girl."

"A painted face, Aunt?" Emma dodged her aunt's scarlet finger.

"If properly done, a man can never tell which is a simple blush and which is applied. With such an extravagant dress, you need some added color. Anyone would."

A few quick applications to each cheekbone and Emma was astonished by her new reflection. Aunt Mabel was right; the rouge heightened Emma's natural flush, and her excitement shone. There was a knock at her door, and she leaped to answer it, unable to hold back and behave like a proper society lady.

As Jack pulled open the door, his eyes widened at the sight of Emma. She felt a smile of satisfaction escape at his reaction, knowing her vivid gown had indeed arrested his attention.

"Emma?" A spark lit in his eyes but was quickly extinguished. "We're merely going to the office, my dear. It is, after all, a mine." There was such questioning in his tone that Emma's anticipation over her new responsibility fell away like the fuzzy bark of a redwood in spring.

"I thought there might be investors in the office. I was prepared to receive anyone of stature who might enter," she explained. She brushed her gown, and the expensive fabric spoke to them both. "Do you want me to change, Jack?"

He studied her momentarily, looking back at her aunt and then to Emma again. "No, I suppose you'll be fine. The walk is mostly paved with rock, and you can take the carriage back if it proves too much for you. Or your dress." Jack's eyes flickered over her figure again, but she couldn't read his assessment.

"Good-bye, Aunt." Emma closed the door behind her and followed her husband obediently. He shortened the stride of his long legs to match hers, and she smiled at him gratefully.

❉ ❉ ❉

The brick and serpentine building matched that of the house but was far less grand in stature. The foundation was an entire floor, and steps led up to the main office, which was high in case of winter snow.

Inside, a large map dominated the center of the room,

with elaborate drawings showing the underground tunnels that burrowed beneath them. Two offices flanked the map room, each with a separate grand, redwood desk. An open room held four small pine desks for the office workers. Jack provided little explanation and no formal introductions. He kept his eyes lowered to the floor, as though he were embarrassed by her presence in front of his employees.

"That's my office there, Emma. You can use it for the day." He looked to one of the female secretaries at a desk. "Get Mrs. Grant the ledgers. I'll be at the mine." And with that, he was gone. Emma watched his strident exit and, forcing a smile to her face, turned toward the secretary.

"Hello, Mrs. Grant, and welcome. I'm Eleanor Jenkins. My husband is the foreman down on the scales." Eleanor placed several large black books on Jack's desk, while a small child scurried across the office. "That's my son, Max. He likes to hide. I hope he won't bother you."

"He shall be no trouble to me. I love children."

"We're hoping to see a schoolhouse built in town soon, but until then, I'm afraid he must come with me," Eleanor explained apologetically.

"Don't fret, Mrs. Jenkins. Max will not bother me," Emma assured her. Inwardly, Emma wondered how long it would take to get the schoolhouse functioning. If she were allowed to teach, it would probably be only temporarily and, because of Jack's wish that she not teach at all, a schoolteacher would have to be found.

"We haven't heard much about you. I'm honored to finally meet you." Eleanor gave a slight curtsy. "It isn't often we get Boston society women in Empire City. Your gown is simply wonderful." A long, wistful sigh followed.

Eleanor was dressed simply in a black wool skirt. It appeared rough and uncomfortable and was topped by a starched white shirt. Not so much as a decorative pin finished the outfit.

Emma suddenly felt like a true peacock in her fancy attire. "I shall dress more appropriately tomorrow, Mrs. Jenkins. I thought I might be entertaining my husband's colleagues today," Emma explained, although she knew it was unnecessary. She opened the large black ledger book, grateful to change the subject. "My husband says the accounts are not up to date. I'm hoping to help him get them organized."

"Yes, ma'am. Your husband has a penchant for the mines so he doesn't always see to the ledgers. I'm afraid the rock is in his blood."

Emma laughed. "It would appear that way."

❄ ❄ ❄

The ledgers were an unintelligible mess, and Emma had a renewed sense of purpose. Jack may have had no use for her as a wife, but as an accountant, he was desperate for her.

The morning disappeared into the afternoon, and Emma's growling stomach caused her to search for Jack. Besides, she had discovered something in the ledgers that she felt he would want to know about right away.

She peeked her head out of the office. "Eleanor, have you seen my husband?"

"He must still be at the mine, Mrs. Grant. It's not like him to show his face until the quitting bell. Your husband works as hard as any miner, ma'am."

"I'll be at the mine." Emma lifted her rustling skirt and started toward the stairs.

"But, Mrs. Grant—"

"Don't fret for me, Eleanor. I'm quite strong."

"The mine is a dirty place, Mrs. Grant. Certainly you don't want to wear such a fine gown to—"

"Never mind the gown, Eleanor. I shall be gone but a few moments."

"Well, at least take Max with you. He'll show you how to get there. Max!"

The little boy peeked out from behind a desk. "I get to go to the mine!" He jumped up and down.

"Yes, but listen to me, young man. You take Mrs. Grant to the hoist house and come right back, do you understand?"

"Yes, Mother." Max looked up at Emma with big, chocolate brown eyes in sheer wonderment. "Are you a princess?"

Emma laughed and bent lower. "I'm most certainly not a princess. I'm actually a teacher. Or I used to be, before I married Mr. Grant."

"Someday, I might go to school," the six-year-old boasted.

"I certainly hope so, Max." Emma spoke with conviction. Although she had already applied much energy into setting up the future school, her true hope was that Jack would see her gift and allow her to actually teach one day. There was nothing like the pure light in a child's face when he first grasped the written word.

Max led Emma toward the wooden shack that housed the main entrance to the mine. The little boy didn't take his awe-filled gaze from Emma, and she couldn't help but see the irony in his wonderment. *If only Jack looked at me with such eyes, there would be a school at the mine presently.* Emma grinned at her thoughts.

Once in the hoist house, Emma introduced herself to the miners, their names all familiar now from the payroll. She looked at the long train of cars designed to transport miners to and from the bowels of the mine. The shaft was lit with a single electric light that shone for about one hundred feet, then disappeared into pure darkness. It was impossible to imagine that not only did the wood-supported framework go beyond the black, but it literally went on for miles.

"I'm looking for Mr. Grant."

The hoist man nodded. "He's in the mine, ma'am. We've got an emergency down there. A broken leg, we think." The hoist man lowered the cars, allowing more men to go into the depths.

Emma could hear nothing of the miners below. It was impossible to believe there was any form of life beneath her, other than the bugs that crept through the blackened earth.

"Is Mr. Grant attending to the man?"

"Yes, ma'am. Took some boards down to set it and get the miner up here."

An explosion rocked Emma's foundation, and she felt herself sway. "What was that?"

"Just a little dynamite, Mrs. Grant. Someone must have found a vein of gold. Common occurrence, nothing to worry about."

"Of course not. Where's Max?" Emma looked around her. The miners did the same, but the little boy had vanished. Emma ran to the door, thinking he might have returned promptly as his mother had asked, but something told her Max wouldn't have been anxious to get back. There was no sign of him on the path, and she had a clear view to the mine office.

Emma looked to the empty rail, and her eyes drifted shut. "Did Max get into that train?"

The hoist man shook his head nervously. "No, ma'am. I would have noticed."

They all might have noticed if they weren't staring at her bright gown in the middle of the mine shack. The sunlight seemed to highlight it like a full moon on a clear night. Her appearance practically screamed for attention.

Emma began to fret. The thought of returning to the offices without little Max at her side made her ill. The cars returned to their resting spot, and Emma scanned them frantically, to no avail. Max was nowhere to be found.

"Where did this car come from?" Emma demanded.

"Station eight." The hoist man pointed to a system of wires that were attached to bells at one end, then ran into the shaft of the mine. "When the bell rings, I send the cars down on a signal."

"Do you know where my husband is?" Emma asked hopefully, thinking he might have Max.

"Yes, ma'am. He's at station seven."

Emma hesitated only a moment. "I want you to send me to station eight." Emma hoisted her skirts and climbed into the ore car. She took one last look at her beautiful gown before shrugging at its probable loss. Gowns could be replaced. Max couldn't.

"No, Mrs. Grant. I can't let you go down there. Mr. Grant would certainly have my job."

"I'll take full credit for any trouble I cause. Now, please, Max will be frightened if he's down there."

The hoist man spoke again. "I can send a man down."

"Max might hide from a man. I'm sure he had no idea how dark it would be in the mine. Please, we're wasting time!"

"If you insist on going, I've got to send a man down with you. No one goes into the mine alone." The man signaled to another, and soon a miner appeared in full garb. "We'll both lose our jobs over this," he mumbled, but Emma's expression ensured that complaints were futile.

The miner placed a metal hat, fitted with a kerosene candle, atop her head. "I'm Henry, Mrs. Grant. You'll need to wear this, but we'll wait to light the candle. Don't want to waste any fuel, just in case."

Emma prepared for the long journey into the mine by closing her eyes. The car jolted, and she felt the descent into the darkness. When she finally had the courage to open her eyes, she could see nothing. Not the hand in front of her face, or the car she was riding in, or the bright hue of her gown. There was nothing but blackness. Cold, unfiltered darkness. *Dear Lord, be with me,* she prayed quickly. *And keep Max safe.*

An eternity passed until she heard voices. "We're almost there," the miner said. "Light your candle," he ordered. She flicked a switch, and the candle roared into a flame. She felt the singe of its heat flick at her hairline. *Is this a bit of what the future holds in store for unbelievers, Lord?* Another explosion rocked them, and she gripped the car with all her strength. The sound of dripping water was everywhere, and the chill of the deep earth pierced her to her innermost being.

"You want to go back up, Mrs. Grant? This is no place for a lady."

"This is no place for anyone, but no, I don't want to go back. I want to find Max."

"You're the boss," he grumbled. "At least until I lose my job."

Emma's heart pounded, and the idea of ever seeing the light of day again seemed to fade with each passing second. Yet, somehow, she felt a comfort in the dark hole. Down here in the deep, she couldn't be seen making some irreparable society mistake.

"Max!" She called quietly as they approached the station, which consisted only of a dim light that shook on and off. "Max." Emma clutched the side rails.

A small voice finally answered. "Here, Mrs. Grant. I'm here."

Emma tore herself from the train, springing onto the tracks below. Falling against the rock wall, she squealed in pain. She rose quickly and turned, shining her light on the young terror-stricken face. She tripped again on the loose quartz and heard her hem tear as she clambered to get her footing.

Keeping her eye on Max, she finally pulled the boy into the train and hugged him tightly, rocking back and forth. *Thank you, Lord, for protecting little Max. Thank you!* She tugged on the hanging wire violently. Soon their position reversed, and the ore train was pulled back up toward the gaping hole of light.

CHAPTER SIX

*J*ack clutched a letter on pale lilac stationery to his chest, gazing over it at his sleeping wife. Her blue dress hung in filthy shreds at the bedpost, and the sight of it incensed him. "Mary! Mary!" he roared.

"What is it, sir?" Mary, the maid, curtsied at her entrance.

"Get that gown out of here!" He paused before adding, "Burn it!"

"Sir?" Mary questioned. "It is such a beautiful gown, perhaps I could sew—"

"I said burn it! I don't ever want to see it again." He dropped his head in his hands, wondering what would possess such an obviously intelligent woman to fish a wandering child out of the mines. "You had no business there, Emma. None at all." He spoke quietly and calmly now, wishing she'd wake up and give him a sign. Upon her return to the house she had collapsed, and no one had heard a sound from her since.

He shook his head and opened the lilac letter. The return engraving read *Mrs. Katherine Blanchard,* and oddly enough, it was addressed only to him and not Emma. He would have recognized Katherine's perfect script anywhere, and her perfume wafted toward him as he pulled out the contents. He stared at the flowery writing, almost ashamed of his longing to read her words, with his wife lying so close by and in such a state. But he had to know why Katherine had abandoned him, why she'd allowed Emma to come in her place.

Without thinking, he inhaled the entrancing scent, which reminded him of her soft lighthearted laugh and their carriage rides in the park. He forced such thoughts away. Of course, her new name could only mean one thing. Katherine was married. *And more importantly, so am I.* He unfolded the letter.

Dear Jack:

Painful recollections motivate me to correspond. I do hope this letter finds you well and adjusting to life with my sister. As you will probably conclude, I am a married woman now. My husband is a banker who possesses a marked intelligence. He is well known and quite respected in the Boston area. Although he is nearly sixty, he is a man of many triumphs who treats me well, and I am most happy. Pray forgive me for relinquishing our courtship as I did, but Emma is far more suited to life in California than I would have been. She never did care for the great pleasures that the city so aptly provides.

Most affectionately yours,
Mrs. Katherine Blanchard

Jack crumpled the paper into a tiny wad. He tossed it into the fireplace and watched it burn with relish. *Mrs. Katherine Blanchard, indeed.* Emotions tugged at his heart. Emotions he didn't want to face. Emma had been right about her sister. East Coast society had slapped him again, this time with him willingly positioning his cheek to be struck.

Reaching into his pocket, he pulled out the ruby ring—too tangible a reminder of Katherine, at the moment—and set it down on the nightstand. *A wife who is more precious than rubies . . . does such a creature exist?*

Emma stirred from her peaceful sleep, her dark-lashed eyes fluttering open. She stared at him and blinked. Again and again, as though he were an apparition. "Jack?"

"Emma!" He took her hand into his own and felt the damage the rock wall in the mine had inflicted. Her hands were rough and blistered. Turning them over, he saw how pink and raw they were. "What were you doing in the mine? You could have been killed."

She clutched his hands tightly, wincing at the pain. Apparently, her fall had hurt more than her hands. "Jack, how is Max?" She struggled to sit up but fell into her billowy feather pillow again.

Jack struggled to maintain composure. "The boy is fine, Emma. Now tell me, why didn't you listen to my men?" His anger masked his fear.

"I went in because I was afraid that Max had wandered in, and he would have been afraid to come out. His mother said that he likes to hide, and I worried he'd get lost in there if I didn't go." She laid the back of her hand on her forehead. "I feel so dizzy."

"One must get used to the depths of the mine. It's hardly for a lady's constitution! I hope you learned your lesson. You should have let one of the men go after the boy!" He wouldn't have forgiven himself if something had come of her. As much as he was exasperated with her willful nature, he was grateful for her safety. Perhaps he should have let her teach, as she had so desired. Maybe then she would have stayed out of trouble. But the idea evaporated as soon as it came. *No wife of mine will teach.*

"I'm sorry, Jack. It was my fault Max went into the mine. I upset the men's routine, so no one was paying attention to the child!"

He stared into her sincere eyes. Although exasperated, Jack was also intrigued. What kind of woman would venture into the depths of the mines to save a child? The question both haunted and exhilarated him.

"It wasn't your fault, Emma. The men knew better than to let you go down. Mrs. Jenkins should have been watching her son!"

"Max was leading me to you, Jack. It was my fault."

"I want you to promise you'll never enter the mine again."

"I promise," she answered in a whisper. "If the children had a place—"

"I'll see to hiring a schoolteacher for the school presently. To keep Max and the other children out of trouble."

Now what can I do about you? Jack added silently. "My mother is coming to California to celebrate Christmas with us. She'll expect a welcoming."

Sophisticated hardly described Emma and her courageous, willful spirit. He knew what his mother would think of such an attachment, and his dreams of approval and esteem from the East Coast evaporated as he gazed into his wife's pleading eyes.

Still, something about her vitality charmed him. Her entering the mine, although foolish, proved that she was not as compliant and quiet as she appeared. A ribbon of excitement clearly dwelled within.

He looked down at the perfumed envelope in his hands. Emma would have to be told the rest. "I've had a letter from your sister."

Emma's colorless expression showed no reaction, but she avoided his gaze. "Yes?"

"She is married now and sends her best wishes for our future together."

"Whom did she marry?"

"I suppose the gentleman she was engaged to when you left Boston, Emma." He wished Emma wouldn't taunt him further with his black memories.

Emma shook her head. "Katherine was not engaged when I left the city, Jack."

"Whatever do you mean, she was not engaged? You came here with the express message that Katherine was to marry another."

"Yes, Katherine was to marry another, but no one in

particular. She wished to stay in Boston, and she had ample opportunity and suitors to do so. Unfortunately, it was not the same for me." Shamed, Emma looked away. "Must you remind me why I'm here? Must you always blame me for our circumstances?"

Emma's tears hit him in a place he had forgotten existed—his hardened heart. Her tears tortured him as he sat alongside her on her canopied bed. The lilac color of the room suddenly sickened him, reminding him of his foolishness over a woman who had probably laughed at his very existence.

"I do not blame you, Emma. You are far different from what I imagined in my wife, but that is not to say I blame you. I have already grown accustomed to the house being managed so well, to the servants attending to my needs before I know I have them, and even to your cheerful face across the breakfast table." He wanted to add that he'd grown accustomed to her warm gazes and cheerful heart, but the words stopped in his throat.

He hated to see her in pain after her ordeal, and her need for his approval struck his heart. She was no different from him. Without another thought, he moved closer and kissed her lips. Gently at first, and then growing firmer. Emma returned his kiss eagerly, and Jack acknowledged for the first time that God did know best. He had given him a wife who respected him.

"Now I must see to the miner who broke his leg." Jack stood up, uncomfortable and uncertain of what this exchange of affection meant to him. Was he beginning to love Emma? Or was he simply trying to forget the awful letter and the terrible simpleton he'd been concerning her sister? He needed time. "You need your rest." He set the envelope down on the nightstand.

"Jack, wait. I need to tell you some news." Emma forced herself up. She grimaced as she used her freshly cut hands to do so.

"What is it? Don't sit up."

"It's the ledgers. You've been entering the profits in the wrong column! Somehow, the columns were reversed, and you've been entering money from profits into the expense column. From the investors, you've done a proper job of detailing the accounts, but from the gold itself, there were many mistakes because the column had shifted. We have enough money to pay off the investors, Jack."

We. He suddenly liked the sound of that. His wife had done what he'd been meaning to do for months, only he hadn't had the time to check it. Being married to her may not have been the desire of his heart, but it had a distinct advantage. He could trust another to look at the books.

❋ ❋ ❋

Emma watched her husband leave with mixed emotions. She reached for the lilac envelope that lay on her nightstand. Her sister's familiar perfume overpowered the stationery, and Emma crinkled her nose in aversion. "Katherine, you never did learn moderation," she said aloud. The envelope was addressed to Jack only, and its contents were missing. Beside the envelope was the ruby ring that was to have been Katherine's wedding ring. Emma picked up the classic jewel and studied it. Perfect in every way and from every angle, it only reminded her of Jack's misplaced affections. Did his kiss mean *anything?*

Aunt Mabel entered her room, and Emma lifted the ring toward her. "Here it is, Katherine's wedding ring. My husband apparently forgot it."

"Perhaps he wanted you to have it, Emma, but didn't know how to give it to you." Mabel fluffed Emma's pillows and poured a fresh glass of water. "Here, drink this. You're pale as a ghost."

"Jack had a letter from Katherine today. She's a married woman. According to this envelope, she must have married Mr. Blanchard."

"The old banker? Well, gracious, I hope the man's money lasts longer than he's bound to."

"Aunt!" Emma chastised, before breaking into a giggle. "Jack says she wishes us the best. What will you tell her when you go back, Aunt Mabel?"

"I won't tell her that her sister had to be fished out of a mine like a mole."

"Aren't you the least bit curious what was down there? I mean, there are literally thousands of tunnels below us. Doesn't that intrigue you in the least?"

"No. And any well-bred woman should have no thoughts as to what happens in a man's world, especially the world underground. What were you thinking?"

Emma heaved a heavy sigh. "I wasn't thinking, I suppose."

"Emma, if you're to be a proper wife to Jack, you've got to think about what he really needs in a wife. Katherine is grace and elegance. Now you and I both know it is a front and that her terrible temper cannot be bottled for long, but Jack doesn't. He only sees what Katherine wants him to see. It grieves me to see you give in to these fanciful whims and lose his respect in the process. He will fall in love with you, Emma, but you must learn to live the life you've been prepared for. Traipsing around with the miners is not acceptable."

"I forget myself here." Emma replaced the ruby ring on her nightstand. "There's no watchful eyes of the city matrons or theaters where I can wear the wrong gown, and yet still I manage to make a scene. Perhaps I'm doomed."

"You are quite capable of performing your duties as a society wife, Emma."

"I suppose I will get my chance. Jack just announced that his mother is coming. She'll arrive soon and stay through Christmas."

"Perfect. You can invite some of the investors from San Francisco, and we'll have a lovely celebration."

Emma sat up straight. "No, we shall have a ball. A Christmas ball. One that will rival anything Boston or New York has planned. I'll have my chance to prove my worth to Jack."

Aunt Mabel laughed uproariously. "Anyone who thinks

you ordinary has never spent an hour with that enterprising mind of yours."

Emma knew it would be improper to confess her husband's kiss to her aunt or to explain how it made her feel. But somehow, it had changed everything. "Jack wished to have a society wife, and I intend to give him one the likes of which Empire City will never see again. The virtuous wife in the Bible is never idle. I have been far too idle."

Her husband can trust her, and she will greatly enrich his life. Oh, Lord, help me to enrich Jack's life!

CHAPTER SEVEN

*J*ack, I've seen to everything. The guest list is full of
your business contacts from San Francisco. Since your
mother and the renowned Mrs. Trainor will be here, I
daresay our little party shall be the talk of society."
Emma's elation could hardly be contained. Jack's approv-
ing smile sent her heart racing.

"It is already the talk of Empire City. The people at the
train station had nothing else to speak of." An unfamiliar
voice caused Emma to turn. The sound of the crush of
expensive silk halted as a courtly middle-aged woman
appeared in the dining-room doorway. Emma would
know the eyes anywhere.

"Mother!" Jack stood and enveloped the woman in a
firm embrace. Mrs. Grant turned her face aside and
allowed him to kiss her briefly before eyeing Emma.

"This must be our Katherine." Mrs. Grant approached
Emma, the rustle of her gown shifting quickly. Upon
getting closer, all sound ceased, and an eerie silence
besieged Emma.

Humiliation reigned in Emma under the haughty stare of her new mother-in-law. Her overwhelming disapproval could not go unnoticed. *Jack's wife is supposed to be a blonde. Blonde and beautiful, so who is this brown-haired woman?* The questions may as well have been asked aloud, for Emma heard them as clear as the California stamp in motion, crushing rocks into slivers of quartz and gold.

"My wife's name is Emma, Mother. Emma, may I present to you my mother, Mrs. Ellery Grant."

Emma steeled herself against the frost and took the remaining steps between them. "Mrs. Grant, it is such a pleasure to have you in our home. I only wish you'd have let us know of your exact arrival date. I would have seen to your passage here."

Jack's mother gave a trifling laugh, "Of course you should have, but then I would not have seen things as they truly are now, would I?" The familiar but, oh so unfriendly, evergreen eyes bore through Emma. It was the same objection she'd once seen in her own husband's eyes, which were now softened by their growing friendship.

"I'll see to your room immediately, Mrs. Grant. We have a luxurious suite in the clubhouse, but I wouldn't think of having you anywhere but in the main house. I'll see to it presently."

"See that she's put in the lilac room, Emma." Jack's order racked Emma's emotions. *If his mother is to be put in my room, where exactly does he expect me to go?*

"Certainly," Emma said aloud without further conjecture. Of course, Jack would want his mother to have the finest room with the view.

Emma broke away from the pair, breathing a huge sigh of relief. The air was stifling in the dining room. She shut the door behind her but heard the loud whispers immediately. She willed herself to leave, but her feet were planted to the redwood flooring as if nailed down themselves. Her mother-in-law's shrill voice was heard plainly.

"Who is this Emma? Whatever happened to Katherine? *Katherine*, your great love. I must admit it wasn't like you to speak so fancifully of a woman. Dare I ask how Emma came to be my daughter-in-law?"

"Is Father here?" Jack obviously wished to evade the subject, but Mrs. Grant would have no part in his avoidance.

"Your father still feels as I do; California is for barbarians who cannot make it on the East Coast. I'll never understand your giving up your birthright to live in this godforsaken country. Although I must admit, your estate is very grand . . . but, of course, it hardly takes the place of a New York house on the right avenue." She clicked her tongue. "And mining, Jack, really. Such a filthy, low-level occupation."

Emma could hear the shifting of the full gown and the pointed steps Mrs. Grant took as she spoke, and something within her wanted to rescue her husband. To boast of his mining conquests and tell of his financial success. She reddened with vexation but continued to listen at the door, like a common scullery maid.

"I am honored you have graced us with your presence, Mother, for the holidays, especially in light of Father's feelings about the West, but you must realize that I have the outdoors in my blood. I could never be fulfilled living in the confined quarters of New York or, heaven forbid, an office."

"You might have seen to it that you were married to a woman of more refined culture." Mrs. Grant's crisp tone grew in volume. "Your wife's gown is woefully out-of-date."

Jack laughed. "You're wrong about Emma, Mother. She has a very good upbringing. She is Katherine's sister. Everything I wrote about Katherine's history is Emma's own. I feel quite honored she's come. It was hard enough to get my own mother to visit."

"I should have seen to it you had a proper bride, Jack. Emma possesses little of the feminine qualities I would have sought for you. New York is filled with beautiful daughters of once-rich businessmen hoping to find a successful match. She obviously brought little into the marriage if Katherine had nothing. Certainly someone with more . . . well, more handsome features might have been better for your investors. But then you always were so impetuous. I can't imagine what attracted you to such a plain girl."

Emma closed her eyes in agony and fell against the paneled wall. The words spoken aloud were far worse than earlier implications. Being compared to Katherine was one thing, but being ruled deficient simply because of her appearance was heart wrenching. Jack's steady voice interrupted her dark thoughts.

"Emma is an excellent wife, Mother. In her short time here, she has already balanced the ledgers, inquired into setting up a school for the miners' children, and managed to run this house like clockwork. What else would I possibly need?"

Emma wanted to break in. *You might need love, Jack. And I could give it to you if you'd only let me.* She scurried up the elaborately carved stairwell, away from the ugly conversation.

The ghastly lilac room was the perfect location for Jack's mother, and Emma was glad to be free of it. Ashamed by her thoughts, Emma couldn't help but think Mrs. Grant would have despised Katherine. Not because the women were so different, but because they were so alike.

"Mary, help me see to my bedroom. Mrs. Grant will be staying in these quarters. I'd like my personal effects moved." Emma entered the lavender room without a care for its loss. It was a daily reminder of her sister, a constant thorn in her side.

"Mrs. Grant?" Mary's round face crinkled in confusion. "This is the mistress's bedroom. You wish me to move your things?"

"I'm referring to Mrs. Grant, Jack's mother. She is here and will be staying in my bedroom for the time being."

"Yes, ma'am. But where shall I take your belongings?"

"Truthfully, I shan't care where I stay. I shall just be relieved to be unburdened of these quarters. It's like living in a French dancing girl's room. Set my things up in the blue guest room for now, Mary." Emma glanced at the gold rock alongside her bed and went to it as though drawn by an unseen string. The ruby ring had long since disappeared from the nightstand, and Emma had never asked of it, but she did have the gold rock. Something that belonged to her, from her husband. Although it was not his heart, it was something.

"Set her nightly things in my room, Mary." Jack's deep voice startled her, and Emma whisked around like a child's top. Mary bowed slightly and excused herself. Jack turned to his wife. "My mother will be staying in the blue room. You may keep your things here, for entertaining and the like, but I am requesting your presence in my room."

Emma could hear nothing over the pounding of her heart. The thunderous beat filled her senses, overwhelming her with fear and longing. She yearned to go to Jack and live as she knew a married couple should, but the suddenness sent a flurry of alarm through her. A mistress should have her own bedroom—what would Mrs. Grant think? And did Emma really care?

Jack cleared his throat. "I hope I haven't made you uncomfortable, but I think we've lived this ruse long enough. My mother's presence is a hearty reminder of that. I did not bring you here as an accountant, Emma."

She felt the blood rush to her cheeks, and she desperately tried to avoid the evergreen eyes, but they searched her out, imploring her to answer.

"Do you have something you wish to say, Emma?"

She forced the words out. "You did not bring me here at all." She was reminding him not out of vindictiveness but out of necessity. She longed to hear a declaration of his own affections, not a list of all the practical reasons for her move.

"God brought you here. Seth Trainor told me that time and time again, or at least he tried to. He says I may not have chosen my bride, but God knew what was happening, and God knows best. It's about time I take an elder's advice and become a proper husband to you." But Jack's words held no conviction, and they lacked the warmth Emma desired.

In his somber expression, she knew he did not feel what she hoped for. In his scrutinizing gaze, there was the feeling of succumbing to the enemy. Was he thinking her worst fears? That she had neither the beauty nor the wiles of Katherine, but that it was time he settled? She prayed it wasn't so.

"I admire you, Emma." He took his forefinger and lifted her chin. "You have become my partner in life, and I have already grown to depend on you in your few months here. I can hardly remember my life without you. Nor do I want to remember a life without you."

She clasped her eyes shut. A woman didn't want to be told she was admired or reliable; she wanted to be loved and cherished, to hear that there was no other woman but her. But she aroused no such passion in Jack, so she vowed to take what he could give. And to do so without complaint. For that is what God was asking of her, that she respect her husband.

"We shall have a lovely family, Jack. I will raise your

children with the best education and love them with all my heart. It shall be my greatest blessing in life." *And sadly, it will be. Just like Leah with her six sons, I will get only what crumbs Jack gives me. Lord, is this how Leah felt?*

"It shall be a blessing for both of us." Jack's hands found her face, and he pulled her into a kiss. But it was nothing like the chaste, quick kisses of their wedding. It was something more, something that held intent.

Emma tried to lose herself in the passion. She returned his kiss with vitality, putting aside what she thought he felt and focusing on her own emotions. She realized that she loved Jack, and her kiss would tell him so. Everything around her soon slipped away—the lilac walls, the missing ruby ring, and especially the bitter memory of Katherine. *I am his wife,* she thought determinedly. *I and only I.*

He swept her from the floor and lifted her with ease, as if she were a rag doll. "We shall share our lives together."

His tall frame hovered over her, and his forest scent overwhelmed her with devotion to him. "I despise this room." Jack scanned the lilac walls.

She giggled at his surprise comment. "As do I."

"Change it to whatever you like. For now, you'll stay in my room—" he paused and corrected himself—"*our* room."

She nodded, unsure of anything she heard, because her heart was still beating relentlessly. Like the machine known as the California gold stamp, continuous and unwavering in its power.

CHAPTER EIGHT

*J*ack's steady breathing beside her at night was a constant reminder that she was his wife. Not in name only, but in every way. She watched him each morning as he knelt in prayer, and she felt the direct results in their life together: his light touch as he pulled her dining chair out, the gentle whispers of "good morning" that started her day, and his sweet kisses. God had finally provided her with a place of her own. A life of her own. Without the luminous shadow of glamorous Katherine lording over her.

Emma spent these first days of December working with the luxury ribbons and fabrics to create wonderful Christmas gifts for Jack's clients, who would be attending their Christmas ball.

One morning, Emma looked at her mother-in-law at the breakfast table and finally pulled herself from her own thoughts. How long had the woman been speaking?

"Mrs. Seth Trainor entertains English royalty, Emma. Although I have never met her personally, from what I understand, she is most welcome in the finest European manors. Your home shall look like a pauper's compared to where she's received hospitality." Mrs. Grant fiddled with her white gloves, which she wore constantly to hide her age spots.

Emma forced away her annoyance. "Seth has taken a special interest in Jack, and their friendship is solid. I'm quite sure Mrs. Trainor will be delighted to see where the nuptials transpired."

"Americans are still not viewed with any great reputation, but Mrs. Trainor has proven herself with the lords and ladies of England. You know, I have garnered my own reputation, and yet . . . well, never mind. I'm anxious for the opportunity to meet Mrs. Trainor. Odd that I should come all this way for the honor."

"Well, since Mrs. Trainor is to dine with us tonight, I think squab will be appropriate. It's one of Jack's favorites."

Mrs. Grant let out a short huff of disapproval. "Squab! Oh no, Emma, my dear. Squab may be fine for the usual people we entertain, but Mrs. Trainor! Surely, we cannot serve such fare."

Emma blinked quickly, trying to digest her mother-in-law's words. Mary had brought a letter on a silver tray, which occupied Emma's thoughts, and she could bear no more.

"Excuse me, Mother Grant, won't you?" Emma stole away to her bedroom, desperate to read the letter before Jack came home from the mine.

Posted from Boston, the envelope bore Katherine's

elegant hand. *What could my sister possibly have to say to me after her behavior?* Emma ripped open the letter without a care as to its condition. She gasped at the contents.

My dearest sister,

Father is convinced that my life in Boston is in need of a change. He thought Christmas with my sister might be just the salve to pull me from my sadness. I'm sure you would probably not have thought me able to travel such a distance, but if Father has not posted a letter and informed you yet, I need to let you know that I am now a widow.

My dear husband departed from this world not long after our marriage. He has left me well enough but had not the resources I anticipated. Life has been such a tragedy, bleak and without hope, compounded by the black gowns I must wear daily. I shall be grateful when my term of mourning is over. I know you think me insolent to have abandoned Jack, but it appears you have done well for yourself in California. (Aunt Mabel keeps me informed.) I should think you have quite forgiven me by now, and so it is in that vein that I know you would expect your dear sister for your Christmas ball. It shall be nice to escape the expected mourning here and resume some type of social life.

I know you will be gracious and make up a room for Cheri (my new maid) and me. Aunt Mabel thought differently, but I told her my sister is not as shallow as all that. Are you, dear sister? I shall arrive December tenth on the train. Please send a carriage around for me.

Your loving and devoted sister,
Katherine

No! No, Lord! Emma slid off the side of her bed to her knees. The letter singed her hands with its lies. *I don't want to forgive her, Lord. This is my home, my home with my husband, and she has no place here, Lord! Please keep her away, please, Lord.*

"Emma?" Jack's steady baritone interrupted her panicked plea. She crumpled the letter in her fist, anxiety building within her.

"Yes, Jack," she answered as calmly as she could.

Lifting her from the floor, Jack eyed her inquisitively. "What, pray tell, are you doing?"

"Praying." *Angrily, but I'm praying.*

"Hmm." He shrugged. "What's wrong, my dear?. Has my mother been that awful today?" He gave a sideways grin.

"No, Jack, your mother is fine. I just received a bit of bad news."

"I'm sorry. What is it, Emma?" he asked evenly.

"Katherine's husband has died. She's a widow." Emma watched her husband carefully for a reaction. Whatever he felt, it was absent from his expression, and he responded without emotion.

"Well, you said he was of an age where that was a possibility. I'm sure your sister will remarry within a suitable time. I'm sorry for the man, naturally."

"She's coming here!" Emma blurted.

"Who's coming here, dear? Surely not your sister."

Jack's Adam's apple delved suddenly, and his ruddy shade faded to a milky tone. Widening his eyes, he asked, "Whatever for?"

"She's coming for the Christmas ball."

"You invited her to the Christmas ball? Emma, I don't think—"

"No, I didn't invite her. She saw Aunt Mabel's invitation, apparently. She has written that she is arriving next week, with instructions to provide a carriage from the train depot."

"No." Jack's eyes thinned and the evergreen disappeared, as it was known to do when he was upset. "It's not proper for a widow to attend such a lavish celebration. I'll not have my reputation sullied by her appearance."

Emma stared at her beloved. How she had grown to love his strength and his calm in the middle of any crisis. But she knew his wounded pride had not completely mended, and she ached. She ached that Katherine still had the power to harm him, and she ached that her own love for him had not overcome that pain.

Emma finally let out her breath. "I'll send a telegram immediately, Jack. Of course, you're right, Katherine has no business traveling for pleasure as a widow."

After a long pause, Jack spoke again firmly, "Send her nothing. It's her right to do as she pleases. If she wants to travel across the country by train, it is her choice, not ours."

The lump in Emma's throat felt like an enormous pinecone lodged within. *How could he be so formal? How could he allow Katherine to enter into the life they were building together?* Emma unconsciously rubbed her stomach. *I'm carrying your child, Jack. Don't you understand?* He said nothing, however, and she wouldn't tell him. Not until she was certain.

Jack pulled the door shut behind him, closing his eyes in agony. *Katherine.* How could he bear to see her again? He had abandoned her lock of hair and photograph somewhere in the mine, literally tossed everything that reminded him of his lost love, but seeing her face-to-face was another thing altogether.

Emma. Sweet, loving, and loyal Emma. His wife. No matter how their marriage had come to be, Jack now loved her more than he thought possible. But did he love her enough? Did he love her enough to forget she was not his first choice? His pride forced him to be convincing, to show Emma that their guest would mean nothing to him. Guilt resonated with his own wavering conviction.

He pulled his grandmother's ruby ring out of a hidden safe in the wall and studied the flawless jewel. It shimmered brightly, its deep red a mere shade of his own heart and what he had once felt for Katherine.

He hadn't been able to give the ring to Emma, and now he chastised himself for his error in judgment. But would he still feel that way when he saw Katherine's blonde locks as she danced at his Christmas ball, reminding him of what he had originally desired? *Sinful. Those are sinful thoughts. I love Emma, Lord. I love her, so why must I be tempted with what might have been?*

Tell her. The admonition came quietly, a mere whisper in his head.

"Jack? Whatever are you doing in the hallway?" Mother Grant crossed her arms, showing her agitation. "Are you and Emma all right?"

"Emma's fine, Mother. I'm just beginning to think this Christmas ball may not be in my best interest."

"Nonsense. Emma has invited the finest society. You'd be an imbecile to overlook such a triumph. I must say, for as quiet as she appears, she has quite the connections. Perhaps you did fine for yourself, Jack."

Quiet. His mother's way of saying "not beautiful." Jack seethed. When would his mother realize what he did, that Emma's beauty went far beyond the surface? "Emma is beautiful, Mother. I'm sorry you haven't seen it yet."

Mrs. Grant laughed. "Well, Son, I'm glad she has managed to convince you of her loveliness. As you may have noticed, Empire City is not exactly teeming with eligible society women. It's only natural you think Emma beautiful. I'm just warning you: when the guests arrive, her appearance may take on a less brilliant hue." Mrs. Grant patted her coiffed bun.

"I'm delighted you've come to California, Mother. I know Emma has been thrilled with your company and the daily teas that you share and the help with the Christmas plans, but I must ask you to stop chipping away at my bride. It was hard enough for her to leave Boston—and her life there—behind." Jack recalled Emma's longing glances toward the schoolhouse she'd set up recently.

Mrs. Grant tossed a hand at her son. "Nonsense. She would have been an old maid in the city, and she knows it. Now don't misunderstand me, Son. I think Emma is a fine wife for out here in the wilderness, but San Francisco society is one thing. Mrs. Trainor is quite another."

"Emma is the reason such society is coming here, Mother. The Christmas ball was her idea."

"I must admit, your wife possesses an element of surprise under her exterior, but Mrs. Trainor is not fooled by the average mistress, Jack."

"Emma isn't trying to fool anyone."

"Of course not, dear. I'm just saying, appearances are important. Naturally, it shouldn't be as such, but it's the case. Why, in New York, when a—" she stopped and foraged for a word— "when an *average* girl gets married, it's almost always assumed she came with a healthy trust."

"I'm due at the office for a few moments, Mother. Please, find something to do, and leave Emma be. She's had a difficult day. Mary can get you settled in the library with a nice book."

"Jack!" His mother took his hand, clasping it tightly between her own. He searched her green eyes. His mother's former glory was still readily apparent. Adelaide Grant had been a beauty in her day, and it was a history she wore like an expensive brooch.

"Yes, Mother." Jack exhaled loudly.

"Beauty fades. I know this only too well." His mother

moved in closer, speaking in a hushed voice. "Your father had a young lady before me: did you know that? She was the plain sort, but filled with the right connections, and a wile that cast a spell over your poor, innocent father. But in the end, my charm and appearance were more than he could turn away from, so he chose me. Grace and the good opinion of others were too important to him to risk choosing the wrong woman. I'm just trying to prepare you for the ball. Are you ready to face the fact that you may have made a mistake?"

CHAPTER NINE

*T*he crisp December morning loomed large with possibility. Mrs.Trainor would arrive that very afternoon, and Emma would have something else to concentrate upon. Something other than her sister's slated arrival.

Mother Grant clapped her hands over her morning crepe, like a delighted child on her birthday. "You know they say Mr. and Mrs. Trainor have toured Europe many times and that their estate rivals the gardens of any English manor!" She lowered her voice as though sharing a great secret. "Amity Station is simply exquisite, from what I've heard. The New York *governor's* wife raves about it—she says it's an absolute fairyland!"

Emma looked admiringly at her husband. "Nothing rivals the gardens of the cottage as far as I'm concerned. I could wander the rose arbors endlessly. I should wonder that you've never ventured past the front porch, Mother Grant. It's quite a sight to behold."

Jack coughed, obviously trying to change the subject before it became heated. "It seems odd you and Mrs. Trainor are of the same society and have not met, Mother."

"But I shouldn't wonder, Jack; New York is a big city." Emma tried to show respect, but the elder woman only turned her wrath to Emma.

Mrs. Grant lifted her chin, as though talking to a slow servant girl on the verge of unemployment. "Emma, New York is not like Empire City. We don't simply have one great house and one great lord of the manor. It is strange, however, that we should come to the *wilderness* for such a meeting. A country house, no less," Mrs. Grant said, followed by a click of her tongue.

Emma knew, in fact, that Mrs. Grant was delighted at any opportunity to meet Mrs. Trainor. It was the sole reason for her journey to California—and the "wild," as she called it—that she might be included in New York's inner circle after meeting the respected Mrs. Trainor. Jack simply smiled and flicked his newspaper.

Their morning breakfast had become a ritual of mirth in the home. Inevitably, the elder Mrs. Grant said something to provoke her son, and he continually ceased to acknowledge it. Their customary daybreak peace was soon shattered by a loud banging at the front door.

One of the miners rushed into the room. "Jack! Jack! Explosion in the mine, explosion in the mine!" Harley's red face was apologetic at the sight of the women, and he removed his hat. "It's bad, sir. Men below."

Jack threw his napkin on the table and was off like a

runaway mine car. It was the call every gold explorer expected but one that Jack had managed to avoid thus far. Emma gasped for air and excused herself, dashing to the door behind her husband.

"Good heavens, where are you going, child?" Mrs. Grant asked in a snipped tone. "Mrs. Trainor arrives today."

"I need to see to the accident, Mother Grant. Anything could be happening in that mine right now. I want to be there. For Jack and for his men."

"Oh, they'll be fine, for heaven's sake. Mining is dangerous work, Emma. That's why it pays so well. Send the kitchen staff if you're so concerned. Now come and let's discuss the final floral arrangements for the entry hall. Mrs. Trainor will probably not set foot into a home without a proper entry arrangement."

Stunned, Emma stood at the front door of the palatial mansion. The California stamp had stopped its vicious pounding, and the ominous silence announced business was not as usual. Overcome with emotion, Emma wanted to dash to the mine, but reality struck her with strange swiftness. *Jack doesn't want me down there. He wants me here, tending to womanly things, seeing that the Christmas ball is an event to impress his critics.* Her heart sank a bit deeper. *Being the society woman he thought he was marrying.*

Fear struck at her heart, and Emma realized her mouth was completely dry with anxiety. She bowed her head in prayer, but her mother-in-law soon roused her from her conversation with God.

"Emma! Emma, get out here, please. We really must see

to the final details. Mrs. Trainor will be arriving within hours. It is your duty as mistress of this house to be prepared for your guests. I know you're concerned, but our place is here. What would Jack say?"

The final admonition startled her from her prayers. *What would Jack say?* Seth Trainor was his most important investor, not to mention Jack's good friend. Seth would be at the mine after his morning walk, and he'd want to know his wife was cared for. Emma had a responsibility to her husband, and today it included small details like seeing to the floral arrangement in the entry hall. As ridiculous as it seemed, appearances were the very reason Jack had taken a wife. If Emma ever hoped to fulfill his desires, she needed to attend to the minutiae.

Emma rose slowly, praying for the strength to pull off her duties and let God look after Jack. She looked at her mother-in-law and knew instantly she could never be like Adelaide Grant. She *had* to know what was happening and, more importantly, to prevent Jack from heading down the mine shaft himself. She opened the front door and scampered down the steps, running toward the hoist house. Her mother-in-law called out after her, but Emma hiked up her skirt and kept running.

A crowd of miners gathered outside the mine entrance, all of them with their hats to their chest. Emma's heart jumped at the sight. She made her way through the throng of men to the pulley man operating the cars. She looked at him hopefully. He only shook his hanging head.

"We can't get to 'em. Mine collapsed. Don't know if they's dead or not."

"Where's Jack?" She clutched the man's shoulder, and a puff of mine dust forced a cough from her.

Harley nodded, pointing his chin the direction of the mine. "He went down manually with Mr. Trainor."

"What do you mean? Jack's in the mine?" Emma screamed.

"Yes, and he left word that you were not to be here, Mrs. Grant. He said you had fine company coming today, and you were to see to them. He gave strict orders to send you back to the house."

Emma's mind raced. She had promised Jack she wouldn't go into the mine again. She had promised him and, for his sake, she would go back to the house. But her mind would remain there. Down in the depths of the mine where the only man she ever loved was trying to save others. Unconsciously, she rubbed her stomach and thought of the innocent life she must protect. She took in a deep breath, whispering a prayer.

She gathered what small strength she still possessed and turned back toward the house. "Send word to me. Let me know when you hear of anything. Do you understand?" Emma's firm voice echoed in the cold hollow of the mine entrance.

"Yes, Mrs. Grant. We'll send word."

The great clock ticked loudly in the front parlor. It marked the hours which felt like eternities. It was now four o'clock in the afternoon, and still no word from the mines. Emma paced the room, wiping her damp hands on her red silk presentation gown.

"Emma, do sit down. You're going to soil your gown with that infernal walking."

"We should have heard by now, Mother Grant. The sun will be setting soon."

"The sun makes no difference in the mine. It's still as dark as night."

Emma gazed at her mother-in-law. For all her stark words, Mrs. Grant's face was blanched. Clearly, she was as worried about her son as Emma was for her husband.

The sound of a carriage coming up the rock path broke them both from their unstated fears.

"Mrs. Trainor is here." Emma drew in a deep breath and practiced her smile.

"Very good, Emma. We'll see to our guest." Mrs. Grant stood and followed her to the great doorway. "It will be good for us to concentrate on our guest," she repeated, as though to convince them both.

Emma opened the door herself just out of sheer habit, rather than letting the servants see to their duty. Emma plastered a smile on her face and prepared herself, as Mrs. Trainor stepped out of the ornate conveyance sent to bring her from the station. The New York society woman was dressed exquisitely in a fine jacket of midnight blue velvet over a coordinating silk taffeta gown. Even in her fifties, she was obviously a woman of carriage and grace. She stepped forward with a warm smile.

"Emma, my dear." Mrs.Trainor held out gloved hands and grasped Emma's tightly. "I feel as if I know you already. Seth has done nothing but rave of your hospitality during his long stay here. He insisted I come for Christmas."

"I'm so glad you came, Mrs. Trainor," Emma said honestly, for Mrs. Trainor's warmth felt like a cozy hug. "Your husband was the first person to welcome me properly to Empire City. His giving me away at our wedding will always hold a prominent place in my heart." At the mention of her wedding, Emma felt her smile wane and the tears coming. She blinked several times, hoping to will them away, but it was no use. The quiet and impending darkness enveloped her with a renewed sense of doom.

The two older women were swept up in conversation and didn't notice Emma's heart on her sleeve. For that, she was thankful. Just when the ache became unbearable and her smile was actually painful, two figures approached on the darkening path. Although it was late in the afternoon and the sun had disappeared behind the great redwoods, she would know her husband's masculine outline anywhere. Relief was like a cleansing stream washing over her.

"Excuse me, Mrs. Trainor." Emma dashed toward her husband. She unabashedly ran into her husband's arms, kissing his cheek. "Oh, thank God, thank God, you're all right, Jack! I've been worried sick. The men were supposed to send word."

He pulled her close; then he released her immediately.

She noticed he was staring directly at his mother. Emma turned to see her mother-in-law's face steeped in quiet admonition.

Even in the dimming light, Emma saw her husband's scarlet face. His embarrassment at her exaggerated show of affection felt like the final nail in her coffin. *When will I ever learn to control my emotions?* Elation was replaced by humiliation over yet another social blunder. This one, in front of the couple Jack most wanted to impress.

Seth Trainor laughed. "Now, Jack, *that* is what I call a welcome." Seth raised his voice, calling out to his wife, "When was the last time I was welcomed home in such a way, Mrs. Trainor?" The older man grinned and went toward his wife, but Emma noticed Jack's expression remained stoic.

Mrs. Grant stood in the drive with arms crossed and eyes thinned. She said something in confidence to Mrs. Trainor, and the New York socialite nodded in agreement.

Emma's heart sank. This had been her chance to make Jack proud, and she'd destroyed the opportunity. And Katherine would arrive on the heels of another social blunder.

CHAPTER TEN

The day's long efforts left Jack grimy and tattered. His emotions from the tragic circumstances of the mine exploded within him, and he couldn't fathom spending the evening in idle conversation. He praised God for Emma, and her uncanny ability to make guests feel welcome on her own. He didn't even fear his mother's impertinence when Emma was present to make things easy. Seth and Mrs. Trainor would be well attended to, and he felt his shoulders relax at the knowledge.

As they approached the manor, he took Emma's arm, taking notice of her appearance for the first time that day. Stunning in a deep crimson gown with a gathered waist, Emma appeared to be everything he expected in a wife. Her hair was swept into a coil, with elegant ringlets falling around her oval face. He questioned how he had ever thought her anything less than magnificent, for she was as beautiful as any woman he'd ever met. More beautiful, in fact, because her beauty ran deep within her.

"I'm sorry, Emma. I fear I wouldn't be good company

this evening." He knew his wife would be disappointed, so he spoke gently, belying the turmoil that raked inside him.

"No, of course you're tired." Emma agreed. "I'll have Harrison bring you a tray shortly." She touched him lightly on the chest.

Jack took in a deep breath. The apprehensive, awkward woman who had stepped off the train from Boston was slowly disappearing. The sweet helpmate who sought his praise at every turn was fast evolving into what he *said* he wanted. A socialite wife. A mere ornament on his arm to impress the Eastern bankers and lawyers.

He longed for the former Emma. The one who clung to his every word and looked upon him with respect. The one who wasn't content to sit about and order gowns, but rather offered ledger expertise and was still willing to enter a dark mine to rescue a precious child.

The Emma he married wanted to teach the workers' children, to see them educated in the ways of God's Word, but he'd worried over the appearances of things. *It isn't right for a society woman to be seen in the miners' barracks*, he'd said. He stifled a laugh. Emma had still managed to plan the development of a school and even hired a teacher when he'd forgotten his pledge, but she hadn't technically gone against his orders. Jack had been thanked for his generosity with the children, but he was owed no such thanks. Emma cared for others, while Jack cared what others thought.

Coming home from the mine, Emma's overzealous hug had made him feel like a prince, but his mother's harsh

stares had reminded him of his wife's misplaced enthusiasm. He shook his head. He'd left New York because of
those exact rigid society standards, and here he was, invit-
ing those very rules and the people who lived them into
his home. He wanted to show Emma how he really felt, to
envelop her in the tightest embrace, but his aspiration for
appearances won out. He was sick at the thought.

Jack studied his wife and smiled his warmest smile.
Then he climbed the ornate mahogany stairs and closed
his heavy bedroom door behind him. Filling the claw-foot
tub with scalding water, he wasn't in his room for five
minutes before there was a knock. "It's okay, Harrison. I
can handle things myself tonight," he shouted, not wanting to be disturbed even by his butler.

"It's me, Jack. May I come in?" Emma's soft voice broke
through the door, and Jack nearly ran to open it.

"Emma! The Trainors—"

"Are doing just fine, Jack. Mrs. Trainor is a very
discerning woman. She announced dinner would wait
until I had spoken with you. Even your mother could not
defy the woman. There's something about her that
commands respect. Your mother may not be so
impressed after all."

Emma giggled softly, and Jack was delighted at the
sight. He embraced her. So thankful that she'd made her
excuses and come to him, especially after his rudeness on
the path earlier. Why had he let her go because of his
mother's harsh expression?

In the dim electric lights, the green in her eyes sparkled

like a brilliant emerald touched by gold. Emma's very being seemed to light a room when she entered it. He grasped her by the arm, gently tugging her into their private chambers, ignoring any discussion about his mother. "Emma, I hoped you'd come."

"I know something terrible happened in the mine. I could tell by your face. I'm dreadfully sorry for my unspeakable behavior. I was just so worried. I shall be certain to apologize to the Trainors and your mother, of course."

"No, Emma. It was me who was wrong. Let the matter pass." He cupped her chin, tilting her face up toward him. Emma looked away, and Jack knew his earlier coldness caused her response. "Emma, please accept my apology. I was wrong."

Emma nodded. "Tell me what happened in the mine, Jack."

He broke away from her, falling onto the settee. "Two men were buried for a long time this morning. The explosion didn't hurt them too badly, but they were unconscious when we found them. Doc isn't sure they'll make it to Christmas."

"Who?" she asked. Her eyes darkened with foreboding. Although he'd forbidden her to enter the mine, Emma kept careful records of the ledgers. She knew each man, his family, and how many children he was responsible for. The names would hit her with severity.

"Orville and Micah." Jack didn't look at her while he stated the names. Orville, his new overseer, the one Emma had fought for. Something as simple as educating the man's children and Jack had denied it for appearances' sake. Now they might be fatherless. Guilt ravaged him. Still, Emma said nothing to make him feel worse.

"Jack, we have to trust that they are in God's hands now and that they'll be okay. God knows their situation. We can pray together that he will be merciful and bring healing. But in the meantime, I'll have soup sent to the barracks posthaste. If the barracks are not warm enough, I shall have the families moved to the clubhouse." Emma rattled on more directives for herself before absently kissing him on the cheek and exiting.

Jack closed his eyes, praising God for his wife and feeling the loss as she left the room. *My heavenly Father, you have truly provided for me, and I've been too blind, too prideful to see it. Emma is the woman for me; she always has been. That's what you've been trying to show me all along, isn't it?*

Jack only hoped his revelation hadn't come too late.

Emma scurried about the kitchen, trying to focus on tasks instead of the emotion she felt. *Jack is just upset right now. His loving embrace didn't mean anything. Don't get your hopes up, Emma.*

Jack's caring glances and soft touches made her want to blurt out her good news of their child, but she only had to remember his cold glances on the path and his mother's disapproval, and truth hit her like a sudden icy wind. She was his wife, nothing more. The woman who mistakenly showed up on the westbound train one morning.

Orville Sack's and Micah Johnson's families were attended to immediately. She ordered warm soup and extra blankets be sent and that the families' well-being be given top priority for the night. She then drew a deep breath and prepared to be the perfect hostess. Opening the kitchen door, she smiled as broadly as possible without spilling the tears she hid behind her carefree expression.

Mrs. Trainor met her with quiet laughter. "Oh, my dear, you must not take us so seriously. Look at you, you're a grain bag of nerves. Come sit down with us." She patted the seat beside her. Mrs. Grant shot Emma a warning gaze, and Emma stood frozen. Sensing Emma's trepidation, Mrs. Trainor insisted.

Emma took her place between Mr. Trainor and his wife. Mrs. Trainor smoothed her hand over Emma's and smiled warmly.

The elder Mrs. Grant cast daggers in Emma's direction. *"I'll* attend to dinner. It's running far too late. Our guests must be starving. Emma, we do eat a bit later in New York, but this is bordering on absurd, my dear. We wouldn't want Mrs. Trainor to feel slighted. After all, she is our special guest."

"Of course, Mother Grant, but the kitchen is short staffed at the moment. They are attending to the men who were hurt in the mine today." She smiled reassuringly at Mr. and Mrs. Trainor. "It will just be a few moments, I promise."

"Emma, would you come here a moment? I'd like to speak with you in the kitchen." Mrs. Grant fluffed her watered-silk gown in the doorway. She looked like an angry peacock with her feathers outstretched.

Emma's own temper flared. "I've only just come from the kitchen, Mother Grant. The staff has assured me everything is on schedule." Emma turned her attention back to Mrs. Trainor.

"Emma!" Mother Grant called sharply, as though it were possible Emma had missed her earlier beckoning.

"Mother, Emma is entertaining our guests. May I assist with something?" Jack's deep voice shook Emma. Her husband's appearance was like a soothing, wool wrap on a cold winter's day. *He cared enough to come downstairs.*

"Jack! You should be resting." *But I am so elated you're not.* Her husband's thoughtful eyes met hers, and Emma felt his gaze in the pit of her stomach. Dressed in his finest sack coat, something had changed. Gone was his callous front, and Emma felt as if she could see into his very soul.

Jack mysteriously escorted his mother to the kitchen, and Emma turned her attention back to Mrs. Trainor.

"Your husband cares a great deal for you, Emma." Mrs. Trainor said.

"Mr. and Mrs. Trainor, I owe you both an apology for my behavior this afternoon. I was simply so excited to see my husband, I did not think of my actions."

"Emma, my elder brother fought in the War between the States," Mrs. Trainor said. "I remember all too well when he walked up our path in Virginia. It was as though I was seeing a ghost. There is no room for decorum when such emotion is present. I understand the relief you felt, and it does my heart good to see a young couple so in love."

Emma swallowed hard and looked at her wringing hands. Is that how she and Jack appeared? If only Mrs. Trainor knew how cordial and careful they were with one another. Two strangers with fleeting moments of affection.

"You forget I know how you came to be married, Emma. Jack confided in me how your marriage came to be," Seth said.

Emma straightened. "Then you know Jack doesn't really love me." The admission felt like a boxcar of gold lifted off her chest.

"I know no such thing, Emma. Jack cares a great deal for you," Mrs. Trainor whispered.

Seth nodded and leaned in. "I've spent quite a bit of time with Jack, Emma. He's not a man to wear his heart on his sleeve, but his love for you is apparent."

Emma forced a smile.

"I think I'll leave you two alone." Seth rose from the settee and took a cigar from his pocket. "I'll be in the library if anyone wants me."

Mrs. Trainor leaned in, speaking quietly. "It isn't an accident that your mother-in-law and I haven't met in New York, Emma." Mrs. Trainor lowered her voice yet again, coming ever closer. "When I was a young girl in Virginia, I was courted for a time by Jack's very own father. My father was wealthy, and he had the means to make Ellery Grant's dreams come true."

Emma's eyes popped open. "Were you engaged to Jack's father?"

"Nearly so. It was quite scandalous at the time. Everyone assumed we'd be married, and when we weren't . . . well, you can imagine the gossip. I thought I'd be a spinster after being dropped by Virginia's premier bachelor. Even my father's money failed to impress the other men when they knew I was Ellery Grant's castoff."

Emma's mouth dangled in surprise.

"Then," she said wistfully, "Seth came along. He was a simple preacher's son, impressed by my knowledge of Scripture. We knew immediately."

"But Seth *did* love you, Mrs. Trainor. He married you for love. I fail to see the connection between Jack and me. I didn't have several suitors as you did, Mrs. Trainor. I would have been a spinster."

"Ellery Grant took one look at Adelaide Hemmingsworth, your mother-in-law, and dropped me like yesterday's crop. I would have been a spinster as well, if God hadn't intervened."

"Does Jack know about his parents?"

"No, and I don't think even Adelaide remembers. Not to this day. She had her heart set on Ellery, and I daresay she never thought twice about whom he was promised to. Not until I became part of New York's elite society, and I bet that would fail to impress her if she remembered me." Mrs. Trainor stood.

"I shall keep your secret, Mrs. Trainor."

"I see in your eyes all the fears and insecurities I felt in those awful days when Ellery left me. But now I know. I know that God doesn't make mistakes when it comes to wives and husbands, even though people often do. God can take what we think is a wrong relationship and create from it a good marriage, if both partners are willing to do their share to make it work. God is watching over you and Jack, just as he has watched over me and my precious Seth."

"Katherine is to arrive soon. She's a widow, and Jack may fall victim to her beauty again, just as his own father did." Emma's fears welled up greater than before.

"I think you underestimate your husband. And God."

Emma contemplated the advice as Mother Grant and Jack returned. Emma stiffened at their entrance. Mrs. Grant took special pleasure in making the announcement for her daughter-in-law. "Dinner is *finally* served."

CHAPTER ELEVEN

*J*ack didn't dare look Emma in the eye. "I must go into
town today." He fiddled with the horses' tethers
nervously, something the grooms had already seen to, but
he didn't want his wife to suspect anything about his
quest. "Last-minute details I need to see to before the
Christmas festivities tonight."

She came alongside him, an air of desperation in her
voice. "Everything's been done, Jack. We're having fresh,
wild turkey with all the trimmings. I've hired extra staff
from the miners' wives, had them trained in etiquette. The
gatehouse is overflowing with guests from San Francisco."
Emma shifted uncomfortably. "What have I forgotten?"

"I'm quite sure you've seen to everything, my love, but
I have something special planned for the ball. The house
looks and smells lovely. The wreaths and bows are
delightful, my dear."

"I'll come to town with you; let me get a wrap." Emma
started toward the house.

It broke Jack's heart to disappoint her. "No, Emma. I

need to go to town alone. You'd be bored with all my ridiculous errands."

"Not if I were with you, I wouldn't. I could stay in the
general store with Mrs. Maher until you were done."

Jack dropped his facade of seeing to the horses and drew
Emma into his arms. "Seth was right, you know. I'm one
lucky dog, as he likes to say. Most wives wouldn't give
their husband's errands a second thought."

He watched his wife blush and breathed in her soft,
floral scent. Never had he met a woman who worked so
hard and always managed to be fresh as a California
poppy. She snuggled her face into his neck and, rather
than worry about appearances, he placed a soft kiss on her
neck.

"You're beautiful when you blush." The gentle curve of
her shoulder awoke his senses.

Emma looked up at him, her eyes wide, bright, and
hopeful. A light blanket of new snow glistened under the
morning sun, providing the perfect backdrop against her
amber morning gown and creamy complexion. She was
the picture of health, with rosy cheeks and a fuller figure
of late. More womanly than when she'd first come to
Empire City.

Taking her face into his hands, he bent to kiss her. Not
his reserved proper Victorian kiss, but one which he felt to
his boots. Closing his eyes, he felt for her lips again.
Firmly, he pressed his mouth to hers, desiring her with
renewed passion.

"Let me come with you," she pleaded.

"Now, Emma, we have a multitude of guests for the ball. Someone must stay here and play host."

"Your mother—"

"My mother might alienate my entire investor base. Stay here and see to it that our mine continues." He kissed her forehead.

Emma clutched his hands as he turned to leave. "Katherine comes in today."

"Yes, I know. I plan to pick her up on my way home." He tried to say it with no emotion whatsoever. "You said her train gets in about noon."

"Jack!" Emma's face contorted. She had been especially attentive since the mining incident, afraid to let him out of her sight, but today he knew why she appeared worse. Still, his errand needed to be done alone, and picking up Katherine would only upset his wife. He intended to lay down the law with Katherine before she ever entered his home.

"Emma, everything will be fine. I'll be home by one-thirty unless the train is late. I promise." Jack squeezed her hands and let her go. As the carriage pulled away, he watched his beloved wife gaze after him until her outline disappeared from sight.

❊ ❊ ❊

Emma observed the black carriage fade to a tiny spot like a retreating insec, as if staring after it might turn it around and bring her husband back to her. "Oh, Jack," she wailed to the great trees. "Why? Why couldn't you just send

213

Harrison to pick Katherine up?" Emma hated to admit it, but her sister was a seductress, and Emma feared her husband might fall victim to Katherine's carefully calculated charms. She wanted to protect him, to protect *them*. A new life depended on it. As if their precious baby agreed, Emma felt a tiny flutter in her abdomen.

At least I shall have someone who loves me. Just as Leah did. Oh, Lord, if Jack does not come back to me, please let this baby be enough for me. Let me constantly seek your will, unlike Leah, who tried so desperately to please Jacob but did not ask for your help. Lord, let me please you and be a good wife to Jack, too. Emma's gaze fell to her hand. The hand that wore her plain gold wedding band. It had been months since she'd seen the exquisite ruby ring. Would Katherine return to the cottage wearing it?

"Emma! What are you doing out here? You'll catch your death of cold." Mrs. Trainor took Emma by the shoulders and led her back to the house. It was then that Emma realized her toes were completely numb. Just like her heart.

Mother Grant met her at the door, her disapproving scowl already in place for the long day ahead. "Tonight is the social event of the year, and you are out gallivanting in the snow in your tea slippers. Don't you have the good sense to put on a pair of boots?"

"That is quite enough!" Mrs. Trainor's gentle voice took on a harsh tone. "You have ridiculed this poor girl since our arrival. Her gowns are not the proper color, her hair is not the latest fashion, and the dinner is late. I could go and on! I think Emma is an elegant hostess, while I find your behavior most appalling." Mrs. Trainor's grip on Emma's shoulders tightened.

Mother Grant sputtered, but her harsh words remained unsaid. "Mrs. Trainor, I'm only seeing to my son's guests. My daughter-in-law supposedly went to the finest finishing school in Boston, though sometimes she forgets herself."

"It is you who forgets herself, Adelaide."

The room was spinning, getting darker and darker. Emma heard someone call her name just before the sights and sounds faded altogether.

❋ ❋ ❋

Jack finished up his errands and arrived at the train depot. He had a sick feeling in the pit of his stomach. Katherine's arrival could only mean trouble. He needed his privacy for the errands, but he was glad for the excuse to leave Emma home. It would be hard enough to face Katherine after she'd humiliated him, but if it pained Emma, he couldn't bear to see it on his wife's face.

The train whistled into the station right on time. Jack waited at the Pullman car. Strangers stepped off, and he looked about to see if Katherine would arrive coach. From the front of the train she finally emerged, a vision in blue. It was the first thing he noticed, because propriety statedthat, as a widow, she should be in black.

She was still as beautiful as ever. Blonde ringlets framed her face, and she wore an extravagant feathered chapeau, a perfect indigo color that matched her violet eyes. Oddly, Jack was unmoved by her glamorous presence. Witnessing Katherine's entrance was like peering at a lovely painting or a fine piece of lace handwork. He had to acknowledge the beauty, but it didn't affect him in any emotional way.

"Get my trunks now!" she shouted, and her beautiful face twisted in annoyance. She yanked her skirt boisterously. "You'll get no tip from me! Nor should you expect one."

"No, ma'am." A young porter followed her out, obviously trying to please her. He tipped his hat before dragging two large cases from the train.

"Pick them up, fool!"

"Begging your pardon, ma'am, but they are quite heavy."

Jack strode confidently toward Katherine. At the first sign of him, her expression softened. She smiled coyly. The kind of smile that would have sent his heart to racing at one time. Her skin was flawless, and her eyes sparkled with mischief. He remembered why he had been so taken. She had a magnetism that couldn't be described. A beauty that made a man *want* to believe he was the object of her affection.

Gazing at her now, he realized *she* was the only object of her affection. If Jack had ever believed Katherine loved him, he'd been a fool. Just as her rich, old banker had been.

"Why, Jack, I knew you'd come." She touched his hand gently, but it felt like ice to Jack, and he flinched.

"I was in town for errands." Jack's jaw was set. "Is your mourning over?" He nodded his chin toward her gown.

"I am so weary of black. Besides, no one will be the

wiser here in the middle of nowhere." She jabbed him playfully.

"Actually, Empire City is a very conservative city. My business associates are all here from San Francisco, as well." Jack lifted her trunk over his shoulder and led the porter to the carriage. He could hear Katherine's heels clicking swiftly behind him along the boards.

"Well, they shall have to make allowances for me. Black doesn't suit me at all. Besides, if they knew how old my husband was, I daresay they'd bend the rules a bit." She giggled, covering her mouth with a gloved hand.

He glanced at her gown again before meeting her eyes. "As I said, Empire City maintains a proper mourning period. We are not complete heathens because we are on the West Coast."

"Of course not." She waited for him to put the trunk on the carriage, then grasped his hand. "Jack, it's me. Katherine, remember? You needn't be so formal with me. You're not still angry over our tiny courtship, are you?"

"On the contrary, I'm grateful for it. Otherwise, I might never have met your beautiful sister." Jack watched his comment take the desired effect. Katherine recoiled at the mention of her sister.

"Beautiful? Emma? You needn't pretend with me, Jack. I remember what my sister looks like. I know how she likes to pick up dirty street urchins and teach them to read. How she prefers a book to the company of men. In all her spinster years in Boston, I never heard her referred to as beautiful." Katherine rolled her eyes, as though Jack were deaf, dumb, and blind. "Your standards have diminished here in the gold country."

"They were once diminished, I'll grant you that." Jack said with a slight smile. "But I find my tastes have improved greatly." He opened the conveyance door and helped her into the courtly interior.

CHAPTER TWELVE

*E*mma awoke with a cool compress on her forehead. As the pale yellow walls came into focus, she started from her bed. "What time is it?"

Mrs. Trainor and Mother Grant stood over her, worried frowns on both their faces.

Mrs. Trainor gently pressed Emma back toward the bed. "Lie down. There's plenty of time. It's only four in the afternoon. The butler has seen to everything. I've approved the table setting myself. You were very tired, apparently."

"We are so sorry we upset you, dear." Mother Grant's eyes were warm and concerned, an expression that confused Emma.

"We owe you a great apology," Mrs. Trainor agreed.

"Four . . . it's four o'clock? Is Jack home?"

"Not yet." Mother Grant answered. "He should be home shortly. We heard the train whistle at noon. Perhaps he was held up by one of his clients in town."

Emma sprang from her bed, tossing the covers carelessly. She checked her reflection in the mirror and patted some face powder on her sallow skin. She tried pinching her cheeks to bring out more color, but shortly she ran out of patience.

"Emma!" Mother Grant's sharp tone returned. Emma turned out of sheer habit, but her mother-in-law's soft expression hadn't changed. "Mrs. Trainor and I had a long discussion. We're trying to tell you how sorry we are."

Emma tried to be patient, but she felt trapped in the room. She wanted to go after Jack. This Christmas meant everything to Emma. She was carrying the child of her husband, a man she loved with all her heart, but would it withstand Katherine? From Emma's first porcelain doll to Jack's affections, Katherine had courted and stolen everything Emma ever cared for. Emma wouldn't release Jack so easily.

"I must get to Jack." Emma's hand flew to her chest. "I must see to Katherine's arrival. Thank you both! I love you!" Emma dashed down the stairs just in time to hear the carriage coming up from the carriage house. She drew in a deep breath and said a silent prayer. *Please, Lord, please let him see Katherine for who she really is.*

The footman opened the carriage door and Katherine emerged, more beautiful than ever. Emma felt physically ill at the vision and wanted to rush to her washbasin, but she forced her feet to remain planted. *My future depends upon my performance,* she reminded herself.

"Katherine!" Emma walked toward her sister with arms

extended. She tried to hug her sister but was met with a face full of feathers from an overly ornate chapeau.

"Emma," Katherine answered flatly, removing fine leather kid gloves. "Where is the cottage, darling?"

"*This* is the cottage. Jack calls his estate the 'cottage.' Isn't that quaint?" Emma looked to her husband, who avoided her gaze. She tried not to let his reaction throw her. "If he was honest about our great mansion, perhaps Boston would be vacant of all its bankers and lawyers. Speaking of which, I was terribly sorry to hear of your husband's passing."

"Where can I wash up, dear? I'm dreadfully dusty from the carriage."

Emma had spent twenty-four years playing nursemaid to Katherine. She wasn't about to let it start again. "We have a guest room all ready for you. Mary, my maid, will see you to it." Emma lifted her chin slightly and handed her sister off to Mary.

Emma walked toward her husband with trepidation. How would he feel after seeing Katherine's beauty again? After looking into her violet blue eyes under the long and luxurious lashes? Would he even be able to look at Emma again? She kept her face to the ground, hoping he wouldn't notice the vivid contrast. "Is everything okay, Jack?"

"Couldn't be better, my love. I stopped off at the mine for a bit. It seems the two injured men are doing fine. Doc says they'll make a full recovery."

"That's not what I meant."

Jack gave a light laugh and kissed her forehead. "I know." He stretched, standing to his full intimidating height, and something fell from his watch pocket. In the glistening layer of snow glimmered the ruby wedding ring.

Emma's stomach turned. She looked into her husband's guilty eyes, and all the fight fell from her body. She could do nothing else but run.

She ran past Katherine and Mary, past her mother-in-law and Mrs. Trainor, and headed inside to her mistress's bedroom. She locked the door and fell into the corner of the room, catching her frantic breath. Huddling her knees about her, she rocked as she trembled with audible cries. She inhaled deep, choking sobs, and tried to fight the memory of her husband's guilty eyes. The sick feeling returned. Jack would never love her. Never.

Later, as the sun descended, and Emma's room grew dark, she had ignored the countless knocks of Jack and her maid, and after a while, no one knocked further. Emma could hear the quartet she'd hired begin to play and the carolers outside. The Christmas ball was beginning without Emma. Katherine could play mistress of the evening, just as she'd always done when Emma planned a great event in Boston. Jack must have realized his mistake. Perhaps he would ask for a divorce. Emma shivered, thinking about the possibility. Would knowing he had a child make any difference?

Emma whispered, "Oh, precious babe, I love you. I love you so much, and I shall protect you, come what may. No matter what happens with your daddy, I'll see to it that you have the brightest future imaginable. Your daddy may not want us, but he has money enough to make sure we'll be well taken care of. We'll go to Europe. We'll dine with kings and queens, and perhaps you'll marry royalty one day. I shan't allow you to marry without love. I shall see to it whoever marries you will be worthy of you."

A light suddenly flickered, and Emma peered up at Jack's sullen face, which was lit by a single candle. He had unlocked her bedroom door and entered the room. Emma stood up, trying to assemble any remaining shred of dignity left to her.

"Emma!" Jack put the candle down at the sight of her and rushed toward her. He pulled her into an embrace, nearly crushing her. "Emma, you had me worried beyond belief. Why didn't you come downstairs for our guests?"

"I *saw* the ring. The ruby ring. Were you planning to give it to *her*, Jack? To divorce me?" Emma pulled herself away, putting her arms around her shivering frame. "I suppose divorce is not nearly as scandalous in California. Did you believe you might marry me in front of the investors, then toss me aside when you were wealthy enough to do so?"

Jack smiled. "You must know I would never do something like that! And I was wealthy enough to toss you aside from the beginning!" He grinned as he stepped closer.

She pressed her palms out toward Jack. "Katherine can play hostess for you tonight. I venture to say I might never be missed. You shall have the entire evening to practice being married to my sister. I give you my permission."

"Your permission? Emma, you're being fanciful. You've worked for weeks to make this night perfect. Come downstairs and enjoy it! All your handmade works are lit up beautifully on the Christmas tree. It's lovely." He started toward her, but she darted away.

"I ask only one thing." She crossed her arms again, defiantly.

"And what might that be?" He placed a hand on his hip. He looked more dashing than ever in his fine swallowtail jacket with satin lapels and ascot. She turned around rather than look at him. She didn't need the visual reminder of all she would lose.

"I ask only that you see to our child when he or she is born." She stole a glance to catch his reaction.

"Our child? Emma, we're going to have a child?" Jack jumped and kicked his feet together like a backwater farmer. He raced beside her and grasped her tightly. She struggled, but his powerful arms stilled her.

"Emma Grant, you're carrying our baby? Now I shall definitely remember this as my favorite Christmas. Never have I had more to celebrate." His grip threatened to swallow her. "I love you, Emma Grant. I love you with all my heart." His warm expression hardened. "Now get dressed for the ball. You must take better care of yourself." He grinned with a twinkle in his eye. "I also have a Christmas surprise for you. It will not match yours, though."

Emma tried to digest the hopeful words. "You love me?" she questioned.

"Of course I love you." He cupped her face in his hands, and even in the dim light of the candle she could see the sincerity in his eyes. "Emma, there is no other woman for me. There never was. God has made that abundantly clear. When you came here, spouting about Katherine, I thought my heart would remain like ice forever. Then I watched you reading your Bible each day and giving books to the miners' children. I saw you clean up my ledgers, and I knew . . . I knew God had supplied me with more than I could ever ask for in a wife, and I'd been too blind to see it. Just like those who had all the evidence that Jesus was the Christ. They had everything before them but expected something different and missed the greatest gift of all. There is nothing wanting in you, Emma. You are just right for me. God only had to humble me before I could appreciate it."

Emma's eyes narrowed; she was still not thoroughly convinced. "Why did you pick up Katherine alone?"

"You shall find out this evening. Now get dressed properly. I'll put off dinner and describe my wife as fashionably late."

❋ ❋ ❋

Emma descended the staircase gracefully in her new Christmas gown, and all eyes turned. She wore an elaborate dress of black velvet with white accoutrements, and her hair was swept up in a thick coil with tiny seed pearls laced through the silky strands.

Jack gazed at his wife in awe. Gone was the apprehensive, retiring maiden he'd married. In her place was an elegant woman of God, who knew her place in society but, more importantly, her place in his heart. Why had he waited so long to tell her he loved her? Clearly, his words had changed her.

Katherine came beside him, her face stricken with jealousy over the attention Emma was receiving. "You really should send Emma to New York. Her gown is quite out of fashion."

"Emma doesn't care much for fashion. And besides, when you look like Emma, the gown pales in comparison, regardless."

"Low necklines are in for evening, and she's wearing a tucker." Katherine sniffed in disgust.

"Low necklines are inappropriate for my wife," Jack answered stiffly.

"Jack." Katherine tore at Jack's arm, trying to gain his attention. "I am going to stay in California." She smiled, tilting her chin upward. Her blue eyes fluttered open and closed. "Would that make you happy?"

"You won't be staying here, if that's your plan." Jack looked away from his wife and into the sparkling yet calculating eyes of his sister-in-law.

"Jack, you have to understand," Katherine said desperately. "I never loved my husband."

"What a pity for you. There is no greater gift than to love one's spouse."

"You loved me once, Jack. Please, listen to me. I could be an excellent hostess alongside Emma for you. You know, charm your associates when needed. I would allow her to remain as she is. The truth is, I have no money to go back to Boston. My husband left me penniless."

"I shall be happy to provide you with train passage back to Boston." Jack smiled at his guests, talking through the side of his mouth. "And should you play your tricks with one of my colleagues, I shall eagerly tell them of your mourning period, or lack thereof." He let his eyes meet hers.

Katherine's cold stare was glacial. "You wouldn't!"

"I was a fool, Katherine. I will not have you make a fool of my investors. More importantly, for Emma's sake I will not have you remain here. Excuse me." Jack nodded and went to his wife's side. He picked up a crystal candy dish and clinked the side with a strawberry fork. "Attention. Attention!"

❄ ❄ ❄

The buzz of conversation died. "It is my pleasure to welcome you to our home, and I ask you to lift your glass to my wife, Emma, who is responsible for making the cottage warmer than it's ever been."

"To Emma!" the crowd shouted. Emma felt her heart skip a beat. With all eyes on her, she looked to the floor as her husband continued.

"This morning when I was in town, I saw many of you, but I was quite secretive as to my quest." Jack pulled Emma a bit closer. He pulled the largest Christmas cracker Emma had ever seen from the tree. She didn't recognize it, but it was wrapped with a shiny red paper.

"Where did this come from?"

Jack continued to address their guests. "When I selected my wife, I wanted her to have a scarlet ruby, because as the Bible says, a virtuous woman's worth is far above rubies. That is what my grandfather always said about my grandmother. Emma—" he handed her the cracker, and she popped it open with a jolt—"my grandfather brought this ring to America for her Christmas gift. Sadly, he passed away during passage, but this ring made it safely. My grandmother always knew how my grandfather loved her, just as you shall know how much I love you."

Inside the cracker was the great ruby ring. Its scarlet color shimmered brilliantly in the candlelight. "The tradition continues, Grandfather." Jack took the exquisite emerald-cut ruby ring, held it to the ceiling momentarily, and then slipped it on Emma's finger.

Emma's heart pounded at the thrill of the Christmas ring on her hand, but Jack picked up the silver fork and clinked the crystal again.

"I wanted to add to my grandfather's Christmas tradition. I want to tell my wife every Christmas how she is worth more than I can form into words. I have failed miserably until now. I had this commissioned for her by a goldsmith in San Francisco—" he pulled out a black velvet box and held it up for all to see—"and it arrived today, just in time."

Jack opened the box. An intricately designed necklace made up of several red rubies danced before Emma's eyes. The chandelier caught several of the stones and delivered a dazzling show of reflective light.

Emma's hands flew to her mouth. "Jack!"

He kneeled in front of her, quoting from the Bible. " 'Who can find a virtuous woman? for her price is far above rubies.' "

The sting of tears intensified, and Emma swallowed the lump in her throat. Gazing at him, she saw all the love and trust she'd ever hoped for, that she'd ever imagined. She reached down and touched his cheek, and in front of all their guests, he stood and kissed her. She felt his kiss to the depths of her soul.

The gathering clapped wildly, and Emma felt her face race with heat. She looked about the room and then into her husband's deep evergreen eyes. She was loved. And *everyone* knew her worth was far above rubies to the man of her dreams.

A Note from the Author

Dear Reader,

I hope you have enjoyed reading "Far above Rubies." It is a story that is close to my heart. My husband and I are both very practical people, and I have often thought of myself as Leah rather than Rachel. As time and trials have touched us, I have grown to realize that God could not have selected a more perfect partner for me or for my husband. Focusing on God's will has allowed me to appreciate who my husband is, rather than on who I thought he'd be.

I would encourage you, whether in a marriage or happily single, to remember that God is the completer of us; no person can fill that void for you.

May God richly bless you in your walk.
Kristin Billerbeck

About the Author

KRISTIN BILLERBECK is the popular author of four Heartsong Presents novels and has written novellas for several Barbour anthologies. "Far above Rubies" is her first HeartQuest novella. Her novel *To Truly See* was a Top Pick in *Romantic Times* magazine and ranked #5 by readers among Heartsong Contemporary novels for 1998. *Meet My Sister Tess* was ranked #3 by readers among Heartsong Contemporary novels for 1999, and *The Landlord Takes a Bride* was voted #4 Heartsong Contemporary novels for 2000. Kristin also has pieces in *Storytellers' Collection* and *Storytellers' Collection II* (Multnomah).

Kristin and her husband, Bryed, have served as Sunday school teachers and leaders of an adult fellowship class, and they are currently working with The Highway Community, a ministry designed to reach a postmodern society near Stanford University in California. Kristin and her husband have four children—three boys and a baby girl.

Kristin welcomes letters written to her in care of:

TYNDALE HOUSE AUTHOR RELATIONS
P.O. Box 80
WHEATON, IL 60189-0080

or you may e-mail her at KrisBeck@aol.com. Visit Kristin on the Web at www.KristinBillerbeck.com.

Memory to Keep
GINNY AIKEN

Rejoice in the Lord your God! The Lord says, "I will give you back what you lost to the . . . locusts."
JOEL 2:23, 25

CHAPTER ONE

BRAES, ISLE OF SKYE, SCOTLAND, 1887

O ch, lassie," groused Cook as Grace Carlisle wound little Rory McConnell's bright red scarf around his neck. "That wind is sharp enough to cut a wedge of cheese, an' yer takin' our wee bairns into it." She clucked her displeasure.

Rory's grin dipped southward as the three-year-old shot an alarmed look at his governess.

"Aye, that I am," Grace answered with a wink to the boy. She then turned and tugged his brother Alasdair's crooked cap into place. "But have you ever seen a less likely wedge of cheese than these two?"

Cook rolled her eyes and chuckled. "Ye have me there, lass; ye do indeed. Fresh they may be, but cheese they ain't." Reaching into a large crockery canister that sat on a shelf across the east wall of the large, cheery kitchen, she withdrew shortbread biscuits for the lads. "Well, if ye must, then I guess ye must. Go on with ye. And give them these to keep their bellies happy."

Grace ushered her smiling, munching charges out the kitchen door and into the mid-December morning. As was typical of winter days in this lovely corner of the Isle of Skye, mist covered the Cuillin Mountains and the wind whipped by in a lively rush.

To some, these traits of her new home spoke of bleakness, but Grace had yet to see anything but God's magnificence in her surroundings. From the moment she'd arrived in Braes four months ago to assume her position as governess to Mr. and Mrs. Roderick McConnell's two boys, Grace had found the Isle of Skye a jewel in the rough.

To her, the frequent ring of mist that descended from the heavens protected the island's secrets, secrets it shared only with those who looked beyond its rocky crags and blustery breezes to its wild and wonderful beauty.

"Watch your step now, Alasdair," she called when the impulsive seven-year-old scrambled up a boulder, then leaped off, hollering his glee. "And, Rory, you must not follow everywhere your brother leads. Your legs haven't stretched that long yet."

The three-year-old crossed his arms across his chest and frowned. "I am *too* a good brae lad. Mama said."

Grace's insides melted at the determination displayed in the snapping brown eyes and still-babyish chin. "Of course, you're a big boy—just not quite as big as Alasdair." She knelt at the wee one's side. "Perhaps a mite wiser, too, wouldn't you say?"

Rory tipped his head and glanced at his brother, who somersaulted on the damp grass, yelped, and rubbed his head. A smile lit Rory's face as Grace ran to the older boy.

"Found yourself a rock in the grass, did you?" she asked, checking under the boy's green cap and thick auburn hair. When she uncovered no blood, she made her voice stern—as stern as she could. "Now then. Was that somersault the wisest move?"

"Aye!" Alasdair's chin, sharper than Rory's, jutted. "'Twas not a wise rock to find itself a home right there." So saying, he trotted back, dug out the offending stone, then stuffed it in his coat pocket. "I'll put it in its right place soon enough."

Knowing the boy, Grace feared that the rock might well end up in the collection of oddments that Ellie, the laundress, regularly returned to the nursery. Alasdair's pockets always yielded bounty.

For a few minutes, the threesome walked farther. Then, finally reaching her destination, Grace studied the panorama spread before her with her usual admiration and awe. The wild beauty of it swept over her soul, overwhelming her.

"Oh, Father God," she whispered as the boys chortled at the freedom their outing afforded them, "you are so wise and wonderful. You knew just where to bring me when I feared I had nowhere to go."

During those final weeks as she finished her schooling at Miss Morrissey's School for Young Ladies in Edinburgh, Grace had wondered what would happen to her. It seemed no one needed a governess, and that was the best line of work for a respectable, unmarried, schooled young woman. For the past nine years her trust fund had covered her living and schooling expenses, but now there was scarcely enough in the account to cover the cost of travel to a new position, should she need to secure one.

Each time anxiety threatened, however, she did as her parents always had; she turned to God in prayer. When Grace was a young girl, he'd provided for the Carlisle family while they'd answered his call to the mission field in China. They had sent Grace to Miss Morrissey's School in Scotland, knowing that she would not only receive the finest of educations, but that she'd be safe from the dangers of rural China. Then, when Grace was ten, her parents had been caught in the middle of a clash between rival warlords. They'd been killed. And although Grace had cried until she could cry no more tears and had missed her parents' presence every day, God had continued to provide for her. He'd used the trust fund Papa had established in her name with Mama's inheritance.

After finishing her studies, she was blessed with a surprising position. When the McConnells' former governess eloped with a visiting wool merchant, the family had needed a replacement straightaway. Miss Morrissey sent one of her star pupils—Grace.

Upon her arrival, Grace had been surprised. All her

fears about what she might find disappeared. As soon as she saw this mysterious and hauntingly beautiful island off the western coast of Scotland, she felt at home. "Welcome," it had called.

Now she checked on her charges, noting that the boys had resumed the construction project they'd begun earlier in the week near a lonely pine in the meadow behind her. She smiled. They were fine lads indeed—mischievous, intelligent, and loving. They were a joy to teach.

Fighting the wildly whipping wind, Grace made her way to the craggy rock outpost that afforded her the most splendid view of her new home. Her slate flannel skirt roiled around her ankles, and her cape caught an occasional gust to billow out behind her. But these were mere annoyances. To worship God in this natural—if uncommon—chapel, she'd gladly don itchy woolen stockings and thick petticoats, heavy leather brogans to protect her feet, mitts, and scarf.

Just then a blast of air flung her cape's hood off her head, tugging tendrils of her hair from their moorings. They frothed before her eyes, then backward as the wind continued on its path behind her. Grace drew the folds of her navy wool cape more tightly about her.

As the splendor of God's creation surrounded her, she let her voice express the words of one of her favorite, richest songs of praise. To the one who'd made her and led her to this bit of his earth she sang, "How great Thou art! How great Thou art . . ."

❋ ❋ ❋

The wind blew sharply against Andrew Fraser and the aging mount as they headed inland from the coast of the Isle of Skye. He ducked his head against his chest and shivered. "A seaman belongs on deck," Drew said, as he nudged the horse's sides, "not on the back of a rented horse, crossing a forsaken, misty rock."

What *was* he doing there? Why had he even agreed to this absurd journey? to carry out his father's last wish? The father who had barely noticed his existence for the last nine years?

As these thoughts swirled in his head, grief rushed in, making his head throb and knotting his gut.

Drew dragged in a breath of damp, icy air. It tasted of the loneliness he'd felt when reality had hit him in his fifteenth year. Cheerful Ada Fraser, his beloved mother, had left the Fraser home to stay at the mission with the Carlisles. She'd wanted the comfort and safety of fellow Scots while her husband's extended buying trip separated the family. His mother and Mrs. Carlisle had been great friends. And in that supposedly safe haven she'd died, as had the infant she'd carried in her womb. That infant would have been Drew's only sibling.

When Drew's father, Daniel Fraser—or "the Captain," as everyone had called him—heard the news about his wife, he'd plunged into a dark hole of misery. It was a place from which he had never managed to rise, with his lone companion bottle after bottle of malt whiskey. Oh, the Captain had continued to run his importing and exporting business quite handily despite the liquor that denied his sense of reality. But what time and energy did his father have for a youth? a motherless lad of fifteen?

Daniel's loss of the woman he'd loved was the only thing that had registered. He had not spared a moment's thought for his son.

So Drew learned his father's trade, joining the crew on one of the Fraser ships—eventually taking over its captaincy. He'd also shown himself adept at negotiating.

And now, at twenty-four years old, Drew knew his life at sea suited him. After all, he could go from port to port, experience new cultures and places, and never have to worry about any attachments. After loving his mother and losing her, he knew how much loving could hurt. He was determined to never allow himself to be hurt in such a way again. So he never lingered long in any one place.

That was precisely what he planned to do on the Isle of Skye—carry out his father's last wish as quickly as possible and then leave the wretched island. His father had begged him to deliver a nine-year-old, belated Christmas gift to the daughter of the missionaries whom Ada had stayed with in China. But in order to do so, he'd have to face the daughter of the couple who had failed to protect their guest, the expectant Ada, from the warring factions. They'd been so intent on saving the souls of Chinese heathens that they'd allowed their guest to be in a place where she could be harmed. And the worst thing possible had happened—she was killed and the babe within her. No wonder his father had never been able to deliver the

Christmas gift himself. His father had harbored too much hatred and bitterness toward the Carlisles. And it had destroyed his life.

Yet, from his deathbed, a guilt-riddled father had given Drew strict instructions: *he* must go deliver the present. After all, it belonged to the daughter, Grace Carlisle. So after his father's death several months ago, Drew had written to Miss Morrissey's School, the daughter's last-known location. He'd discovered that she had hired out as governess to the McConnells.

"Fancy that," Drew informed the unwilling mare as he urged her down the rocky lane leading from Braes to the McConnell manor. "Whereas Father was never able to make himself seek out the girl, here he's made me promise to carry out his chore for him."

It was a bitter draught for Drew to swallow. He'd suffered as much as Daniel after the tragedy. So why should he, the now doubly grieving son, do what the widower never could?

"Because Drew, my boy," Daniel had rasped with what turned out to be one of his last breaths, "ye're a better man than I."

As Drew now urged the mare to a faster pace, he spotted movement on a craggy ledge to his far right. "Fool," he muttered in disbelief, pulling the collar of his coat higher around his neck.

Someone had gone out in this detestable weather and now stood on the edge of a rocky shelf, evidently oblivious to the buffeting gale. He shook his head at such idiocy.

Then, as he rounded a slight bend in the road to the manor, he realized the fool on the ridge was a woman.

Outlined against the smoky mist, her dark garments stood out sharply as the wind clawed at their lengths. Her skirt swirled close to the ground, while her cloak filled like the sail on his mainmast. Yet she stood her ground against the power of the gales.

He continued his unwanted trek to his meeting with the Carlisles' daughter, his attention now riveted to the woman on the rocks. A sudden gust threw back the hood on her cape, revealing her profile. Delicate and feminine, yet tall and willowy, she appeared scarcely older than a child. Still, to stand so firmly against nature, to hold her ground against such a force, she had to be more. As he watched, she lifted her face into the wind and, incomprehensibly, twirled in the tempestuous air, her movements light and graceful, seemingly joyful.

"Must be mad," he reasoned. Spying the stone facade of the manor up ahead, he clicked his tongue at the uncooperative horse. Then the reality of what he was about to do hit him: He was about to meet the daughter of those responsible for his mother's death. How would he handle it?

"Whoa," he said softly, and the animal complied with this command much more readily than with any previous order.

Drew knew himself a coward. He'd suspected it when he'd left the gift intended for Grace Carlisle back at the room he'd taken in Portree. He'd begun to fear it when

243

he'd willingly allowed the stable owner to saddle for him what had to be the worst horse in town. And, as he'd come closer to his destination, certainty had filled his gut.

He no longer had any doubt.

Andrew Fraser was a coward. He feared coming face-to-face with the lass whose parents had cost him his family. He did not know if he was civilized enough to control his rage and not seek justice . . . or perhaps revenge.

❄ ❄ ❄

The sound of children's laughter dragged Drew from his bleak thoughts. Ah . . . the Carlisle chit's charges, no doubt.

Time to get on with his difficult errand.

As every bit of his being rebelled, Drew nudged the horse toward the curving drive in front of the imposing stone house. Old, perhaps as much as a pair of centuries, so it boasted mullioned windows and a turret to boot. Massive chimneys huffed smoke out into the cold air, giving proof of its habitation.

Truly, the location was desolate. Drew shivered and thought longingly of the South Seas. "Naught to be done, old lass," he informed the again-slowing nag. "A man must do what a man must do."

He dismounted when he no longer dared stay atop the horse, mere steps from the large front doors. With equal measures of determination and reluctance, he strode up the walkway to a broad stoop flanked by squat stone pillars. Empty iron urns topped the posts, adding to the air of bleakness.

Shuddering, Drew clapped the huge brass knocker. The sound echoed—

"Can't!" cried a child from behind Drew.

"Of course I can," scoffed another. "I'm older than ye."

"I'm faster," the first retorted, closer than before.

Footsteps approached from inside the house. Drew debated for a scant second whether to satisfy his curiosity about the children with whom the daughter of careless missionaries had been charged or whether to seek warmth for his poor bones.

His decision was made for him. As the door swung inward, a pair of whirling dervishes shot past him and into the grand entry hall of the McConnells' manor house. Instead of children, all Drew saw were splashes of red and green.

The tall, spare woman who'd opened the door frowned. "Och, those bairns. I despair of seein' them walk. 'Tis runnin' they're always after, an' across the waxed floors with the holidays approachin', no less."

At a loss, Drew merely stood in place.

Rushed footsteps approached from his left. "I'm so sorry, Mrs. Oswald," said a feminine voice. "I had no idea they were headed inside. Why, a moment ago, they were racing each other over the brae, while the next . . . they were gone."

The softly burred words rang an uncomfortable bell in Drew's mind. This woman sounded a bit too much like his mother.

Slowly he turned, moved aside, and studied the

newcomer. A bulky navy cloak obscured her body and contrasted with the fair skin at her slender neck. Her cheeks glowed rosy from their contact with the wind, while her chestnut hair, free from the restraint of many pins, lay in silky strands across her forehead, loose locks down her shoulders, and a meager knot at her nape. Silver eyes sparkled despite the lady's subdued tone.

The dark cloak looked familiar, and if her weather-kissed looks were anything to go by, Drew might wager he'd seen this stranger before. Unless he was much mistaken, this was the woman he'd seen on the ridge, the one who'd danced with the squalls and gales.

This woman was—

"Miss Grace!" cried one of the scamps who'd caused the current controversy with their romp across the entry hall.

She hurried past Drew, smiling at the child. "Not so fast, Alasdair. You've fashed Mrs. Oswald with your wild dash through the house. Please apologize."

So it was true. This was Grace Carlisle.

His quarry.

His nemesis.

Scarcely more than a girl.

As he watched, she removed her outerwear and folded the garment over her arm. Her movements were efficient and elegant, with no fussing, no wasted energy to them.

She wore a plain white blouse and a dark skirt, somber clothing befitting a woman in her position. Yet those silver eyes glowed from within, as though a hearth warmed and burned behind the cool color of the irises.

Despite himself, Andrew was intrigued by the missionaries' daughter. "Miss Carlisle?"

She spun around. "Oh, my. I hadn't noticed you standing there. Hello. And who might you be?"

Mrs. Oswald shook her head disapprovingly. "Naught
but trouble, I'd say. Who'd come a-knockin' at a proper
house an' not introduce himself?"

"One who was verra near bowled over by a pair of lively
lads," Grace answered while perusing her charges, who
were peeking between the balusters of the curved oak
staircase. "Please forgive Alasdair and Rory, sir. They
dinna seem to have their manners with them this day. And
because of that, they must go straight up to the nursery
and stay there until they find them. Can't have proper lads
running loose with no manners a'tall. Go on, you two. Up
those stairs now."

As the scamps reluctantly marched on their way with
nary a cross word, unexpected admiration filled Drew. The
governess hadn't lost her temper, hadn't frowned, hadn't
even scolded the boys. Yet they'd known they'd trans-
gressed, just as well as they'd learned it from Mrs.
Oswald's criticisms.

"Congratulations," he said. "You have a way with children."

The rose in Grace's cheeks darkened. "Thank you. It's
not so hard if you love them a bit."

Her gentle words sent a shaft of pain straight to his
heart. Aye, he once knew what it was like to be loved. Ada
Fraser had loved her son wholeheartedly, never bothering

to temper her affection with the detachment proper society expected.

And then . . . her love was gone. Her life was spent, spilled on foreign soil. All because this woman's parents had failed to protect their guest.

Now before him stood Hugh Carlisle's daughter. The daughter of the family who had taken away his family. Unbidden, rage bubbled up in Drew. How dare Grace smile so innocently? How dare she speak with such a sweet, soft voice? How dare she live so freely when her parents' actions should burn in the deepest corner of her heart?

"I'm Andrew Fraser, Miss Carlisle," he said. "I wonder if my name means anything to you?"

When she paled, he sought to feel satisfaction, but instead felt a hint of disconcerting concern. She swayed as if weak and frail, yet he'd seen her withstand the bluster of the winds without a twinge.

"I see you know my name—"

"Oh, dear," she murmured, cutting off his words. "Of course I know your name. I've often thought of you these many years. I've wondered . . ."

As her words trailed off, Drew arched a brow.

She breathed deeply and set her shoulders, the air of fragility leaving her. The woman on the ridge had returned. "Aye, I wondered how you'd taken the frightful news. I knew you'd been with your father aboard his ship, and I knew it would take awhile before either of you heard word. I wondered how it'd be for a lad. If it would hurt the same as it had me."

"Losing one's mother is the same, regardless of one's gender," he said, his voice more biting than even he'd expected.

She winced. "Aye, I suppose 'tis true. But you had your father with you, while I . . . I had neither left."

The glitter in her eyes was no longer that of their silver color. This sparkle owed its hue to the presence of her tears.

Drew had to work hard to stay focused on what he had come to say. "That, Miss Carlisle, is where you're wrong. I lost my father the very day I learned of my mother's death. I lost him to his grief and to the easy comfort and forgetting in a bottle. You were sheltered at school, as you'd been even while your parents lived. I lost *everything* when my mother died."

A mix of bewilderment and compassion spread across Grace's face. She reached across the space that separated them and tentatively placed a hand on his arm. "I'm sorry to hear that, sir. I know just how you felt. Mama and Papa were all I had. When they died that day, I lost everyone, too. A school is no mother, no father. I'm so sorry for the grief you've felt, for the sadness you clearly still feel. It's hard indeed to lose someone you love."

Drew stared at the hand on his coat, marveling at the lightness of her touch . . . and the depth of its effect on him. Had her soft hand turned his years of anger to shame? Or had the gentle words she'd offered done so?

"Tell me," he said more gently. "Don't you still feel . . . sadness, as you said? Don't you still mourn your loss?

Doesn't unfairness burn at you until you fear you might go mad—"

Drew caught himself. It wouldn't do to reveal so much to a perfect stranger.

The governess slipped her cloak from her right forearm to her left, smoothly allowing herself to remove her touch from his arm. At that instant Drew knew the loss nearly as deeply as he'd known its presence.

"I'll always feel the loss and the sadness, Mr. Fraser. But the unfairness?" She shrugged and stepped back, putting some distance between them. "God never said life would not be unfair, you know. He merely said he'd walk us through it if we just trust and obey. That burning you speak of, why, if I'd allowed it to take root in my heart, it would likely have been the end of me."

So Miss Carlisle was indeed coldhearted, as her parents must have been to allow what they had. "What kind of daughter are you, then? You don't want justice for the way your parents died?"

Again she studied him with those disconcerting silver eyes. "God is just, Mr. Fraser. I'm certain that in his time and in his way, justice will indeed be served. In the meantime, I serve him, not some feeling inside me that insists I seek to right those instances where I've been wronged."

"Perhaps you do not see the events quite the same as I do."

"How can I see them other than as they happened? Two godless, greedy men allowed their wants to control their conscience. They fought where innocent folk lived. Rage blinded them and, in the heat of their contest, my mother and father, as well as your mother, were killed."

Drew nodded knowingly. "Just as I thought," he said sarcastically. "You only see one side of the events."

Grace shook her head, dislodging yet another silky brown tendril from its mooring. It slipped past a cheek that looked as smooth and rich as cream. "There is naught more to know, Mr. Fraser. They died tragically, but with the eternal hope of their faith in Christ. We live. And how we do so counts. Would that I could serve my Savior as they did."

There it was. The faith he'd known would soon be flung in his face. Bitter words began to pour from him. "What kind of a savior do you serve, Miss Carlisle? If it's the one your parents did, then you serve an ineffective one. What kind of powerful God would allow his servants to expose an expectant mother to the danger of warring factions? What kind of powerful God would let his mission be destroyed? And what kind of witness to a powerful God would fail to take another man's wife, heavy with an unborn child, entrusted into his care, back to the safety of civilization when the trouble first hit?"

Grace Carlisle recoiled at Drew's vicious words as if she'd been struck. Aye, he'd gone too far this time. She looked ready to drop. But he couldn't seem to help himself.

Almost unconsciously Drew reached for her, afraid she might faint. But once again, that deep well of strength made its appearance. Grace straightened and held her head high.

"The verra same God, Mr. Fraser," she said, her voice shaking with pain and perhaps a drop of anger, "who gave you the freedom to choose such hateful words. The same God who'll forgive you for saying them if you but ask. The same God who healed my pain and gave me a reason to live. The same God your mother loved."

Once again, shame filled Drew; he knew his actions would have shamed his gentle mother as well.

Who was this slip of a woman? Who was she, really? What gave her the strength to dance in a Scottish windstorm and then withstand one of words?

Although he hadn't rightly known why he had decided to leave behind the box that had set him off on this difficult trip, Drew was glad it sat in his room back in Portree. Grace's ability to overcome grief and anger and bitterness piqued his curiosity.

As did the fire behind her silver eyes.

He wasn't quite ready to bring his errand to a close yet. Not until his curiosity was satisfied.

CHAPTER TWO

After Andrew Fraser left, Grace continued with her routine automatically, her mind on their encounter. What had brought this rather good-looking, black-haired man with a heart of hurt to her new home? Why had he sought her out now, after so many years? And so close to Christmas, when people tended to stay close to the hearth of home and those they loved. The questions would not let up, regardless of the number of times she turned them over to the Lord. What could cause a man to retain so much rancor over a tragic accident so many years after the event?

Grace, too, had initially felt shock and deep anger. She had grieved the deaths of her parents. At times her pain had been debilitating, and she'd wondered if she could go on. The grief had seemed to cycle, sweeping keenly over her during times she'd traditionally been with them, including the winter holidays. Even now, she still ached with loss, especially when something—a phrase, a scent, a wisp of song—reminded her of her parents. But the years of dealing with the pain had also brought her to a first-hand knowledge of the endless love and bountiful provision of the heavenly Father, almighty God. After walking through the fire of loss, she now trusted God's promises, holding to them as a lifeline. And she looked forward with joy to a reunion with her loved ones in heaven.

Andrew Fraser evidently held no such hope, even though Grace knew his mother had been a devout follower of Christ. Mrs. Ada Fraser had been a frequent visitor at the mission house in the Shantung Province when her husband's business interests sent him on long trips aboard one of his merchant ships. The letters Grace received at Miss Morrissey's School from her mother had often made reference to the woman's presence and, particularly, her commitment to sharing the Good News with the Chinese.

Could Andrew Fraser, the son of such a godly woman, have reached adulthood without coming to know the Savior? Or had he turned his back on the God his mother had served because of her death?

With a flash of insight, Grace wondered. Had God brought Andrew to her, after all these years, to have a part in his healing? in his reconciliation with God? Would she ever see him again? He'd left without any indication. Grace now rued the fact that his hurtful words had so stunned her that she hadn't thought to ask him much of anything.

Not that the McConnell boys experienced any such reticence. "Miss Grace, who was that man?" the older of the boys asked as the door to the large nursery closed behind her. "Why was he so stroobly?"

"Stroobly?" she asked. "And what would that mean, Master Alasdair?"

"You ken," he proclaimed with childlike wisdom, "his forehead all down, an' his lips all puckered up as if he'd sucked on a green persimmon."

"Hmm . . . ," Grace murmured. "He did look a wee bit stern, but he was discussing sad, sad things. Perhaps that's what you're calling *stroobly*."

The boy shrugged. "No matter, Miss Grace. He looked mean. An' he was not verra mannerly, either. He just showed up at our door all stroobly-like."

"I cannot argue with you there," Grace answered, setting out the materials for the boys' ciphering lesson. "But since I know naught more than you do about Mr. Fraser, I suggest we get on with a discussion of *your* manners, laddie."

Alasdair rolled his golden brown eyes. "All I did was come inside. 'Tisn't my fault Mrs. Oswald is such a prune."

Grace had a time keeping her face straight in the light of such candor. "Now, Alasdair, that's precisely what I meant. Referring to an elder by such a rude name is not what a proper, mannerly lad ought to do." Grace arched one brow and narrowed her other eye. "Especially one so distressed by a visitor's poor manners."

"But 'tis verra true, Miss Grace." The obstinate chin jutted farther out. "You would not want me to lie aboot it, would ye now?"

The sly twinkle in the dancing brown eyes warned

Grace that time had come to end the discussion. "I do believe, Alasdair, 'tis time for you to march downstairs and apologize to Mrs. Oswald for whatever additional work your dash into the entrance hall may have made for her. Then you must help clean it up."

Slender arms crossed over a boyish chest. "'Tain't her house, Miss Grace."

Grace winced at, but prudently chose to ignore, the otherwise forbidden *ain't*. "'Tis her job to keep it sparkling. And you'd just been wandering the brae. Have you had a good look at your boots since coming indoors?"

A giggle drew Grace's attention to the younger brother. "Dirty, dirty, dirty," sang Rory, holding up a filthy boot.

Alasdair's bluster faded. He muttered something conciliatory in a reluctant voice and opened the room door. "But I don't hafta like it, do I, Miss Grace?"

She smiled. "No, son, God's Word does not say we will always like doing what is right. It only says he will bless our willingness to obey. Honoring our elders is something the Father calls us to do."

A deep sigh followed; then the door closed.

"Stroobly, Miss Grace," echoed Rory, his brown curls bouncing as he punctuated his pronouncement with a nod. "The man's stroobly."

Despite her earlier protestation, Grace had to admit her charges were right. Andrew Fraser's visit had left her with the impression of a very "stroobly," troubled fellow indeed.

Would she ever learn why he'd come so far after so long?

❋ ❋ ❋

Drew stared at the dirty old crate he'd hauled halfway
across the world. Logic insisted he hire out a cart and
driver and have it delivered to Miss Carlisle first thing in
the morning. Then he could go back to the sea and his own
business. But as he sat in the overstuffed armchair in his
rented room at the inn in Portree, staring at the steam that
rose from a bracing cup of Earl Gray, he knew he wasn't
likely to do so.

The curiosity that had driven him this far had merely
grown stronger after meeting the missionaries' daughter.

His initial encounter with Grace Carlisle had made him
want to know more. Although not everyone would call
her a beauty, a loveliness seemed to shine from her soul
and through her smooth creamy skin. Even though her
wealth of silky brown hair had surrendered any
semblance of a coiffure during the tromp out of doors, it
shone with health and vitality. And the pair of clear gray
eyes that had met his directly . . . well, their silver depths
reminded him of a mirror. He couldn't help wondering,
silly though it seemed, if the emotions he'd seen flit
across them had been not so much hers as a reflection of
his.

"No," he scoffed, rising and resuming the pacing he'd
begun when he'd returned to the inn. Even after he'd said
those hard words to her, he hadn't spied even a hint of
anger or outrage in those eyes. Instead, he had identified
grief . . . and something else. He certainly hoped it hadn't

been pity; if Miss Grace Carlisle thought him in need of pitying, she'd gotten the wrong impression.

Justice was what Andrew Fraser craved. But he had no idea how to achieve it. Or from whom to extract it.

Two innocents—one not yet born—had lost their lives because of a religious idealist's negligence. One could, of course, add his father's death to the tally, since the elder Fraser began to die the day he learned of his wife's and unborn child's fate.

Still, nothing altered the truth. He had been rude; he had acted shamefully toward Grace Carlisle. His mother would have been mortified, since she'd taught him better than that.

Surely he owed her memory an attempt to rectify his abominable loss of control. He'd visit Miss Carlisle once again. Right away—tomorrow, even. This time, however, he would keep his temper under control. And he'd try to learn what more, if anything, she knew about the nine-year-old tragedy. Perhaps there was something that would be able to bring him a measure of peace about his past so that he could move on with his life.

Her lack of anguish baffled him. Perhaps her equanimity came from information to which he was not yet privy rather than from an appalling coldness of heart, as he'd first thought. Yes, he'd go back, and when he had satisfied his curiosity, he would bring his errand to its conclusion.

Once he learned how Grace Carlisle had managed to set aside the roiling pain of loss, he would hand over her belated holiday gift.

✳ ✳ ✳

"Miss Grace!" called Maude, the upstairs maid, as she threw open the nursery door the next afternoon. "Yer gentleman caller is back. Och, and he's a bonny one, too."

Startled, Grace didn't immediately grasp the meaning of the girl's words. "Gentleman caller . . . ?"

"Aye," said Alasdair. "'Tis the stroobly fellow again. I can see his old yellow horse from this window."

Grace's heart skipped a beat as she hurried to the boy's vantage point. Andrew Fraser's nag stood tied to a post in the front yard. What had brought him back again? And would his mood have changed?

"Settle down, lads," the flustered Grace urged her charges, feeling anything but settled herself. "I'll be right back. I doubt Mr. Fraser will be staying long."

His bitterness remained clear in her memory, as did the compassion she'd felt for him. He still grieved his initial loss and, from what he had said, it seemed he also
credited his father's decline to that long-ago tragedy.

As she hurried down the curved front stairs of McConnell Manor, Grace smoothed her hands over her navy skirt, checking that her blouse remained neatly tucked in. Skimming fingers revealed only a few strands of hair wisped beyond the anchoring pins.

"Good afternoon, Mr. Fraser," she said from the parlor doorway. "I'm surprised to see you again."

A hint of ruddiness crept over his chiseled, tanned cheekbones. "Before I even left yesterday, I knew I'd behaved dreadfully. I owe you an apology, and I've come to deliver it."

His forthrightness caught her by surprise, and she sought to hide her reaction by gesturing him toward the coffee-hued velvet settee near the hearth. "Your pain was clear, Mr. Fraser. I assumed your sharp words stemmed from your feelings."

He shrugged and sat, his tall, broad form dwarfing the elegant furnishing. "You're right, of course," he said. "I cannot deny my grief, but that does not excuse my attack. My anger isn't with you." He paused a minute, then continued, unsteadily. "It's with your father."

"Indeed, Mr. Fraser." Grace cocked her head. "You hold Papa responsible for those deaths. 'Twas a pair of warring heathens who killed your mother—mine, too, as well as Papa himself."

With her words a brittle glitter sprang into his eyes. "He must have known what was afoot. Why would he stay? Why would he force two defenseless women—one expecting a much-wanted child—to stay in a place where they had no protection? Can't you see his foolish actions caused their deaths?"

Grace gasped. Although she knew Andrew had an obviously skewed and flawed understanding of the events, it nonetheless hurt her to hear his accusation. "Papa was anything but foolish, Mr. Fraser. He was a committed man of God and well knew what his calling to spread the gospel might cost."

"What good did talking to the Chinese about the gospel

do him? He wound up dead—they all did. Besides, the Chinese remain the heathens they've always been," he finished bitterly. "I know. I spent time in the Shantung Province myself."

Grace took a deep breath. "It depends, of course, on how you view good. Mama, Papa, and I view good as doing God's will, despite the price or the immediate outcome."

What looked like hatred narrowed his eyes. "Price, Miss Carlisle? My mother's life was too high a price for your father to pay for his calling. Especially since it wasn't his coin."

"Do you not feel that your mother's commitment to her Savior had any bearing in the situation?"

He rose and began to pace. "You cannot possibly expect me to believe a woman carrying a child would choose to expose herself to certain death."

The man was obstinate—and sadly mistaken. "Of course, she would not do that—she didn't do it a'tall. Your mother shared my parents' commitment to take the gift of salvation to those who had never heard of the Lord Jesus. She especially loved the girl children scorned by their families simply because they were girls."

He glared at Grace. "She didn't love them any more than she loved the babe that died inside her. She wouldn't have traded it for one of them."

"'Twas never a matter of trading. She chose to obey God's command to go forth and share the Good News of Jesus. She chose to visit Mama and Papa, just as they chose to stay in a dangerous land for the sake of Christ."

He fairly spat the word, "Madness."

Just then the mischievous Alasdair peeked around the doorway. Inches below his head appeared the equally impish Rory. "Miss Grace," said the younger McConnell, "will we not go oot today?"

Relieved by the distraction, Grace rose. "Of course, we will. And we'll do so straightaway." Turning to her disturbed guest—if one could consider Andrew Fraser her guest at all—Grace said, "As you can see, I'm quite busy. The lads require my attention, since they are my responsibility. You must excuse me. This has been . . . most unusual, I must say."

Andrew nodded and absently waved. "I can see I have again handled this matter poorly, and you're right. I cannot keep you from your duties any longer. Thank you for your time, Miss Carlisle."

Grace gestured him toward the front door. As he stepped ahead of her on his way out, he added, "It has been an unusual experience indeed."

Closing the door behind him, Grace leaned against the solid mahogany slab. She felt buffeted by the vilest storm.

"Dear Lord," she whispered, "that man is hurting. He needs your comfort and healing touch. He also needs to lose the scales over his eyes." Compassion welled within her, even though Mr. Fraser had hurt her and maligned her beloved parents' memories. "Father, send someone who can share with him your goodness, someone more able than I, someone who will show him that obeying you may not be easy, but 'tis always best."

Alasdair skidded to a stop before Grace. "We're ready."

"To the brae!" cried Rory, his cheeks pink with excitement.

And thank you, Father, for these lovely imps. They're a joy to watch. They're just what I need to clear away today's sadness.

"To the brae, then," she agreed, looking forward, as always, to the exhilaration she experienced each time she went to the wild and wonderful bit of land. It had become like a private chapel to her, the place where she felt closest to the Lord, where nothing interfered with her worship of the Father.

❋ ❋ ❋

A short mile's ride from the McConnell manor, Drew again found his mind whirling with myriad questions brought to life by one Grace Carlisle. There was something about her, an indefinable quality that he somehow found familiar. He couldn't shake the feeling that Grace and his mother had a lot in common.

Again, in the face of his bitterness, Grace had remained pleasant, even when he knew he'd offended her by tarnishing her precious father's memory. She'd disagreed with him, made her point most succinctly, but her demeanor had revealed a certainty that disarmed him.

What was it about Grace Carlisle he found so disquieting? so intriguing? so reminiscent of Mother?

The only thing the two women had in common was the connection through the elder Carlisles, and they had been nothing if not religious zealots. Grace had said his mother shared her parents' faith and commitment to Christ. Could that possibly be the similarity he found between the woman who'd mothered him so sweetly until her death and this composed, gentle stranger?

No, of course not. It must simply be a matter of Grace Carlisle being the first Scottish woman he'd spoken to in . . . good night! It had been years since he'd had a conversation with a woman from the British Isles. No wonder Grace reminded him of his mother; he recognized that distinct quality of Scottish womanhood in the missionaries' daughter.

Content with his assessment, Drew nudged his horse in the hope of a livelier gait, but the old nag would not be swayed from her plodding pace. Resigned to his fate, he took the time to study the landscape around him. The Isle of Skye boasted a certain craggy majesty, rough and natural, straightforward and sincere. The sky, visible now that the earlier mist had burned off, covered the world in a steely blanket, suggesting the approach of a winter storm— snow perhaps. Yesterday's winds had somewhat calmed, and despite today's occasional brisk gust, he didn't have to battle the piercing sharpness that had accompanied his arrival yesterday.

He smiled—reluctantly, at that—remembering his first glimpse of the rather charmingly wind-tossed Grace Carlisle at the McConnells' front door. No, in truth, that had been his second glimpse of her. Drew turned to look back toward the cliff where she'd stood yesterday, wind-swept and hauntingly feminine. To his amazement, a

cloaked figure again stood on the edge of the outcropping.

He tugged hard on the nag's reins. Did Grace take to the
fields every day? In this inhospitable climate? Why would
she do something so wretchedly uncomfortable?

Surely indulging a pair of rambunctious lads didn't
require one to fight inclement elements every day. He'd
assumed her agreement with the wee one had been for the
purpose of ridding herself graciously of his own unwanted
presence. But maybe he was wrong. What drew her to that
spot?

His curiosity got the best of him as he stared at the
woman he'd come so far to meet. Clicking his tongue,
he kneed the nag in the direction of the crag where
Grace stood, a slender beacon in wind-rippled wool. As
he approached, he took note of her closed eyes and
her expression of pure joy. She stood still, firm against
the strong breeze, apparently impervious to discomfort.

Was she daft? Did the McConnells know they had
entrusted their scions to a possible madwoman?

The closer he came, the more vividly he remembered his
two exchanges with Grace. No, she couldn't be mad.
Rather she was different from every other woman—and
any man—he'd ever met.

"Miss Carlisle!" he called when he'd succeeded in cajol-
ing his horse up the slope adjacent to the outcropping.

She turned, gray eyes wide, revealing her surprise. "Mr.
Fraser. I thought you'd be nearly to Braes by now."

"So I would have, but a number of questions made me turn back."

She stiffened. "Questions?"

Seeing the change in her posture, he adopted a harder tone. "A multitude of them. Beginning, of course, with your dispassionate attitude toward your parents' deaths."

Miss Carlisle gasped. "You think me dispassionate? Why, Mr. Fraser, I assure you I feel most deeply my parents' loss—your mother's death, too. How could you arrive at such a mistaken opinion?"

"Your demeanor. I do not bother to hide my grief over the events of nine years ago, yet you seem quite cheerful, as though nothing of import had ever happened to you." Yet as he said the words, Drew winced inwardly. Would he ever manage to speak to this woman in anything resembling his normal polite manner? Those who knew him well would hardly recognize him the past two days. He'd delivered that last little discourse in a very pompous fashion.

Miss Carlisle cocked her head, and the hood of her cape slipped off her hair. The wind coaxed fine tendrils to dance with it, again softening her features. As her scrutiny lengthened, he grew increasingly uncomfortable. He cursed the earlier impulse that had led him to this moment.

"I must admit," she finally said, "I have a few questions for you as well. I find it puzzling that a strong, and what I would assume to be an active and busy man, should live in the past as you do."

It was Drew's turn to gulp a sharp breath. "I do no such thing."

"'Twould seem so, Mr. Fraser—"

"Call me Andrew, or better yet, Drew. Most do. Or if you must, Fraser. Even Captain, as my sailors call me. But Mr. Fraser? I'm certain that's a doddering old barrister or banker in Edinburgh—certainly not me."

A hint of a smile played over her lips. Splendid. Now he'd managed to make a fool of himself. Captain Andrew Fraser, boor and fool.

"Very well, Andrew," she said with a nod, "if you'll indulge me a moment, I'll explain myself. Nine years after the loss of your mother you've tracked me down to accuse my father of an atrocity he did not commit. We'd never met before yesterday, and I doubt we shall ever stumble across each other's path in the future. It would seem you've nurtured your anger to the point where it has festered into a ripe bitterness you cannot hide. And yet you appear a powerful, more than likely successful, man. I also consider myself successful, since I love what I do. I also loved my parents, but I grieved their deaths a long time ago and allowed God to salve my wounds."

"God," he spat.

"Aye, God. He held my hand through the days when I despaired of ever again noticing the gold of the sun, the laughter of those around me, the blessings the Father showers me with daily. And believe me, there were many of those desolate days, as many as only a girl of ten can suffer when she is orphaned."

He shook his head in disgust. "I can see you're as blinded by faith as your father was. Can't you see that's

267

what caused it all? That trust in a God who doesn't care. Who only takes the best of those who love him and gives back nothing in return. Certainly not protection or safety or . . . or anything that might have saved—"

"That's precisely what God gives," she cut in. "Salvation. Perhaps Mama and Papa lost their earthly lives, but they were certain of their eternal future. God's Word gave them every reason to trust."

"To trust a God who then abandoned them."

Again those intelligent gray eyes studied Drew. Yet again, discomfort struck, making him shift in the saddle. Dreading what Miss Grace Carlisle might utter next, Drew fought the urge to turn the nag toward Braes, pay someone to carry out his belated errand, grab his unpacked satchel, and bid this forsaken Isle of Skye farewell.

But something in Grace's expression held him back. Something in her keen perusal. Something in the concern she revealed, in the understanding she'd expressed, in the lack of ugliness in her response to his churlish behavior.

After what seemed an eternity, she spoke softly and with deadly aim. "Tell me, Mr. Fraser, was it God who abandoned you, or you who turned your back on him?"

CHAPTER THREE

*E*arly the next morning, Drew entered the small
bakery in Braes. He nodded to the haggard woman
setting a sheet of dainty sweets on the counter. "Good
day."

She wiped the back of her hand across her forehead,
pushing scant gray hair out of her eyes. "Mornin', sir."

"I'm looking for Angus McNee. I was told I might find
him here."

Wariness sharpened her lined features, then lodged in
her faded blue eyes. "What would ye be wantin' with
him?"

"I've an errand I need run, and the innkeeper said
Angus would be glad of a job."

A flush colored her cheekbones and her shoulders stiffened. Pride seemed to abide in the woman. "Nae, Angus
ain't here, but I can get word to him. He's my boy." She
clamped her lips tight, drew a deep breath, and nodded.
"He'll be glad of a job—well paid, ye ken."

Indeed the pride of the Scots Highlander and Islander

lived in Mrs. McNee. "I would have it no other way," said Drew. "If he's not here, then how soon will he receive my message? I'm in a hurry to leave—"

"Good day, Mr. Fraser—er, Andrew," said Grace Carlisle as she approached the counter, flanked by her lively charges.

Drew spun to face the person he'd hoped never to see again. In fact, she was the reason he'd asked his host to recommend someone to carry out his unwelcome task. Drew wanted to escape the Isle of Skye with at least a scrap of unexcoriated—ever so gently and politely—skin left to him. The missionaries' daughter had a rapier-quick tongue when it came to asking questions.

"Hello, Miss Carlisle," he responded.

As she slipped the hood of her cape from her shining brown locks, the light from the lamp on the wall to her left illuminated her eyes. Drew shifted his weight on his feet and glanced at Mrs. McNee in the hope of a swift reply to his question.

Grace was swifter. "Did I hear you say you're leaving our fair isle?"

"Fair?" He glanced out the front plate window at the leaden sky. "I'm afraid your notion of fair doesn't quite match mine. I find tropical sunshine and balmy breezes more fair than overcast skies and gale winds."

"The Isle of Skye is an acquired taste, I'll grant you," Grace answered with a knowing smile. "But once you've acquired it, it's one you cannot imagine going without."

Drew shook his head. "I doubt I'd acquire it even after living a lifetime here."

The governess removed caps from a brace of curly heads. "You'd be surprised, sir," she said. "I've been here but four months, right lads?"

The two looked at each other and shrugged.

Grace's smile broadened. "Go on," she said, prodding each in the back. "Choose a sweet for yourselves and then tell Mrs. McNee which kind you'd like her to pack for your mama's gift. Remember, Christmas is only a week away."

The boys scampered off in search of treats. Grace nodded at Mrs. McNee's questioning look. "If you could please make up an assortment of Mrs. McConnell's favorites for us," she added, "we'll come by on the twenty-third to pick it up."

"Aye, miss," said Mrs. McNee, turning toward the lads.

Grace sighed, her eyes on the older woman, compassion brimming within. "'Tis a pity," she murmured.

Drew felt he'd missed something in the conversation. "A pity?"

"Aye, that it 'tis. The McNee family's situation makes me so terribly sad."

"And what might that situation be?" Drew asked, resigned to the further delay in his search for an errand boy.

"In a word, they're destitute. They were turned out of their croft with naught but the clothes on their backs. And their Granny Nell's not well, at that."

"They can't be totally destitute. Mrs. McNee is here, working."

271

Grace's eyes shot shards of silver. "A family of eight cannot live on what little she makes, especially without a roof over their heads."

"I still don't follow. Why were they turned out?"

"Back rents, as usual."

"Well, there you have it."

Grace shook her head vehemently. "No. Their landlord couldn't—or wouldn't, one cannot be sure which—extend them any more leniencies; he turned them out so he could rent the land to a more viable tenant. Which means the old tyrant wants more for his scrap of land. What some call 'capitalist sheep farming' is more lucrative than small farms, where the crofters have grazed their stock for years. And although the dear Lord loves the animals he created, I daresay he would side with his children rather than with ever so many more sheep. Compassion and Christian charity would have the landlord wait at least until the spring, don't you think?"

Drew waved and whispered, "It has nothing to do with religion. It's a matter of business. The landlord is the owner of the land, after all. If his tenant cannot meet his obligations, then the owner is free to find one who can. You cannot expect a businessman to carry out his affairs based on charity. Soon he'd be a charity case himself. Besides, Mrs. McNee has found employment. I'm certain the others in the family will too."

Grace's cheeks pinkened. "What you fail to realize, Mr. Fraser—"

"Andrew, remember?"

"Aye. What you fail to realize, Andrew, is that McNees have worked that croft for generations. A new landowner has bought the entire area and is changing the way the locals have always lived. That land . . . why, it's their very life."

"I'm sure that given time, and with sufficient effort on their part, they'll recover and flourish in their new positions."

Doubt dimmed the liveliness on Grace's face. "One can only pray that is so."

At her mention of prayer and the fact that Mrs. McNee had now returned to the counter, Drew recognized this as the time to beat a prudent retreat. "Mrs. McNee," he said, "as we were discussing before Miss Carlisle arrived with the lads, I have an errand I need carried out, and I'd like to hire your son to do it. Please have him call for me at the inn sometime today."

With a teary sniff, the former farmer-turned-candy-maker nodded. "I'll have him do that, sir."

Drew clapped his hat on his head, then turned to Grace. "Have yourself a pleasant day, then, Miss Carlisle."

"Have a blessed day, Andrew," she responded, a spark returning to her eyes.

Drew hastened to the door, certain of only one thing. Though delicate, feminine, and pleasant, Grace was a formidable woman. In spite of his better judgment, he paused to listen as she addressed the young McConnells.

"I'm sure you'll like that one, Rory. It looks as though

Mrs. McNee dusted it with cocoa. And Alasdair, you must choose. Indecision will not win you two sweets."

Gentle humor underscored her words, and Drew turned reluctantly for a last look at the missionaries' daughter. She'd bent her slim, caped figure at the waist to bring her closer to the level of the lads' eyes. Although she'd reproved the elder of the two, she'd done so in a kind and instructive way. The boy pointed to one, then another confection, finally returning to the first one he'd indicated.

"That one," Alasdair said. "If I must choose only one."

Grace's laughter rang out in the shop, bringing an unexpected ray of sunny warmth to Drew's heart. At the same time, his stomach dove toward his toes. In that instant he realized, to his astonishment and dismay, that mere curiosity and puzzlement weren't all that kept him coming back to the intriguing Miss Carlisle.

It was attraction, pure and simple, powerful and complex.

Drew didn't know what to make of this startling development. But he did know one thing.

He had to get away from Grace.

❋ ❋ ❋

A note awaited Drew when he reached his room at the inn. His presence was requested at McConnell Manor that evening. Mr. Roderick McConnell, who'd made his fortune in textiles, would enjoy discussing the current state of commerce with Captain Fraser.

Collapsing into the armchair by the window, Drew

stared at the heavy vellum sheet as though it were a many-headed monster. That morning he had determined to hire Angus McNee to deliver Grace's gift so he wouldn't have to see her again. Then, as he had gone to find the boy, he'd found her instead.

After yet another discomfiting exchange with the woman, he'd renewed his determination to leave. His escape, however, was now endangered by a summons from a wealthy Glasgow merchant. Wise businessman that he considered himself, Drew didn't know if saving his pride and what might remain of his sanity was worth losing significant potential business.

Disgusted by his double-mindedness, he stood and flung the invitation on the bed. He'd never been a coward—until a day or two ago. "That's unacceptable, old chap. I'm not about to let that bold-speaking woman turn me into one again."

He'd go. He'd speak with McConnell. *Then* he'd leave Skye. He doubted McConnell invited his children's governess to business dinners anyway.

Or so he fervently hoped.

✵ ✵ ✵

As Grace tucked Rory into bed later that evening, Maude's knock at the nursery caught her by surprise. "What is it?" she asked.

The maid's brown eyes widened. "Dinna ken, but the missus would like ye at dinner tonight. Ye'd best hurry, too. There's to be a guest, I hear."

Placing a kiss on the sleepy lad's brow, Grace straightened and frowned. "Me? At dinner? How very odd. I wonder why they would want me there."

She followed Maude into the hallway. The younger lass shrugged. "Maybe there's another missionary passin' by."

"Maybe," Grace said, "but 'tis a week before Christmas, hardly a time one would expect them to be away from their mission . . . or visiting out here." She shrugged. "Oh, well. It won't do me any good to dawdle and wonder. I'd best go refresh myself. Thank you, Maude. Tell Mrs. McConnell I'll be down shortly."

Grace neatened her too fine, too straight hair and made sure her plain blouse and skirt looked passable. She didn't own formal gowns of the sort the lady of the manor wore in the evening, but her employers wouldn't expect her to appear in such garments.

When her thoughts again turned to the possible reasons for her summons, she forcibly turned them elsewhere. When they unerringly returned to that day's meeting with Andrew Fraser, she knew it was time to seek help.

"Father God," she prayed, "these have been troubling days. Sad as it is to live without a family, I've been able to do so because you've filled my empty spaces. Why have you allowed this man with his great pool of grief and rage to find me now? I can't seem to say anything to help him see clearly, and all he's done is bring back to me the sadness of nine years ago. Help me keep my eyes on you, Lord, not looking to the past with its old troubles, nor peeking into the future, which is sure to have troubles of its own."

After a soft "Amen," she closed her bedroom door and descended the massive stairs to the large entry hall. As she stepped toward the dining room, Mr. McConnell called out, "Miss Carlisle. We're in the parlor. Won't you please join us?"

Grace entered the well-appointed room and, for the first time in her tenure at McConnell Manor, failed to notice a single detail. Instead her eyes flew straight to the familiar male figure leaning against the mantel.

Maude's description of Andrew Fraser as a bonny man was indeed more than apt. Dressed in a navy-colored suit, its brass buttons embossed with anchors, the captain made a powerful impression on a woman. Tall, broad, and strong-featured, he looked capable and most appealing. For the first time, she noticed how green his eyes glowed in the firelight, how black his hair shone.

"Good evening," she said to no one in particular, her voice ridiculously breathless.

A strange sensation in her middle made her wonder if she could possibly be hungry again—she'd supped with the lads upstairs just a half hour ago. She found it hard to focus on the feeling inside her, since her eyes and attention remained riveted on the McConnells' guest.

"I wish you'd mentioned your friend's visit," boomed Mr. McConnell in his deep bass. "It just so happens I'm particularly interested in silks at the moment."

Grace tore her gaze from the man by the mantel and nodded to her employer. "Silks . . ."

"Come, dear," said Mrs. McConnell, patting the settee at

her side. "Sit with me awhile. You must be tired from running after my two scoundrels."

Automatically Grace approached the indicated spot and dropped down beside the scoundrels' mother.

"'Tis most fortunate Henry went into town today," continued Mr. McConnell, evidently oblivious to the incomprehensible state in which his governess found herself. "An' not just because he had to fetch my stallion's repaired reins. He learned of Cap'n Fraser's presence in town, and of his connection to you, m'dear. Of course, we had to have your friend for supper."

"My friend . . . ," Grace voiced, aware only of the man in question.

Mrs. McConnell's plump hand patted hers. "And wouldn't you know it? The lad's in the Asian goods trade. Why, he and Mr. McConnell have so much to talk about. Dinner shall be a most fascinating time, don't you think?"

"Fascinating . . ." Then the conversation bubbling around Grace sank in. *Fascinating?* Oh, dear. She'd been reduced to a gawking adolescent in the past few minutes, and her employers expected the evening to prove fascinating? Nae, 'twould most likely prove awkward, embarrassing, discomfiting. . . .

Why had she never before noticed what a fine figure of a man Andrew Fraser truly was? Why now? In front of the two who paid her modest but adequate income? How was she to keep from making a fool of herself?

Andrew cleared his throat, and Grace stole a peek at him. She noticed the foreign ruddiness on his cheeks.

"After such a proclamation," he said, his tone rueful, "I'm afraid my conversational skills are sure to disappoint. In fact, Miss Carlisle can tell you I tend to place my feet in my mouth on a regular basis. I can only hope not to offend."

Her eyes flew to his. An unspoken apology seemed to shine there, reminding her of their previous encounters. "I'm not offended," she answered, recognizing how pointed some of her comments to him had been. "And I hope I haven't offended either."

"Do tell, Grace, dear," said Mrs. McConnell, her interest clearly piqued, "how did you two come to know each other?"

Andrew winced, evidently as uncomfortable as she. Taking pity on him, Grace smiled. "Our parents were acquainted while we were children."

"Aha!" bassoed Mr. McConnell. "Childhood sweet—"

Thankfully Cook's silver bell chimed, cutting off Mr. McConnell's hideously erroneous assumption. Grace's cheeks burned in mortification. She stood and started scurrying in the direction of dinner—and hopefully, the end of this indeed embarrassing evening.

Mrs. McConnell would have none of it. "Grace, dear. Wait for the captain. I'm sure he'd love to escort you in."

No! He wouldn't. Grace was as sure of that as she was of her own unwillingness to be escorted. But propriety commanded her to smile and behave civilly.

Nothing, however, demanded that she look at the man whose shoes had entered her lowered range of vision.

"Miss Carlisle?" he asked.

279

Raising her gaze only a minute increment, Grace saw navy wool. She slipped her shaking hand through the curve presented and gingerly laid her fingers on his forearm.

The warmth she found there made her catch her breath. Beneath her touch, she felt his muscles tighten.

Grace risked a look up . . . and found green eyes filled with puzzlement and . . . something strange and unfamiliar.

Andrew cleared his throat, then said, "Shall we?"

They entered the dining room.

During the interminable meal, Grace played with her unwanted food in a way reminiscent of the children she'd earlier put to bed. How she longed to retreat to her small room next to the nursery.

But, no. The McConnells' kindness—and business interests—forced her to stay put. And while she tried to think of the children and the upcoming holiday, Andrew's voice made clear thought of anything but him impossible.

She realized his initial arrival a few days ago had caught her off guard. She'd been out to the brae with the lads. Andrew had scarcely given her the opportunity to catch her breath before raking up the embers of her long-ago tragedy.

It seemed reasonable that she had hardly noticed the man who'd done so, as focused as she'd been on the memories he'd brought back to life. And his accusations . . . she'd been flabbergasted by his outrageous charges and yet moved by the evidence of grief that had led him to do so. Unfounded, of course.

But now, tonight, she'd had a chance to really look at Andrew Fraser. Undoubtedly, the silly, girlish part of her liked what she saw. The mature, womanly part of her recognized her need to regain control. It would be foolish even to acknowledge this unwise attraction.

As the men spoke, Grace learned how well versed Andrew was in matters of commerce—at least, that was the impression she got from Mr. McConnell's appreciative response to the younger man's ideas and suggestions. Most considered her employer a commercial genius.

At long last, Cook sent out the trifle. When neither man wanted any, Mrs. McConnell urged them to repair to the library and their cheroots. "I'm certain Miss Carlisle and I have had more than enough of business talk for one night."

Grace saw her chance to escape.

Standing, Andrew said, "I'm afraid, Mrs. McConnell, I do not smoke. Besides, it's growing late, and since I'm unfamiliar with my surroundings, I'd best be heading back to the inn. I thank you for a splendid meal—"

"Nonsense, lad!" cannoned Mr. McConnell. "You cannot stay at the inn a day longer when we've plenty of guest rooms here. Right, Mrs. McConnell?"

Grace might have hoped for help from the feminine quarter, but apparently, her employer hid a matchmaker's heart within her matron's bosom. With a sly wink at Grace, she said, "Indeed, Mr. McConnell. I can have Maude make one up in no time. Then the captain can stay with us for the rest of his visit."

"But—" argued Andrew.

"But—" objected Grace.

"Tell me, laddie," said Mr. McConnell as if neither had spoken, "how long has it been since you've celebrated the Lord's birth among family? An' don't tell me a band of sailors can compare with this." He gestured to the elegant dining room with its suite of mahogany furnishings, the crackling fire in the hearth, the untouched yet delightful-looking trifle in its footed crystal compote, the two women in their chairs.

"Nae, my men don't compare with your gracious company, nor does my ship compare with your home, but—"

"How lovely!" chirped Mrs. McConnell. "It's settled, then. You'll stay with us through Christmas Day—surely you won't sail off to some untamed sea before then, will you?"

At Andrew's dazed shake of the head, the woman went on. "Isn't that perfectly delightful, Mr. McConnell? This way the captain and our dear Grace will have plenty of time to catch up on old times."

A shudder ripped through Grace. The last thing she wanted was to spend more time discussing deaths and greedy, insurgent warlords with Andrew. The awkward evening had degenerated into a veritable nightmare.

She'd do best to leave. "If you'll all excuse me, I think I hear Rory crying—"

"I'll see to the bairn," offered Mrs. McConnell.

"And I'll go with her," added her spouse. "Why don't

you see our guest to the door, Miss Carlisle? I'm sure that rather than stay here tonight, he'll want to return for his things to the inn—I would in his place. Then he can come back to us tomorrow after clearing his account."

After a brisk shake of masculine hands and a motherly kiss to the captain's lean cheek, the McConnells vanished from the dining room. If Grace had earlier found the evening uncomfortable, that discomfort paled before this.

"Well," Andrew said after a bit, "are they always like that?"

Despite the flush on her cheeks, Grace released the chuckle that bubbled up. "I assure you not. True, Mr. McConnell is said to always get his way, and Mrs. McConnell is a disciplined mistress of her home, but . . ."

They again fell silent. Finally Andrew gestured toward the door. "I really should be on my way."

Grace preceded him into the hallway, then led him to the entry hall. "I understand. And I'm sure you don't appreciate the way you've been set up to spend your holiday with a group of total strangers. Especially not when one of them brings you nothing but painful thoughts."

When he didn't answer, Grace cast a glance over her shoulder. To her surprise, he looked bemused.

"What is it?" she asked.

"I just realized that I didn't once think of the past during dinner."

His gaze snagged hers, and he extended his hand in a gesture of farewell. Grace took it, and the warmth of his fingers winnowed through her arm, then flew straight to her head.

Oh, dear. "I—I'm glad, Mr. Fraser—"

"Andrew, remember?"

Grace could do no more than nod. They stood in the large silent room, staring at each other, holding hands in an unexpectedly thrilling clasp.

As she stared into Andrew's green eyes, Grace realized that even if he left right now, never to return, they'd forever be bound together. Not only did they share a tragedy; they now shared this unexpected and baffling attraction. The sparks in the eyes staring into hers left her no doubt. Andrew felt it, too.

He came closer.

She waited.

The clock chimed the quarter hour.

Reality crashed through Grace's daze on the wings of an appropriately timed note. She dropped Andrew's hand as if it burned. "Good night, Mr. Fraser," she said, emphasizing the title. *"Captain,"* she added, just in case he had missed her intent.

Without waiting to see him out the door, she bolted up the stairs, aware of his scalding gaze on her back every step of her retreat.

CHAPTER FOUR

*G*race spent the next two days in prayer and avoidance. For the most part, she managed to miss meeting the McConnells' guest. She didn't count the odd
glimpse she caught of him as she dashed through the halls
in pursuit of her charges as a meeting of any sort. Nor did
she count the evening that she, the captain, and all the
McConnells had formed a circle around the piano and
sang the carols of Christmas. The music had rung through
the house, uniting the carolers in lighthearted cheer.

Inevitably—and predictably—her absence from the
dinner table didn't satisfy Mrs. McConnell's desire to play
Cupid. Early on the third morning of Andrew Fraser's stay
at the manor, Maude brought Grace another summons.

"The missus wants ye in the morning room, Miss Grace.
An' last I heard, bonny Cap'n Fraser was with her. Lucky
you," she added, a trace of envy in her words.

Grace would gladly have traded places with the younger lass. "I'll be down in a flash. Keep an eye on these two
for me, please. They're to make their beds, then do their

lesson. Alasdair knows what to do, while Rory can play with the wooden letter blocks."

Maude sighed. "Some of us never get the good luck, Miss Grace. Go on. See what the missus wants with you and the cap'n."

Grace shuddered at the thought. The recognition of the attraction between her and the man downstairs had shaken her. And although by now she'd almost persuaded herself that it was due to nothing more than an overblown sense of compassion in the face of his grief, a niggle of doubt remained.

Perhaps facing him in the light of day would erase that doubt once and for all.

Grace prayed it would be so.

"Good morning, Mrs. McConnell," she said, entering the blossom-upholstered room.

Perched amid a cluster of cabbage rose–bedecked cushions, her employer beamed. "Good day, my dear. I haven't seen you since we sang carols the other night. When Mr. Fraser said he hadn't either, why, I knew that had to change. After all, he really is *your* guest rather than Mr. McConnell's."

Grace sent Andrew a reproachful glare. "Oh, not at all, Mrs. McConnell. I have a job to do, one I love, and that takes all my time. I really don't have the freedom, or the need, to do anything but watch the bairns—something I'm most happy doing, you understand."

"But Mr. Fraser came this far just in search of you."

"And he did in fact find me," Grace said ruefully.

"Indeed," Andrew concurred, a sudden twinkle in his green eyes.

Why, the wretch seemed to enjoy her current discomfort! What was he up to?

"There you are, Miss Carlisle," exclaimed Mr. McConnell from the doorway to Grace's right.

She spun to face her employer, and the gleam in *his* eye sent more dread through her. "Were you looking for me, too, sir?"

"Aye, I was indeed." He strode to Andrew, shook the younger man's hand in greeting, then went to sit at his wife's side. "I'd think it a pity if we sent Andrew back to sea without ever showing him any of our fine isle, don't you?"

Not really, Grace thought, especially since she knew what the visitor truly thought of Skye. "And . . . ?"

"And neither Mrs. McConnell nor I can escort him on a tour today. We've a commitment with the Reverend Waite—have had for weeks now. 'Tis the day for our yearly Christmas luncheon with him and his wife. Her plum pudding is not to be missed, you see."

Grace did *not*. "But, the laddies—"

"Can use a day of leisure, don't you think?" Mr. McConnell cut in. "In several days it will be Christmas Eve, so we plan to trim our tree this evening. I say, let the boys build up some excitement for the approach of the sweet baby Jesus' birth. Let them start rejoicing today."

"Oh, they have been, sir, they have," Grace hastened to say. "You should visit the nursery. We've decked it with greenery and ribbons, and Alasdair and Rory have been roasting chestnuts at the hearth every chance I give them. Besides, we've been reading the Advent story daily. They know full well what we honor these days. No need to go gallivanting over the Isle—"

"No need to belabor their lessons, either, dearie," Mrs. McConnell countered, then dragged herself out from the depths of her overstuffed floral nest. "Besides, you have been working yourself ragged. 'Tis time you enjoyed a day of relative ease. Go on, do the honors, and have a good time. Henry will drive you wherever you'd like."

Grace was well cornered, and she knew it. "Very well. I'll go ready the lads."

"And yourself," ventured Andrew, the beginning of a smile causing the corners of his lips to twitch.

"How could I forget?" Grace responded, then exited the room as quickly as she could.

✳ ✳ ✳

Hours later, in the close confines of the McConnells' fine carriage, Grace feared she might suffocate. Between the ebullience of the boys and the interested questions of the very large man seated across from her, she didn't know which way to turn for a brief respite of prayer.

She'd asked Henry to drive them to medieval ruins on the other side of Portree. While the males investigated the remains of the structure, she spent the time scrambling after the McConnell lads, intent on preventing any major accident.

The four tourists took their midday meal at an attractive establishment in Portree, and that event demanded all her concentration. One could not accuse young Rory McConnell of being a tidy eater.

They then strolled around the town itself, the boys growing more excited each time they spied evidence of the upcoming holy day. When they came across a church with a splendid nativity scene in its yard, the lads begged to play with the animals.

"It's not ours," Grace responded, trying to lead the two away from the fascinating display. "Come along. Let's see if we can find a candy shop."

But the boys' tummies were full from lunch, and their wheedling continued. Fortunately for all, the pastor, who'd been on his way out, allowed the lads to approach and touch the pieces under his—and Grace's—watchful eye.

To her relief, the time spent exploring Portree passed in relative ease. The children's delight—and Andrew's discourse with them—filled in any potentially awkward moments. Soon enough the time to return to McConnell Manor arrived. Understandably, the lads fell asleep the moment the carriage wheels began to roll. The silence between Grace and Andrew lengthened, deepened, and became intolerable.

Casting about for a neutral topic of conversation, Grace asked, "Have you and Mr. McConnell been able to do business?"

"Aye," answered Andrew. "It appears we'll sign a

contract for a rather large shipment of Oriental goods—silks, to be exact."

"I suppose, then, that you're chafing at your delayed departure. You must be anxious to be off to your exotic ports in search of those goods."

He smiled. "I'll admit the weather here doesn't encourage a lengthy stay, and I am fascinated by the sights, smells, and sounds I find around the world."

"I don't remember much about China," Grace then commented, "but I can recall how I drove Mama mad with questions about every last little thing I saw. I wonder if by staying with her and Papa instead of returning to school I might have satisfied my curiosity."

As she uttered the words, Grace realized how close she'd come to dangerous conversational territory. When Andrew shook his head without a contorted expression, she dared to breathe again.

"I can't know about you," he answered, "but I can tell you I still thrill when I sail into a new port—even old familiar ones charm me each time I return. It's what keeps me on the seas."

Grace tried to imagine what it must be like, constantly changing location, spending weeks—months—at a time on the water. She didn't succeed. "I'm afraid I'm too land-locked. I prefer my travels few and near at hand. One time to China seems to have cured me of any desire to wander the world."

"I, on the other hand," said Andrew, a faraway look in his green eyes, "cannot imagine always seeing the same sights, the same folks. It would strike me as terribly boring—if you can forgive my saying so."

"Oh, there's nothing to forgive. You've every right to your opinion." Grace measured her next words. "As I understand it, you prefer to live in a constantly fleeting and changing way instead of settling where you might build something that could last. You don't see yourself putting down roots, as one might say."

Andrew laughed. "I can't see myself as a sturdy oak. I'm more a will-o'-the-wisp, touching down where fancy strikes, then dancing off to a brand-new fancy."

The spark of excitement in her companion's eyes made Grace wish she shared his enthusiasm for grand adventure. He appeared so vital, so energetic, brimming with such glamorous desires, that by comparison, her longing for a home seemed simple and far more mundane.

But as she glanced out the window at the rocky terrain of her new home, she was reassured. "The bulky stones of Skye are very comforting to me. The crags aren't likely to shift or change, just as God always stays the same. I must admit I feel very close to him here, in this beautiful and sturdy land."

She stole a glance at her companion, wondering how her reference to the Lord had struck him. Andrew's features remained reasonably blank, so she went on. "Besides, I like being part of my neighbors' lives, even when those lives, like the McNees', aren't easy or charming. I'd like to think they know they can count on me to help in any way I can."

This time Andrew's brows lowered. Before he could

question her, Grace continued. "I also like knowing that I have many years to look forward to while the McConnell boys need me. That I'll be here to watch them grow into good young men and send them off to higher learning. After that . . . well, perhaps I'll find another family somewhere nearby who'll need my services. I feel certain that God has brought me here to stay."

Although she'd expected him to respond, Andrew remained quiet, evidently considering her words. He turned to the window at his side and continued to ride in silence, seemingly mesmerized by the passing scenery.

After a few more minutes, he leaned closer to peer through the pane. "What's that?" he asked.

"Where?"

"On the field. It looks like another ruin. I didn't realize there were medieval sites so close to the McConnell home."

"Nothing so fascinating, I'm afraid," Grace answered. "And far more painful. Those are the remains of a cleared croft. Years ago, during the worst of the Clearances, the sheriff and constable sent out delegations to forcibly remove tenants for the landowners. Here on Skye, the Macdonalds were the worst. The Sutherlands were as bad on the Highlands. Before these landowners considered a removal complete, they had their agents burn the home to ensure complete compliance with the eviction."

Andrew's eyes met hers in an intense gaze. "You find comfort in a land where others have found ejection and what you have called merciless treatment? Like the baker whose plight you pled to me? How can God be a part of both those circumstances?"

That's when Grace knew that Andrew Fraser was intelligent indeed. "The God of Scripture was not responsible for the Clearances. Human greed accomplished that. The landowners demanded higher rents, and the crofters couldn't meet them when the prices of wool and kelp went down."

"Human greed, you say?"

"Aye."

"Is that how you would see all forms of commerce? What I do?"

"Not if you treat those you do business with in a fair and compassionate way. Do you give fair value for the goods you acquire to later sell?"

"Always."

"Do you call in debts when you know your debtors cannot pay you? Simply to justify a more beneficial arrangement with another? Do you show no mercy to those who ask for it?"

"I can't say I've ever been in that position. I handle all my transactions on a ready-money basis."

Grace waved aside his equivocation. "How about your sailors? Do you show mercy to those who find themselves in unfortunate straits?"

"I would like to believe I always do."

"But do you? And why?"

"Why?" Perplexity bloomed on his features. "Why . . . because it's right."

"What makes it right?"

"Why . . . it just . . . is. That's all. Right is right, and wrong is wrong."

She allowed herself a slight smile. "So you agree with me that there are certain moral standards one is obliged to live up to."

"Of course."

"Well, Andrew Fraser," Grace said triumphantly, "I'm pleased to see your godly mother managed to instill in you solid biblical ethics. Therefore, you must agree with me that the McNees' landlord should have waited until a more merciful time before turning them from their home. And furthermore, you must agree it was indeed greed that compelled his action and not God's lack of provision or anything the like that left that family destitute. Certainly, it wasn't a matter of good business sense."

To Grace's delight, her companion's jaw gaped. He snapped his mouth closed, then frowned. He shook his head, his eyes widening. "I . . ." he started, then fell silent again.

Finally he laughed out loud. It was a hearty belly laugh that rang through the carriage, causing the sleeping boys to stir. Grace wondered if his peculiar response to her argument meant he was laughing at her or conceding to her.

Would she ever know?

❆ ❆ ❆

Grace Carlisle had done it again. Drew didn't quite know what to think of her . . . other than to admire her powers of logic. He hadn't agreed with her convoluted argument—

or he didn't think he did—but he acknowledged her ability to build a case on her own terms. And, if one followed her train of thinking, it almost— almost, mind you—made sense.

But to break down business affairs to something akin to a religious sermon . . . that was practically laughable. That wasn't, however, why he'd laughed in the carriage earlier that evening. He'd laughed at the sheer delight of watching an intelligent woman best him in a conversation.

It had never happened before.

Grace challenged his thoughts, to say the least. She was the first woman who'd ever done so. He couldn't keep his gaze from straying to her time and again. She fascinated him.

And she'd managed to make him forget, for hours at a time, the bitterness he still bore her late father. The man had been negligent all those years ago. He'd failed to protect Drew's mother. That failure made him culpable in her death. Nothing would ever change that fact.

But he'd come to realize that it didn't involve Grace.

And Drew was glad. Undoubtedly he was attracted to the missionaries' daughter. In many ways. He liked her quick mind, her intelligent eyes, her bright smile, her silky, misbehaving hair, her skillful handling of and love for the McConnell boys.

He wondered how the seagoing men of his ship would react to her gentle but purpose-filled tactics. He laughed, then flushed when everyone in the McConnell parlor faced him, questions in their eyes.

"Come now, do share the humor with us," Mr. McConnell urged.

"Er . . . ah . . ." Drew scrambled mentally to find something reasonable to say. "Ah . . . well, I'm thinking how different this holiday has turned out in comparison to my more recent ones."

As he'd expected, he was bombarded with questions about his travels. Everyone's interest was obvious, but especially that of the young woman whose gray eyes fluttered from him to the mischief makers attaching candles to the lower branches of a vast evergreen. She in turn was fastening pine boughs to the balusters with red ribbon.

Although his surroundings were indeed different from those where he usually spent his Decembers, Drew knew it wasn't the location that made this time different from others. Grace's presence did that.

He couldn't stop thinking of her. Try as he might, he'd even begun to dream about the McConnells' governess. If he didn't know better, he might think he was falling in love—with a most unlikely woman.

Words flowed from his lips as he told of the holiday where a multicolored parrot's antics stole the sailors' hearts. In no way, however, did the tale reflect the thoughts that milled in his head.

To his amazement, and no longer horror or dread, he could see himself returning to far-flung ports, Grace at his side. True, she'd said she liked the Isle of Skye. And she'd stated she found it difficult to imagine a life like his, without encumbrance of location or relational ties. But Drew wondered. If she once tried living his way, would she change her mind?

Visions of Grace, parrot on her shoulder, danced in his head.

And then, in a flash, it occurred to him that the missionaries' daughter would make him a splendid wife.

❊ ❊ ❊

"Ach, Rory, lad," Grace whispered. "That candle must stand a wee bit straighter than that. Otherwise we might set the tree afire when we light it."

Although she kept an eye on the boys, Grace found her attention fixed on Andrew's tales of past Christmases. She especially found the yarn about the lively parrot engaging. It occurred to her she wouldn't mind having such a creature for a pet.

Not that it could ever happen, of course. Not here in Skye. The notion made her chuckle.

When the time to put the young gentlemen abed arrived, she found herself reluctant to leave the gaily decorated parlor with its scent of pine, its lively conversation, and air of festivity.

"Don't be gone long now, dearie," called out Mrs. McConnell as Grace stepped into the hallway. "I'm asking Cook to make a pot of chocolate for us adults. Now that we've worked so hard to make the room look so special, it's time to sit back, sip a cup of cocoa, and enjoy the fruits of our labors."

For the first time, Grace's spirits soared at the thought of returning to Andrew's presence. She stole a glance in his direction and met his gaze. He smiled.

"Aye, ma'am," she answered. "I'll be back shortly."

And she was, feeling like a foolish girl—again. Andrew Fraser did that to her.

❋ ❋ ❋

"Won't you join us on the settee?" asked Mrs. McConnell upon Grace's return, making it impossible for her to sit anywhere else in the room. Of course, the canny woman had made certain Andrew was perched in the middle of that furnishing.

In seconds, or so it seemed to Grace, the McConnells finished their chocolate and began to yawn. They excused themselves and bid their governess and guest polite good-nights.

A hint of awkwardness meandered into Grace's awareness, but her excitement at being with this interesting man soon made it dwindle. "You have the most fascinating tales to tell," she said.

"Anyone who sails the seas can have them, too, you know."

"Ah, but there's the rub, indeed. One must be a sailor. Not everyone is tailored from the same cloth."

"It only takes a desire to leave behind the entanglements of society and follow the hunger for adventure to join a ship's crew."

Grace shrugged. "Perhaps. But some of us are quite happy living on land. We can still cherish the tales the adventurous few bring back. Especially if they're gifted storytellers. I admit, you do weave an excellent yarn."

Andrew smiled. "Am I a fair enough bard that you might find my company less than odious?"

"Why, Andrew! I've never found your company hateful." Grace thought back. "Nae. At the risk of raising troublesome subjects, I confess that your arrival brought back some very painful memories. And it's been difficult to witness your grief. But at no time have I considered you odious."

For a moment, Grace regretted her candor. Andrew's jaw tightened, and he shut his eyes. Then he gave a tight nod. "I can't deny my feelings about the past. But perhaps you've amended your opinion of me. I hope you no longer feel I live in that past. You must have noticed how I've enjoyed the present here with you and the McConnells, and I always look toward a better future."

It dawned on Grace that his stay would soon draw to a close. Only three more full days until Christmas. A pang of sadness struck her. Although Andrew Fraser was altogether wrong for her and she knew she should see his imminent departure as a blessing, she knew she would feel the loss of his companionship. No other man had interested her as much. Even if he wasn't a Christian.

"And where will the immediate future take you?" she asked in a deliberately cheerful voice.

He gave her an odd look. "More than likely, I'll head for Siam first. They have splendid textiles there."

"Siam . . . ," she said, tasting the word.

"A fascinating land."

"I'm sure."

"One you'd find most intriguing."

"I'm sure . . . ," she repeated, uncertain what direction the conversation was taking.

"Would you not like to see it?" he asked, his eyes on her.

Grace thought about it. Although life in Skye fully satisfied her . . . "I can't say I *wouldn't* care to see it," she finally answered.

"Splendid!" exclaimed Andrew, further confusing Grace.

"What is so splendid?" she asked.

"Why, that you *do* still have a desire to venture forth. I think, Miss Carlisle—Grace, if I may?"

At her nod, he shocked her by taking her hand in his. "I think," he repeated, holding tight despite her discreet efforts to retrieve her hand, "that we may be fairly well suited. My dear Grace, would you accept my suit?"

CHAPTER FIVE

*G*race tugged at her ear. "I beg your pardon?" She could have sworn Andrew had asked to court her. "Oh, I understand this must come as a surprise, especially because of the rough beginning we had. But, as you know, as a seafaring man, I don't have a great deal of time on my side. Besides, I'm a man of action. I make decisions on instinct—I'm often forced to do so in order to gain the advantage in business."

What *was* he saying? "I don't understand . . ."

He chuckled wryly. "I'm making a muddle of this, aren't I? You can blame it on my lack of experience in these matters."

Andrew stood and paced back and forth in front of her. "I'm due back to my ship on the twenty-fifth of December. We set sail the next day. And while I never expected anything of the sort, I find I've grown very fond of you in the short time since we met."

Fond? "But we scarcely know each other. . . ."

"Indeed." He stopped directly in front of her and dropped to one knee.

Grace bolted upright. This simply couldn't be happening to her.

He stood and caught her hand again. "Please. Hear me out."

The rational side of her demanded that she run from that parlor as fast and as far as her feet could carry her. But the feminine, easily flattered side of her that had been responding to Andrew in such unprecedented ways kept her in place.

"Very well," she said softly.

"You're an admirable woman, Grace Carlisle, and I'd be a fool to let you slip away."

Slip away? From what? whom? him? He didn't have her— or if he did, she didn't know it yet. "But—"

"Please. You agreed to listen."

She sighed and nodded.

"What I mean to say is that I've come to recognize what a splendid wife you'll make, and I want to be the lucky man who wins you. I know my proposal to court you has come as a surprise—"

"Oh, aye!"

His cheeks ruddied. "Well, yes. I'm known as a swift mover at times, and I suspect I've outdone myself this time. Still I encourage you to consider how well we suit each other."

Grace felt as though her head would fly off in the gale windstorm he'd unleashed around them. "How could you say that? We have nothing at all in common."

Andrew seemed to consider her argument for a minute. Then he grinned. "Precisely! And that's an excellent point.

Opposites are well known to complement each other. What one lacks, the other supplies."

Persistent, isn't he? "They would want to have that so-called lack supplied to start off with, wouldn't you think?" she asked, trying to find her way through this stunning turn.

"I can assure you I'm quite interested in your smile and your unique way of seeing the world."

Dear Lord, what shall I do? What shall I say? "But I don't want you to supply me with a desire to leave the place I've just begun to call home."

Andrew's smile dimmed. "How can you be so sure if you've never gone beyond Glasgow, Edinburgh, and Skye? Aside from that long-ago trip to China, of course."

After yet another brief prayer, Grace tried to put into words what until then had been only feelings. "Because I've always longed to put down roots. I've only been in Skye long enough for a shoot to take hold. I'm looking forward to a future here."

He waved her words aside. "Since you've been here such a short time, this is the ideal time to leave. Surely you can see that the longer you remain, the more difficult it will be to sever your ties."

Grace sighed in exasperation—and dismay. "Oh, Andrew, that is precisely my point. I don't want to sever the ties I'm establishing." Still, the thought of him courting her was anything but distasteful. If only . . . "There is another way, you know," she volunteered.

His eyes brightened. "Oh?"

"Indeed." She took a deep breath for courage. "You could always choose to settle somewhere in Skye. We could become better acquainted, perhaps see if we might in some way suit. God has brought me here, and perhaps he's brought you here for a purpose as well."

"Preposterous!" He turned from her and strode to the hearth. Resting his elbow on the mantel, he slipped his other hand in his trousers pocket. "I'm a man of the sea. I make my living in the import-export market. What would I do on this misty, frigid block of rock?"

Grace shrugged.

"Besides," Andrew added, removing the hand in the pocket and gesturing upward, "what has God to do in this matter?"

Grace gasped. It had taken these blunt words from Andrew to awaken her to reality. Shame burned in her conscience. How could she have entertained such a thought as allowing Andrew Fraser to court her—for even the briefest of moments? *Oh, Father, forgive me for this foolish lapse.*

Aloud she said, "Andrew, God has *everything* to do in every matter of my life. And while I seem to have forgotten that for a short time," she went on, a guilt-induced hitch in her voice, "you've just reminded me of my commitment to God. I want to honor him in all I do, and courtship and marriage is a most important part of a woman's life. I want to base mine on the Lord. I had an excellent example in my parents—they consecrated their union to Christ's service. I can't consider a man who doesn't see a lifelong partnership the same way I do."

Andrew scoffed. "You can't mean you want to marry a man who'd expose you to the kind of dangers your father did your mother—and *mine*, lest you forget."

"Nae, Andrew, I can't forget—you'd never let me. And that's another reason I cannot consider your proposal. Your unforgiveness toward my father would taint our relationship. I will always view my father's actions in the light of obedience to God and the deaths as the wages of the sin of greed."

Andrew came toward her, green eyes blazing. "Obedience . . . sin . . . what does it matter? Your father is to blame for my mother's presence in a dangerous place. You must accept that."

"While you must find the grace that only Christ gives and forgive a man who bears no blame. How could . . ." Her words trailed off before she gathered her courage to speak again with boldness. "How could love grow between us when you continue to hate my father?"

"God is love," he said in a disparaging way. "Forgive us our debts as we forgive our debtors. Turn the other cheek." He shook his head. "Once I believed all that, too. But your father, an avowed man of God, in service to God, cured me of those beliefs. The God you serve took my family and is now taking you as well."

Grace turned and approached the parlor door. Without facing him, she said, "Nae, Andrew. He's not taking me.

He doesn't have to. He's always had me, as I've always been his child."

She left the room, aching, but more certain than ever of the heavenly Father's love.

❄ ❄ ❄

"Fool!" Drew spat as he closed the door to the elegant room the McConnells had given him. "You should have known better, Andrew!"

Like father, like daughter. Religious zealots were all the same. They saw life only through a God-filter. They had such cloudy vision they couldn't recognize how wrong they were.

It took devastation to clear a man's vision, as Drew well knew.

He'd been sadly mistaken about Grace. He no longer believed she'd make an excellent wife; she was far too married to her misguided faith in God.

Without bothering with a light, he sprawled on the plush bed. Well, if Grace was married to her faith, he was married to the sea. Which was where he rightfully belonged, where he'd return as soon as this dreadful holiday came to its end.

He watched the play of shadows in the room as a cloud moved away from the face of the moon. Silver light puddled through the window and outlined a too-familiar, rectangular shape.

"Oh, bother!" Grace's nine-year-late gift.

What was he going to do about the thing? How was he going to explain keeping it for so long?

Drew sat up and glared at the crate that had sent him on this fruitless trek. Would its rightful owner understand his reasons for withholding it?

Grace had expressed some measure of curiosity when she'd said details of his travels held interest for her, so perhaps she'd understand his curiosity about the daughter of the man—

"Best not even think that, old chap," he warned himself.

Very well. Curiosity might carry some weight. But how could he explain his reluctance to turn the thing over even after he'd moved into McConnell Manor?

How could he explain to another when he didn't understand his own motives?

He should have followed his instincts and paid young McNee to deliver the gift instead of hiring the lad and his cart to move Drew to the manor. Then he should have excused himself nicely to the McConnells and gone on his way, never to set eyes on Grace Carlisle again.

But he hadn't been able to do that. Something existed between them, a certain bond he'd been unable to evade. Was it the attraction? that fondness he'd mentioned? Was it perhaps more? Perhaps as much as . . . love?

Or, as he'd begun to fear, did it go deeper than that? Did it hearken back to the past? To her father, her mother, his mother? Could it have anything to do with the one thing that bound them all together? Did it have to do with God?

The miserable crate of weather-beaten wood taunted him throughout the long, sleepless night.

✳ ✳ ✳

For Grace, the next two days passed in a blur of prayer, difficult thoughts, feelings of what might have been, more prayer, and the demands of a pair of happy boys awaiting the celebration of the Lord Jesus' birth. She scarcely recognized herself in the woman who breathed, spoke, and moved with scant thought to her actions. It was Christmas, her favorite holiday, and yet this year she barely noticed. Everything she did seemed rote.

She'd just received her first offer to be courted. More than likely it would also be her only one. And while she'd known it was the right thing to do even as she did it, she felt a great deal of sadness at having to turn it down.

Grace knew herself too well to let an infatuation fool her. It might have clouded her reason for a short time, but eventually, as it did, reason returned. She knew what she wanted; she wanted to serve God with every part of her life. Including her marriage.

Feeling as he did about her earthly, and especially her heavenly Father, Andrew was the wrong man for her. Attraction, fondness, and romantic love paled in the face of serving Christ.

Still she experienced the disappointment; she felt the heartbreak. She'd come to care more for Andrew than she'd been willing to acknowledge.

Had his faith been strong, his relationship with God more like hers, he would have been a good candidate for marriage. He was intelligent, handled himself ably in social settings, seemed to enjoy the company of children,

and challenged her thoughts more than anyone else ever
had.

Not to mention the appeal of his "bonny good looks,"
as Maude often said.

But the matter didn't merit any further consideration.
Things were as they were. And unless some miracle
occurred, Andrew would soon go his way, while Grace
would remain to establish the roots she so longed for.

God would see her through the disappointment, the
sadness. He always had. He always would. He always
knew what was best for her. She trusted him. Even so, her
heart ached.

❋ ❋ ❋

Soon it was Christmas Eve. The day turned stormy,
making the McConnells reconsider their plans to attend
evening services at church. Instead, before supper, the man
of the house read the story of Christ's birth straight from
Scripture.

As the age-old words filled the quiet parlor, Grace let
them salve her bruised heart. She stole occasional peeks at
Andrew and sympathized with his obvious discomfort.
Still, it could do him nothing but good to hear again the
truth of God made man.

Later, those gathered in the McConnell dining room ate
the lavish, roast-goose supper in an atmosphere of excited
celebration. As believers, they awaited the next day, to
celebrate the birth of their Savior.

But tonight Grace was unusually quiet and pensive. She

knew this would be the last time she saw Andrew. He would be leaving the next day to go back to his ship.

As soon as possible, she excused herself to escort her charges upstairs. Yet again, however, Mrs. McConnell thwarted Grace's desires. "You must not be long, dearie. It is the captain's last evening with us, you know."

Actually, that was the best reason for leaving the room, in her opinion, but Grace couldn't very well say so. "I'll be brief," she offered instead.

When she returned to the parlor, a strange sight greeted her. The McConnells had disappeared—not an entirely unexpected situation, if one considered their Cupid-like endeavors. Andrew remained, and a termite's feast of a box sat in the center of the room.

Grace's curiosity took over. "Where did that come from?"

Andrew gave a dry chuckle. "You go straight to the point, don't you?"

HIis presence—and words—disoriented her. "What do you mean? Is it so odd for me to notice a big old crate that has suddenly overtaken the parlor?"

Andrew approached. He took her elbow and led her to the settee. "Please sit. This may take some time."

Grace grew alarmed. "Time? It's late, and I'm quite tired—"

"Please. It's important that you listen. You see . . . that crate's the reason I came to find you."

His statement knocked the starch right out of her legs. She dropped onto the settee. "I don't understand."

"I know." He strode away, skirting the crate, and went

to stare at the glowing embers in the hearth. "It's not your fault. It's all mine."

"But—"

"Nine years ago," he said as though she hadn't objected. His words killed any thought of further speech on her part. "Nine years ago, that box was to have been your . . . Christmas gift."

At Andrew's hesitation, Grace realized this was the first time he'd referred to the holiday by its rightful name. His anger at God and his Son ran deep indeed. Then the import of his words struck her.

"My Christmas gift?"

"Aye. Your parents entrusted it to my father's care on that voyage we took while Mother stayed with them at the mission house. We set sail for England to deliver a shipment of Chinese porcelains, but when we stopped in Marseilles, word of the deaths reached us. Father couldn't bring himself to deliver the box."

"But that was so long ago." And it would have meant the world to the newly orphaned girl to receive something—anything—from her late parents. "Didn't your father return to England after that? Couldn't he have had another shipping company bring it to me? Why did he keep it from me?"

Andrew's shoulders slumped. "Father never forgot whose daughter you were."

Grace stood, anger impelling her. "But I was just a child! You have no idea how lonely and sad I was." She ran to his side, grabbed his arm, and forced him around. "Look at me!" she cried. "I needed something of theirs, a token, *anything* tangible, just then. How could he have withheld it from me?"

Andrew's eyes met hers, then again sought the floor. "He felt your father's actions stole his wife and child from him. He never recovered."

A shuddering breath racked Grace. "You," she said, "you could have made sure it reached me. Why didn't you?"

This time, when his eyes met hers, Grace thought she read a plea for understanding in the green depths. "I had no idea it was in his possession until he died just months ago. One of the last things he did was to insist I carry out his belated duty. He knew he'd wronged you."

The explanation took the wind right out of her anger's sails. "Oh."

He shrugged. "And so I came."

"And so you did. But why did you wait until today to give me the box? You said even your father knew he'd wronged me by keeping it so long. Why would you do the same?"

His cheeks reddened. "At first I was curious about the missionaries' daughter. I'm sure you remember my struggle to understand how you reconciled your tragic past with your cheery present."

"Of course."

"Then, too, you spoke of God and his love. You still do, all the time, and I couldn't accept that—still can't. If God were such a loving God, if he had loved the Frasers so well, he would never have allowed my mother's senseless death. After all, she'd been helping your parents at the mission house, serving the very God who then turned on her."

"Ach, Andrew, we've been over that before." A large lump lodged in Grace's throat, making speech difficult. "I can't make you see the truth you refuse to see. . . . But the box? Why didn't you just give it to me and go back to sea?"

His eyes swept her face with a gentle look. "You. You intrigued me. I wanted to know how, after all that had happened, you could still radiate such joy when you stood on that craggy spit of rock. I wanted to know how you could still love a God who'd abandoned you as a little girl."

"The brae . . . when I go there I feel closest to God. It's where I worship him in complete freedom. I look at his magnificent creation and realize how much he loves me. The God who made that beauty cared enough about me to offer me his love, salvation, and many, many blessings."

"So you say."

"But you don't agree."

"Nae."

"Then why did you stay? I'm sure you could have gone as soon as you and Mr. McConnell came to terms on your business affairs."

Again he gave her that tender look. "You."

Grace's cheeks warmed. "You . . . grew *fond* of me, as you said."

"Aye."

Taking a moment to digest the meaning of his words, Grace turned to the box. "I wonder . . . what did Mama and Papa send me so long ago?"

She approached the splintered gray mess and ran a finger across the wood. Her parents' hands had touched those very boards shortly before they'd died. Even the most rotten one was precious to her.

Testing one slat, she found the wood had held up well against time. It didn't give an inch.

"Here," Andrew said, kneeling by her. "Allow me. It truly is the very least I can do."

With a sharp knife, he began to pry out the nails. They'd rusted in the sea air and presented him with a challenge. As persistent as he'd already proven himself, Andrew persevered, and in time, he lifted the top from the crate. Another box met their gaze, this one with a removable lid.

Instead of digging in, Grace paused. What would the box reveal? Would it be like the mythological Pandora's box and set more troubles free? Or would it offer up a treasure of some sort?

"Oh, Father God," she said softly, as a ripple of anticipation ran through her, "only you know what Mama's and Papa's intentions were. But I trust you . . . in all things."

She reached in and pulled out masses of first, paper, then fabric—silk, according to Andrew. While he exclaimed over the excellent quality of the goods, Grace continued digging through her box. Soon she struck something sharp and hard—and heavy. "Help me," she said to her companion. "I can't lift it from the crate."

The packing material fell away from a splendid doll-house. Grace fell back with a plop. She burst into delighted laughter.

It was Andrew's turn to be puzzled. "What is it? A miniature house?"

Grace nodded. When a salty drop landed on her lip, she realized she'd begun to cry. "It's the dearest thing," she said. "Mama's dollhouse. When I was little, she would only let me play with it and its perfect, tiny furniture when I'd been especially good. I tried ever so hard to behave, because I knew how dear the dollhouse was."

It was extraordinary. The miniature building was perfect in every way. From the graceful turret to the right of the front entrance, to the dainty, thumbnail-sized shingles under the pitched roof—every detail spoke of care and artistry. The tall, slender glass windows graced the front, just as full-sized ones did in Queen Anne–style homes. Perfect steps led to the front door, a lead-glass insert filling its center. When one looked around to the other side, the attention to detail continued.

As Grace stared at the structure, rich, warm memories rushed back, so vivid she could almost hear her mother's voice. *"Treat the pieces gently, my darling Grace. They're precious, just like you."* How often she'd dreamed of touching this house again—the one thing she remembered sharing most with her mama. And after her parents died, she had so longed to see the miniature house again. For she had felt that if she could touch the house, she could touch her mother. But she'd never thought her childhood dream could come true.

The hall clock chimed twelve.

"Isn't God wonderful?" she exclaimed. "What a gift he has given me at the time of his Son's birth. His love and goodness are so clear. . . . He has given me back a bit of my mother in this very special Christmas keepsake."

"But what," Andrew asked, his voice raw with harsh emotion, "has he given me?"

Looking away from her treasure with great reluctance, Grace found bitterness etched on Andrew's face. Her heart nearly tore in two at the sight of his pain. Especially in the face of her renewed joy.

The contrast brought home to Grace the differences between them, why the feelings that had begun to flourish could not grow any stronger.

Then it struck her. Perhaps God had given Andrew something this Christmas after all. But was she bold enough to voice the thought?

Gathering her courage, Grace said, "Perhaps God has brought you to Skye to give you what you've always lacked—a home. Since you proposed to court me, it would seem you don't want to go through life alone."

"Nae, I don't want to live the rest of my life alone. But you're the one who turned me down."

Tears again prickled her eyes. "For good reason. How much love can fill a heart that's as full of hate and unforgiveness as yours?"

Her question had been hard to voice; it clearly was hard for him to hear. Andrew blanched.

Grace went on gently. "I challenge you to consider all you'll throw away if you run from God to the sea."

"What . . . ?" He gulped. "What do you mean? What would I be throwing away?"

"Peace, Andrew. With God. At long last." When he started to object, Grace held out a hand, palm up, halting his words. "Perhaps memories of your mother, good ones, the kind you'd want to keep, as he has given me memories of mine. And maybe even the chance to build a future where you'll make new memories, ones finally free of the taint of the past."

To Grace's amazement, longing shone in his eyes. "What would it take?" he asked.

"Surrender."

"To what?" he whispered.

"To God's love."

CHAPTER SIX

*H*e should have known how Grace would answer his question. Hours later, in his guest room at the manor, Drew acknowledged her consistency—in all matters, Grace Carlisle did indeed consider God.

Again he experienced that odd pang of longing for days gone by, days where faith was simple and untarnished with grief and the feeling of God's betrayal. He hadn't expected to feel this way. The urge had surprised him earlier while he and Grace had spoken. Now it had returned.

But he knew better than to think faith simple. He'd learned.

Still, Grace's certainty in her beliefs was hard to discount. That gentle firmness again reminded him of his mother.

Although he'd now had a glimpse into Grace's capacity for anger, he couldn't fault her, even for that. He and his father had been in the wrong by withholding what was rightfully hers.

He sighed and stood. Hearing yet another burst of wind attack the house, he approached the window and watched nature's fury continue its onslaught, unabated.

Drew understood that kind of rage; he'd lived with it for nine long years. Unfairness made him furious, and what had happened to the Frasers seemed to him the ultimate injustice.

How could Grace feel herself so blessed by the very God who'd treated him and his family so shabbily?

And yet he had to admit that her mother's dollhouse couldn't fail to bring her comfort, to bring back the memories of which she'd spoken.

What memories had he?

It struck him that indeed he had none—or very few. How could that be? How could he not remember more of his childhood? of the times he and his mother had shared?

He did remember, however, something else Grace had said. She'd said the hate he harbored toward her father would keep love from growing between them. Could hatred also block the good memories of his parents that he might otherwise have had?

Unlike Grace, who'd had nothing of her parents until she'd opened her Christmas gift, he had something of his mother's. He'd had it since the day his father died.

With reluctance he reached for his satchel and withdrew the item he had, as of yet, to unwrap. He knew what the sturdy brown paper protected, though. Father had told him.

It was Mother's Bible.

With the wind howling in the background, Drew sat in the leather armchair in the corner of the room and pulled the tabletop lamp closer. He began to leaf through the old, well-worn book.

At the first notation in the margin, a knot formed in his throat. Soon, though, he realized that just about every page had a mark of some kind. Mother had not only read the Bible; she'd studied it, noting those points that most aptly applied to her circumstances.

Hours passed as Drew renewed his acquaintance with the long-dead woman. Finally he arrived at that most familiar prayer of all: the Lord's Prayer. "... *forgive us our debts, as we forgive our debtors* ..."

There it was again. That Scripture he'd flung at Grace as if it had been a weapon of some sort. His mother had underlined the words. To the side, she'd made another of her now-familiar notes.

> I struggle daily to forgive and know I can't. But the Lord can change my will. Forgive me, Father, for my unforgiveness. I surrender to your boundless love.

By the time he read the last word, a film clouded Drew's vision. His sweet mother had also dealt with the pain of being wronged; she, too, had struggled, as she'd written, to forgive.

Unlike him, however, she'd had the kind of faith he'd come to expect in Grace. Mother had prayed for forgiveness. She'd surrendered to God's love.

As Grace had urged him to do.

When he'd first met her, he'd considered Grace a religious zealot, like her parents before her. What's more, he'd rejected the possibility of his mother's believing so completely, so blindly. Now, faced with evidence of her faith, he had to reconsider his opinion.

Drew had to reconsider everything he'd believed for the last nine years.

Downstairs the clock chimed the hour of 4 A.M. Drew was bone tired. He had nurtured his pain and need for justice for so very long. That fruitless exercise finally seemed to have taken its toll. He needed rest, complete rest. But how could he rest when his whole life had just been turned upside down? when he found himself standing on sinking sand?

"Surrender," Grace had said.

Surrender, his mother had written. Surrender to God's boundless love.

He remembered the days of his childish faith. That had been complete surrender.

Exhaling roughly, he dropped onto the bed, the Bible still in hand. His body sank into the embrace of the blankets, the mattress, the pillows. They enfolded him in welcome comfort, and he melted into them.

"Surrender to God's boundless love . . . ," he murmured.

As a tear seeped out from the corner of his eye, he did just that. He prayed for God's forgiveness, even though he didn't understand why God had betrayed his family. He prayed for God's forgiveness, since he couldn't forgive the man who'd caused his mother's death. But like her, he was going to yield—he'd reached the end of his own strength. He couldn't fight a dead man any longer.

"Forgive me, Father, for my unforgiveness," he said, using his mother's eloquent, simple words, feeling them in every fiber of his worn-out being. "Change my will. I surrender to your boundless love."

Then a miracle happened. Grace had told him that once he surrendered to God's love, he'd finally experience peace. And experience it he did. Peace, sweet and enveloping, flowed through him.

He now knew what she'd meant.

As deep, restorative sleep overtook him—for the first time in nine years—he smiled. He finally had come back to Christ, his very own Savior. He had asked forgiveness for his bitterness and attitudes, and Christ had made his heart clean. He couldn't wait to tell Grace he finally understood what she'd been trying to tell him ever since they'd first met. He'd tell her the first thing, come morning.

For Christmas this year, Drew knew that God had also given him, a memory to keep.

❋ ❋ ❋

A few hours later it was morning, and a cacophony of voices outside yanked Drew out of a sound slumber. Disoriented, he rose slowly, then approached the bedroom window. A bewildering sight met his gaze.

Gathered just in front of McConnell Manor stood a number of people carrying heavy sticks, the women outnumbering the men. All seemed to speak at once, hence the noise that had woken him so rudely.

Since he couldn't make out a word, Drew slipped on his shoes, glad he'd fallen asleep in his clothes the night before. Rumpled and still sleepy, he went to see what was afoot.

Downstairs Mr. McConnell stood in the entrance hall, his body blocking the open doorway. Beyond his host, just beyond the front stoop, Drew could see the milling crowd.

"Ye're nae better than Macdonald an' Sutherland, what wi' all the clearin' they did," shouted a thin man, brandishing his stick.

"Aye," concurred a heavyset woman. "An' ye so friendly-like with th' Rev'rend, an' all."

An elderly crone, swaddled in layers of woolen shawl, bent to pick up what looked like a stone from the edge of the walk. Shaking it at McConnell, she cried, "Mrs. Muir's just birthed, ye greedy grabber! Does yer good wife ken ye're after turnin' oot a new mother an' child in the worst gale in years?"

Behind him, Drew heard footsteps on the stairs. With a glance over his shoulder, he saw Mrs. McConnell and Grace run down, hands clasped, evidently for courage.

"What is it?" asked the older woman, as they paused a few risers up.

A distraught-looking McConnell turned to his wife. "Now, dearest. Dinna fash yerself. Run back to bed. I'll take care of it—once I ken what 'tis all aboot."

Drew noticed the man's surprising lapse into heavy

brogue, a sure sign of strain. He also noted the firm set of Grace's round chin.

The governess marched down the remaining steps, across the entrance hall, past her employer, and out the door. Her posture brought to mind the vision he'd spotted on the brae the day he'd arrived in Skye. Miss Carlisle was indeed a formidable woman—a courageous one, too. And perhaps, just perhaps, a foolish one as well.

What would possess her to plunge right into the middle of such a melee?

"Please," she cried, "could someone tell me what is wrong?"

Drew recognized Angus McNee when he stepped forward. "The Muirs have fallen behind on their rents, Miss Grace," he said. "An' yer employer—" the term came out sounding much like an epithet—"sent his man to turn 'em oot of their croft. Mrs. Muir, she's recently had her babe. 'Twould be inhuman to cast them oot into this."

As the boy gestured toward the leaden sky, the wind again made its presence known. Grace shivered, and Drew stepped forward, wishing he hadn't removed his coat the night before.

But the cold didn't stop Grace. "Mr. McConnell," she said, turning toward the lord of the manor, "is it true? Are you turning out those poor unfortunates? At the time of Christ's birth?"

Her voice rose with each word, underscoring her incredulity.

Drew glanced at McConnell, feeling distinct distaste for the possibility—business decision or not.

"I . . . I dinna ken," the man answered slowly, as if he were in shock. "I know naught of this."

Angus stepped closer, fists on hips, expression belligerent. "Ain't Scanlon yer man?"

McConnell nodded. "He handles some of my business."

"Well, sir," said the lad, "'e's been to the Muir's an' told 'em to clear oot by midday."

At that, things turned ugly. The women, following the crone's example, dropped their sticks and bent to pick up the rocks that lined the walk to the manor's front steps. Above the cries denouncing McConnell's brutality came the sound of approaching hoofbeats. A man in the familiar uniform of the constabulary rode in, joining his voice to the general uproar.

A rock flew through the air and hit the carved lintel over the door.

Fear ran through Drew. Grace was in the middle of the mess. She turned toward McConnell, her lips mouthed a plea. She reached for the woman to her left; her prey's intended missile dropped harmlessly to the ground.

The woman Drew loved continued her efforts to stem the riot. As she ran toward another enraged insurgent, a stone found its mark on her temple. Grace crumpled instantly.

As she fell, a hush descended. All went silent except for Drew, from whose innermost being came the roughest, most pain-filled sound he'd ever made.

He flew to Grace's side. He cradled her in his arms, then lifted the lock of hair hiding her temple. A large welt showed where the rock had made impact, the soft flesh around it reddening even as he watched. To his relief, her pulse was evident beneath her fragile skin.

"Fetch the doctor," he cried.

"Aye, Cap'n Fraser," called Henry, who'd come out to witness the commotion in a scarlet wool nightshirt and matching cap. "Straightaway."

"Ah, Grace . . . ," Drew murmured, his heart aching at the sight of her felled through no fault of her own. She'd simply been caught between two groups at odds. . . .

As the thought crossed his mind, the blood in his veins froze. He couldn't breathe; he couldn't move.

He'd heard those very words before. The woman in his arms had uttered them. She'd been speaking of his mother . . . her mother . . . even her father.

As though he'd been pierced through the heart, Drew took in the scene around him. The agitated townspeople . . . McConnell, pasty and shaken . . . his wife, sobbing in the doorway . . . the constable, still on his horse, aware that, for Grace, he'd perhaps arrived too late.

As if a cloud had blown past his eyes, Drew realized he'd more than likely just witnessed a new version of what had taken place on a mission field in China nine years ago.

"Forgive me, Father," he said. Without a shadow of a doubt, he knew he'd blamed his mother's death on a blameless God.

And a blameless man.

The Carlisles and his mother had been no more than innocent victims of others' sins. Greed and rage had killed them all. Grace had been right.

Then a tiny voice made his heart take flight.

"He has," whispered Grace.

"Don't move," he whispered. "We've sent for the doctor. Henry should have him here very soon."

"I'm fine," she said and tried to sit up.

A cheer went up from the crowd. Grace smiled and waved the onlookers away.

Drew frowned. "Nae, you're not fine. A sizable rock knocked you down. You lost consciousness—"

"I'm fine now, and I'd really prefer to go inside." Surprising him with the strength in her slender body, she stood. "I hate to make any more of a spectacle of myself."

He rose and stepped closer to her side. "You did no such thing. You're actually the heroine of the moment."

"How so?"

"Look," he answered, waving toward the front stoop.

There, beneath the nicked lintel, stood Angus McNee, the constable, and Mr. McConnell, all signs of combativeness gone. The three were speaking in reasonable tones, the rebels on the walk watching the tableau, expectation on their faces.

"Listen here," called Mr. McConnell seconds later. "'Twould seem young Angus here is right. I know naught of what Scanlon has been up to, but I've no intention to turn anyone oot today. In the spirit of Christmas, when

God gave his children his greatest gift, I will not have anyone turned oot of the inn, so to speak."

Another cheer sounded out, loud and clear.

The Laird of McConnell Manor smiled. "I'll look into the situation—not today, I'll grant you, but surely tomorrow morning. Go on, head home. Your families need you more than does my front walk. Especially on Christmas Day."

Chuckling with relief, the rioters dispersed, leaving only the McConnells and their guests in place.

With a hitch in her voice, Mrs. McConnell thanked Grace for her efforts, then chastised her for her reckless run into the crowd. "I nearly died myself when I saw you drop dead in that faint. Dearest lass, don't ever do anything so foolish again."

Grace placed a hand on her employer's shoulder. "I couldn't stand and watch the situation grow any worse. Skye—the town of Braes—this is my home now. I've come to care a great deal for you and your family, as well as for the folks who've made me so welcome here."

"Aye, lass," said Mr. McConnell, "'twas a foolish, brave thing you did today."

Cheeks reddening at the generous praise, Grace shrugged. "The Lord's called us to be peacemakers, to live in peace with our neighbors. 'Twas all I did."

"That's why I find life at sea so much simpler," said Drew. "There are less neighbors out there."

Grace turned her lovely gray eyes to him. "'Tis true, but God also called us to be a light in the world. There's not much of a chance to brighten any path when we're running—or sailing—away."

"I haven't run away from anything," Drew stated in his own defense. "I followed my father's footsteps, learning his business, as many other sons do."

As Grace continued to study him, Drew's discomfort grew. What was it about this woman, who always seemed to best him with her logic? With some minor part of his attention, he took note of the McConnells' discreet departure.

As Grace and Drew walked toward the mansion, Grace spoke as if their hosts had never been there, had never left. "But do those other fathers use their business as a means to avoid fulfilling a duty?"

"How do you do it?" he asked, stunned by how true her words resonated within him. "How do you know my thoughts even before I know them myself? How do you know my father as well?"

"I don't know . . . perhaps you reveal more than you realize."

Drew nodded. "I admit, my anger and bitterness have been hard to hide. But this . . . I daresay you're right, as you've so often been these past few days. On the ship, all I need to do is voice an order. My men must obey. Aside from paying them a decent wage and treating them honorably, not much more is required of me."

A gentle smile softened Grace's features, as they stepped inside the house, but she said nothing.

Drew went on. "It takes a great deal more from a man—

and a woman—to live in harmony if he's in constant contact with others. Sooner or later he will be wronged."

"Most often without malice, Andrew."

"Aye, Grace. The Lord showed me that today. The person who threw that rock never meant to hit you. True, they were angry at the situation, but I can't even be sure they meant to hurt McConnell at all."

"'Twas an accident."

"Indeed. You were an innocent victim." Drew breathed deeply, then went on. "My mother, your parents . . . they were innocent victims, too."

Grace approached him, took his hands between hers, and smiled. "I'm so thankful God's shown you this. I've prayed many prayers for you."

He twined his fingers through hers. And within an instant, the action that began as one of comfort turned into something more private, more meaningful.

"You've taught me a great deal in a very short time," he said, gazing into her silver eyes. "Most of all, how right I was to recognize your worth right away. You're a wise woman, Grace Carlisle, and I've fallen in love with you."

She gasped.

"Nae, don't say anything yet." He squeezed her trembling fingers. "I now know it's much too soon to pressure you for an answer. But I want you to know the truth. Last night, with the aid of my mother's Bible, I made my peace with God. I asked him to forgive me for all my years of anger that have sidetracked me from a true relationship with him. As a result, I've found the peace you spoke of.

I need time to come to know him better, know myself better, too. But one thing I know. . . *you* are indeed the loveliest gift he's ever given me. And I'm willing to wait as long as it takes for you to say yes to allowing me to court you. And I'd be remiss if I didn't say I pray that eventually you'll become my wife."

Tears pooled in her eyes. "Oh, Andrew . . ."

"Don't cry—unless there is no chance you'll ever come to feel for me as I do you."

She shook her head. "Nae, these aren't that kind of tears. They're happy tears. I'm so glad you've found peace at last, and I'm honored to have helped you, if indeed I have. God's the only one who can heal the kind of wound you've carried all these years."

Drew smiled. "He is indeed. And it would seem he's made me wiser in these last few days."

"How so?"

"He used a remarkable woman to teach me to recognize a blessing when I see one."

"Indeed?"

"Indeed. For one, I'd never unpacked my mother's Bible. Father gave it to me right after he made me promise to deliver your crate—your 'Christmas keepsake,' as you called it."

"Speaking of the dollhouse," Grace said, "look over there, to the left of the hearth."

There stood the miniature mansion in its entire splendor, radiant in the soft light of day. At night the glow of the fire would probably highlight features not as obvious

332

at first glance. It was much like the attributes of the woman he loved, Drew thought. The woman who'd helped him recognize the blessing in memories restored through words written in a well-loved Bible.

"In the future, anytime I think of your keepsake, I'll remember you," he said. "You're very much like it. As pleasant an exterior as you both have, it's what's not readily visible that charms. You told me that surrendering to God's love would probably restore to me the memories I lacked. And it did. You also said it might offer me the opportunity to make new ones. It has."

Grace blushed. "I can't believe I was so forward. You must forgive my—"

"Hush. There's nothing to forgive. You were absolutely right."

"I was?"

"Aye. And so I'm going to ask you once again, but this time in a different spirit. Grace Carlisle, after whatever period of time the Lord deems necessary for us to become better acquainted and you more certain of your feelings, would you do me the honor of becoming my wife?"

Tears rolled down her cheeks to her smiling lips. "Would I have to sail to all four corners of the earth?"

Drew laughed. "Nae, only to those where your heart would have you go."

"But what of your business?"

"Father didn't make Mother follow him wherever he went. He often took us with him, but that's because she wanted to go. I wouldn't have to go along each time my ship set sail. I own other ships, you know, and I only captain one. Those voyages that I might need to handle myself, well, you'd always have the choice to join me or stay home."

Grace laughed. "I can see where your success in business comes from. You've an answer to every question, and you don't renounce easily."

"In view of that, my dear Miss Carlisle, might we strike a deal?"

"I do believe, Captain Fraser, in view of your sensible offer of time to prepare myself for our upcoming nuptials, a deal is struck."

They sealed it with a kiss.

A Note from the Author

"Memories are the keepsakes of the past." While finishing "Memory to Keep," I drove past a local builder's office and read that statement on his billboard. How appropriate, I thought, and how true.

The weekend before, our family had set up our Christmas tree. Over the years I have collected a huge number of ornaments, not only for myself, but also for each of our four sons. This year the boys' ornaments filled our large tree nicely—I didn't need to use any of my decorations. A fortunate circumstance since, due to an injury, I'd been sidelined from the actual trimming activities.

When the tree was loaded with ornaments, it was time for the angel topper to be put in place. But when the boys went back to the nearly empty box, I heard things like, "Hey! Look what I found," and "Do you remember this?"

Relegated to my pillowed bunker on the couch, I had to wait until they showed me the apparent treasure. Finally I had my opportunity, and yes, it was a treasure . . . a keepsake of our past.

Beat up—cracked, in fact—its sparkle long gone, and its beauty never in much evidence, the boys were thrilled to put on top of our tree the first ornament my husband and I bought after we were married. It's a tree topper, but not a star, nor anything I could define or describe for you, dear reader. It's tall and pointy and red plastic, with remnants of some silver glitter bits—I daresay "ugly" best describes it; it had been the right price at the time.

And still, it's a treasure. It brought back to my husband and me the memory of being young newlyweds with more hopes and dreams than money. And to our sons? It brought back the memories of their childhood Christmases, the many times we celebrated baby Jesus' birthday with cake and punch and the Bible story read over and over again.

I have a feeling our lovely angel will be spending many more

Christmases in the box, while the red . . . *thing* will grace many
more trees to come.

I pray the Lord will bless you and yours with many memories to
keep this Christmas and bring back to you many of the treasures of
our past.

In his love,
Ginny Aiken

ABOUT THE AUTHOR

A former newspaper reporter, **GINNY AIKEN** lives in south-central Pennsylvania with her husband and four sons. Born in Havana, Cuba, and raised in Valencia and Caracas, Venezuela, she discovered books early on and wrote her first novel at age fifteen. (She burned it when she turned a "mature" sixteen!) That first effort was followed several years later by her win-ning entry in the Mid-America Romance Authors' Fiction from the Heartland contest for unpublished authors.

Ginny has certificates in French literature and culture from the University of Nancy, France, and a B.A. in Spanish and French literature from Allegheny College in Pennsylvania. Her first novel was published in 1993, and since then she has published numerous additional novels and novellas. One of her novels was a finalist for *Affaire de Coeur's* Readers' Choice Award for Best American Historical of 1997, and her work has appeared on various best-seller lists. Ginny's novellas appear in the anthologies *With This Ring, A Victorian Christmas Quilt, A Bouquet of Love,* and *Dream Vacation.* She is also the author of the delightful Bellamy's Blossoms series: *Magnolia, Lark,* and *Camellia.*

When she isn't busy with the duties of being a soccer mom, Ginny can be found reading, writing, enjoying classical music while indulging her passion for needlework, and preparing for her next Bible study.

Ginny welcomes letters written to her in care of:

TYNDALE HOUSE AUTHOR RELATIONS
P.O. BOX 80
WHEATON, IL 60189-0080

or by E-mail at GinnyAiken@aol.com.

Visit www.HeartQuest.com for lots of info on
HeartQuest books and authors and more!

www.HeartQuest.com

CURRENT HEARTQUEST RELEASES

- *Magnolia,* Ginny Aiken
- *Lark,* Ginny Aiken
- *Camellia,* Ginny Aiken

- *Sweet Delights,* Terri Blackstock, Ranee McCollum, and Elizabeth White

- *Awakening Mercy,* Angela Benson
- *Abiding Hope,* Angela Benson

- *Faith,* Lori Copeland
- *Hope,* Lori Copeland
- *June,* Lori Copeland
- *Glory,* Lori Copeland

- *Freedom's Promise,* Dianna Crawford
- *Freedom's Hope,* Dianna Crawford
- *Freedom's Belle,* Dianna Crawford

- *Prairie Rose,* Catherine Palmer
- *Prairie Fire,* Catherine Palmer
- *Prairie Storm,* Catherine Palmer
- *Prairie Christmas,* Catherine Palmer, Elizabeth White, and Peggy Stoks
- *Finders Keepers,* Catherine Palmer

- *Hide and Seek,* Catherine Palmer
- *A Kiss of Adventure,* Catherine Palmer (original title: *The Treasure of Timbuktu*)
- *A Whisper of Danger,* Catherine Palmer (original title: *The Treasure of Zanzibar*)
- *A Touch of Betrayal,* Catherine Palmer
- *A Victorian Christmas Keepsake,* Catherine Palmer, Kristin Billerbeck, and Ginny Aiken
- *A Victorian Christmas Cottage,* Catherine Palmer, Debra White Smith, Jeri Odell, and Peggy Stoks
- *A Victorian Christmas Quilt,* Catherine Palmer, Debra White Smith, Ginny Aiken, and Peggy Stoks
- *A Victorian Christmas Tea,* Catherine Palmer, Dianna Crawford, Peggy Stoks, and Katherine Chute

- *Olivia's Touch,* Peggy Stoks
- *Romy's Walk,* Peggy Stoks

COMING SOON (Spring 2002)

- *Letters of the Heart,* Lisa Bergren, Maureen Pratt, and Lyn Cote

- *Elena's Song,* Peggy Stoks
- *Enduring Love,* Angela Benson

HEARTWARMING ANTHOLOGIES FROM HEARTQUEST

A Victorian Christmas Cottage—A collection of novellas centering around hearth and home at Christmastime. Stories by Catherine Palmer, Jeri Odell, Debra White Smith, and Peggy Stoks.

A Victorian Christmas Tea—A collection of novellas about life and love at Christmastime. Stories by Catherine Palmer, Dianna Crawford, Peggy Stoks, and Katherine Chute.

A Victorian Christmas Quilt—A patchwork of novellas about love and joy at Christmastime. Stories by Catherine Palmer, Ginny Aiken, Peggy Stoks, and Debra White Smith.

Sweet Delights—Who would have thought that chocolate could be so good for your heart? A cup of tea and a few quiet moments are all you need to enjoy these tasty, calorie-free morsels from beloved romance authors Terri Blackstock, Elizabeth White, and Ranee McCollum. Each story is followed by a letter from the author and her favorite chocolate recipe!

Prairie Christmas—In "The Christmas Bride," by Catherine Palmer, Rolf Rustemeyer can hardly wait for the arrival of his Christmas bride, all the way from Germany. You'll love this heartwarming Christmas visit with friends old and new from A Town Called Hope. Anthology also includes special Christmas novellas by Elizabeth White and Peggy Stoks.

HEARTQUEST BOOKS BY CATHERINE PALMER

Hide and Seek—The charming town of Ambleside, Missouri, promises the new beginning Darcy Damyon longs for, far from the scandal of her past. Then her employer, Luke Easton, awakens feelings that threaten her newfound peace. Despite their mutual attraction, Darcy knows she can never risk exposing Luke and his young daughter to the dangers that follow her.

Widower Luke Easton just wants to make a home for his little daughter, Montgomery. But the mysterious and captivating stranger forces him to face the empty, lonely spaces in his life. When a menacing figure shows up to settle an old score with Darcy, Luke must risk his growing love for her—and his daughter's safety—as they seek a truly safe hiding place. What they find will require the greatest surrender of all. The sequel to *Finders Keepers*.

Finders Keepers—Blue-eyed, fiery-tempered Elizabeth Hayes hopes to move her growing antiques business into Chalmers House, the Victorian mansion next to her small shop. But Zachary Chalmers, heir to the mansion, has very different plans for the site. And Elizabeth's seven-year-old son, adopted from Romania two years earlier, has plans of his own: He thinks it's time for his mother to marry—and the tall, handsome man talking to her at the estate sale is the perfect candidate. In this first book of a new contemporary romance series, each must learn that God's plans are not our plans and his ways are not our ways.

A TOWN CALLED HOPE SERIES

Prairie Rose—Kansas held their future, but only faith could mend their past. Hope and love blossom on the untamed prairie as a young woman, searching for a place to call home, happens upon a Kansas homestead during the 1860s.

Prairie Fire—Will a burning secret extinguish the spark of love between Jack and Caitrin? The town of Hope discovers the importance of forgiveness, overcoming prejudice, and the dangers of keeping unhealthy family secrets.

Prairie Storm—Can one tiny baby calm the brewing storm between Lily's past and Elijah's future? Evangelist Elijah Book's zeal becomes sidetracked as the fate of an innocent child rests with a woman Eli must trust in spite of himself. United in their concern for the baby, Eli and Lily are forced to set aside their differences and learn to trust God's plan to see them through the storms of life.

Prairie Christmas—In "The Christmas Bride," by Catherine Palmer, Rolf Rustemeyer can hardly wait for the arrival of his Christmas bride, all the way from Germany. You'll love this heartwarming Christmas visit with friends old and new from A Town Called Hope. Anthology also includes special Christmas novellas by Elizabeth White and Peggy Stoks.

TREASURES OF THE HEART SERIES

A Touch of Betrayal—Alexandra Prescott, looking for inspiration for the line of exotic fabrics she is designing, fully expects her trip to Kenya to be an adventure. But an attempt on her life wasn't quite what she had in mind! Anthropologist Grant Thornton wonders what he has gotten himself into when this beautiful stranger suddenly invades his world. Although they seem to have nothing in common, he is drawn to her—and to her unnerving faith in God. And when the hired killer strikes again, Grant finds that there is far more to Alexandra than meets the eye.

The long-awaited conclusion to *The Treasure of Timbuktu* and *The Treasure of Zanzibar,* a contemporary romance adventure series.

A Kiss of Adventure (ORIGINAL TITLE: *The Treasure of Timbuktu*)—Abducted by a treasure hunter, Tillie Thornton becomes a pawn in a dangerous game. Desperate and on the run from a fierce nomadic tribe looking to kidnap her, Tillie finds herself in an uneasy partnership with a daring adventurer.

A Whisper of Danger (ORIGINAL TITLE: *The Treasure of Zanzibar*)—An ancient house filled with secrets . . . a sunken treasure . . . an unknown enemy . . . a lost love. They all await Jessica Thornton on Zanzibar. Jessica returns to Africa with her son to claim her inheritance on the island of Zanzibar. Upon her arrival, she is reunited with her estranged husband.

HEART
QUEST®

HEARTQUEST BOOKS BY GINNY AIKEN

Camellia—Outgoing, compassionate young widow Camellia Bellamy Sprague finds her peace of mind shattered when her trusted doctor decides to retire—in the final trimester of her pregnancy. Worse yet, his replacement is altogether too attractive for Camellia's comfort. Searching for more out of life, Dr. Stephen Hardesty has given up a lucrative future to open a family practice in Bellamy. But his dreams are threatened when the lovely Camellia Sprague refuses to see him. If he can't gain her trust, how will the other townspeople learn to accept him? When a crisis hits the Bellamy Blossoms, Stephen and Camellia are thrown into an adventure that will change their lives forever. Book 3 in the Bellamy's Blossoms series.

Lark—After the highly successful launch of her literary magazine, Lark Bellamy has come home. Rich Desmond's discovery that tempestuous, redheaded beauty Lark Bellamy is back in town shatters his peace of mind. The last thing Rich needs is a supersleuth like Lark searching for answers to his mysterious behavior. When Lark turns her investigative skills onto the mystery Rich is determined to keep cloaked in silence, she uncovers a startling revelation. Can their budding romance survive as Lark reveals more and more of the truth? Book 2 in the Bellamy's Blossoms series.

Magnolia—Magnolia Bellamy can't believe she's just hired a carpetbagger to restore the fabulous Ashworth Mansion. Against her better judgment, Maggie hires the Yankee contractor, Clay Marlowe, whose credentials are impeccable. Clay Marlowe loves a challenge. But he hadn't reckoned on the delicately beautiful Magnolia Bellamy, the project's self-appointed overseer—nor on the meddlesome but lovable ladies of the Bellamy Garden Club! A rollicking, delightful novel from award-winning author Ginny Aiken. Book 1 in the Bellamy's Blossoms series.

Log Cabin Patch—In a logging camp in turn-of-the-century Washington State, a Log Cabin Patch quilt symbolizes the new hope awaiting a lonely young woman. This novella by Ginny Aiken appears in the anthology *A Victorian Christmas Quilt*.